REMEMBER TOMORROW

OTHER BOOKS IN THE ARGOSY LIBRARY:

REMEMBER TOMORROW

THEODORE ROSCOE

COVER BY
RUDOLPH BELARSKI

POPULAR PUBLICATIONS · 2023

TABLE OF CONTENTS

REMEMBER TOMORROW

Through the Forest of Fire they march, the soldier dead whose battle is never finished. For in that Valley of the Somme, vast armies sleep, rousing at night to strike terror to the hearts of the living. And tomorrow is as yesterday, ever alive and remembering.

In the summer after the Battle of Landen, the most sanguinary battle of the Seventeenth Century in Europe, the earth, saturated with she blood of twenty thousand slain, broke forth into millions of poppies, and the traveler who passed that vast sheet of scarlet might well fancy that the earth had given up her dead—

        Taboos, etc. Frazer's Golden Bough.

Accursed Battle Ground, One Day Its Bones Shall Rise, The Captains Be Accused—

        Aftermath of Glory

1

NO BATTLE CEASED

BILL SHEPHERD DIDN'T like it.... The road was lonely, and the dead man stared. He could not have been dead long, his eyes were open and glassy.

Outstretched there in a nest of fresh poppies alongside the road, stiffly horizontal, he resembled a body on display in a bed of floral tributes. But an undertaker would have pried open the clenched fists and sewed shut the eyelids. Bill Shepherd didn't like those eyes, unblinded by the car-lights, staring up at him in glassy fixation. At distance they had showed as discs of green, and he had stopped, expecting a dog.

Perspiration broke out on his forehead as he saw it was a peasant, a farmer in loose blue smock and corduroy, lying face up, dead on a slope of wet wildflowers. Bill Shepherd switched off the engine of his roadster and listened, hoping to hear another car.

Immediately the night sneaked in around him; woodsy silence composed of a thousand infinitesimal sounds, water rustling through grass, a creaking limb, somewhere a tree frog—the silence of a forest after rain, dripping and leafy. Beyond the rays of the car-lights the summer night, drenched after thunder-shower, was an inky oblivion.

There was only visible a short stretch of road—brown mud furrowed by deep coffee-filled ruts—a steamy corridor walled by dark underbrush and the skeletal silhouettes of black trees.

Dead men can be frightening on any road at night, but this Forêt de Feu was different. Knowing what he knew, Bill Shepherd could feel his hair going up. The poppy bed made a splash of orange against a background of charred timber—the peasant's smock was pale blue among the blossoms—the sightless eyes were agate-green—the upturned face glistened, a grimacing death-mask of wet marble.

Bill Shepherd swallowed and looked around.

No use wishing—the nearest village was eight miles back, and another car wasn't coming. He found himself glaring at tire-tracks printed in the roadway ahead. Of course. Some hit and run driver had skidded around that bend, and sideswiped this poor farmer. Pretending his stomach wasn't squirming, Bill Shepherd leaned out for a closer look.

The trouble was—and he'd realized this at first glance—

*There it stood, the Castle of Fire, frowning over
the graves of a hundred thousand dead.*

that body didn't look as if it had been struck by a car. No
muddy splatter or mangling. Rigid frame and staring eyes,
the man might have died there of a fit.

SHEPHERD GULPED. WHETHER he wanted to or not,
he had to climb out and examine that body. He kicked
open the low-slung door and stepped gingerly down into
the mud.

Then it wanted some resolution to cross over to that
poppy-grown knoll. A sweat bead trickled down from his
temple, and cords were ticking in his throat.

It wasn't that he was afraid of corpses—that would be a
laugh after ten years of bodies on stairways, bodies plunging through trap doors, cadavers hanging from chandeliers,
jamming fireplace chimneys, mouldering under beds. Yet
the nearest he'd come to that sort of thing until now was
his typewriter.

The minute he moved away from his car and let the
night close in behind him, all those stories he'd heard today
prowled into his thoughts and made his neck-hairs quiver
in apprehension.

"Bah!" he said aloud. "I've invented enough yarns of my own! Ought to know more than to believe the bedtime stories of these fool Frenchmen!"

He slogged around the front of his roadster. The road was a paste, and his shoes made a sucking sound, sinking to their laces in the mud. Swearing, he forced himself to the poppy knoll, went to one knee beside the body, and tried, bluffly nonchalant, to flex an arm.

The dead man's stare was impersonal, his arm rigid and wooden.

Bill Shepherd thought: "I suppose it's rigor mortis!" and couldn't remember how long it was supposed to be before rigor mortis set in. He could remark no evidence of violence, accidental or otherwise, and he managed to hunt through the man's trouser pockets for something that might identify him.

He found a new St. Christopher medallion and five francs. Then he supposed he'd better take a good look at the dead man's face. Kneeling as he was, he intercepted the lights from the car, and he'd purposely avoided that glassy stare. Leaning to one side, he braved a hasty glance at the dead man's features.

Breath went out of him with a sound of "Hunnnnh!"

He sprang up, looked around wildly, hunting the roadside underbrush and a path that came down through it, glaring about him with frightened eyes. Trees in the background assumed fantastic shapes, dark stumps and jagged limbs were witchlike arms reaching for him out of the undergrowth; he wheeled and shied at a gray hulk crouching in the brambles beyond the poppy bed, a dark monster squatting in readiness to leap out.

Then he saw the crouching hulk was a trench mortar tilted in rusty disuse, its muzzle draped by wild grape, its base buried under a tangle of briar and woodbine. These woods were littered with the abandoned machinery of War—old engines of death left to rust in thickets that were nourished by a compost of human blood and bone. But their harvest time had been 1916—this murder, not an hour old, was out of season.

The peasant had been strangled! Murder-steeled fingers, clenching the man's throat, had left the mark of nails and talons deep-printed in the flesh. A queerish, blue-pink pallor tinted the suffocated face. But in the ground around that body there was no track, no trampling, no footprint other than the peasant's own which came down the muddy path out of the woods.

Black thunder fell down a stairway in the sky and rolled off into smothery silence. He wheeled; jumped for the car.

The road was a channel of liquefied clay, and the old Hispano-Suiza swerved and slewed as he drove in headlong panic, pursued by black shadows and blacker imaginings through the witchy silhouettes of the forest.

"The Forêt de Feu—?"

Memory quoted so loudly in his mind he could almost feel the breath of whispered words in his ear. "But I would not go into those woods at night, *monsieur*. For a million francs—for ten million, I would not go! Because the Forêt de Feu is in the Red Zone, *monsieur*—and there the dead have not yet died. The World War is not over, *monsieur*. The Battle of the Somme is still going on, and the soldiers who died in the Red Zone are still fighting it, and their front line is in the Forêt de Feu!"

2

CASTLE DANGEROUS

IT HAD ALL started that morning in the Paris office of Bertrand et Frer, although the Paris office of Bertrand et Frer looked like the last place in the world for anything like that to start.

Opening the door of Bertrand et Frer, you disturbed one of those sad thimblelike little bells such as announce the advent of a customer in an old maid's notion shop. The jingle, in his case, warned the visitor he was intruding. The quiet wanted to be left alone.

The place was as dim as evening. A skeletal chandelier, converted from gas to electricity, burned one feeble bulb as a sop to the present era. Walls of brown books and a massive table that looked like a casket in a library formed in the gloom.

Bill Shepherd had said, "Hello," to no one in particular, and sat down.

Faint echo of taxi horns in the Faubourg outside reminded him that Paris was still there. The august mahogany door marked *Private* at room's end should at least have acknowledged his presence by opening far enough to tell him to wait. He tried a discreet cough, and nothing happened. Bertrand had died? Or was it Frer?

He contemplated waking up that little bell over the entry once more. He walked to the table and wrote *Silence Please* in the dust. Then he put his hands in his pockets and jangled some coins. This reminded him of the purpose behind his errand, and in abrupt resolution he started toward the impervious mahogany door. He touched the round brass knob with a tentative finger; then heard a murmur of voices beyond the paneling; cocked an ear to listen.

Distinctly he heard a woman's low voice say, "—Château de Feu!"

Bill Shepherd jerked his finger from the knob with the same reflex that sent his eyebrows up. He hadn't meant to eavesdrop, but circumstances alter cases. Deliberately he listened to:

"—Château de Feu. *Oui, oui, oui,* I remind you it is dangerous." The feminine voice blurred into an undertone he couldn't translate.

Bill Shepherd thought: "Now, what the—?"

A reedy voice piped on the other side of the door, "But, *mademoiselle—!*"

"Attend," the low voice cut in firmly, "I remind you it is dangerous. Not a word of this to be divulged, you comprehend."

"Very well, *mademoiselle.*"

Sound of chairs scuffing back on carpet. Rustle of movement. Bill Shepherd returned to his chair. He was lighting a cigarette as the door at room's end began to open.

HE THOUGHT THE woman who came across the threshold recoiled as she saw him, but he wasn't sure. He was only certain, as she passed his chair hurriedly and brushed on out into the hall, that she knew how to wear black, and that her eyes were as interesting as any that had ever given him a look. The bell jingled excitedly at her exit. He had stood up swiftly to open the door for her departure, but her haste had outmaneuvered this gallantry. Holding the door ajar he had a glimpse of her as she reached the street.

A slow grin twitched up one corner of William Shepherd's mouth. The hushed and dim-lit reception room, the voices behind closed doors, ("I remind you it is dangerous—"), the mysterious lady in black—The other side of his mouth went up. *Chapter One!*

No. The thing was really a disease. He was back at his old game again, and of course he was imagining intrigue. Certainly in France there might be more than one Château de Feu.

A voice from the other end of the room said, "Monsieur Shepherd?"

He wheeled, a little abashed.

The figure now occupying the inner doorway looked as if it had just stepped out of one of the older law books on the shelves. It was dry, and needed dusting off and a new binding. William Shepherd was put in mind of a dummy that had been for a long time in the window of a customer's store. Black frock coat that rustled its hem around rusty knee-caps. High stock collar and plush cravat. A black toupee. A face like an old portrait painting with dried-up little eyes behind pince-nez.

Bill Shepherd admitted his identity by a gesture with his cigarette. "I'm afraid I came early. I was anxious to see Monsieur Bertrand about—"

"I am Monsieur Bertrand."

"Je suis très content de faire voire connaissance, Monsieur Bertrand."

"I too am most happy to make the acquaintance of the son of a client who was always to me the most amiable. Your father was regarded not only as client by us, *monsieur,* but, if I may say so, as a friend. In Paris he was more than highly esteemed. Your father was a great, a famous man. We thought of him almost, one might say, as a Frenchman."

Bill Shepherd thought how that would have amused his father—to be called great, famous and a Frenchman. He had a mental picture of the big boisterous man passing ten-dollar bills and champagne around the Moulin Rouge and Zelli's.

Monsieur Bertrand was going on, clearing his throat at just the right place for *douleur:* "Yes, how well I recall his last visit. Two years after the War. Does it seem seventeen years ago? And your mother, she died the same year. It was tragic, yes? It is sad."

Bill Shepherd said rather stiffly, "Yes, it is."

"But," Monsieur Bertrand sighed, "Bertrand et Frer will always recall that most happy association."

"My father always felt, Monsieur Bertrand, that when he left his European affairs in the hands of Bertrand et Frer they were as safe as if he had deposited them in the Bank of France."

"Bertrand et Frer were honored to have been chosen as your father's European executors, and feel confident there is no house in France whose integrity is better able to uphold this trust."

"I'm sure of that, Monsieur Bertrand. Incidentally,

before we get down to business, who was the lady who left your office just now?"

"*Monsieur* wishes to know—?"

"I'm sorry. I don't want to appear inquisitive, but I thought I'd met her somewhere before—Biarritz or maybe Monte Carlo."

"So. But there is no reason why I should not divulge the lady's name. It is Madame—eh—Madame Mallarmier. Her husband was a French officer and a suicide, poor fellow. Left her in many legal difficulties. She happens to be Swiss; perhaps you met her at St. Moritz. She is here to settle the matter of an estate in Switzerland."

"Well, although I don't seem to know her after all, I sympathize with her. I'm here to settle the matter of my own estate in France, and have to do it in a hurry. As I told you over the telephone yesterday, I've come to see about the Château de Feu."

"The—? *Ah oui, certainement, alors.* The Château de Feu. Of course—the Château de Feu. Please come in, Monsieur Shepherd. I am afraid you are going to be disappointed, *monsieur.* It seems there are some difficulties in the matter of the Château de Feu."

BILL SHEPHERD WAS surprised. For the last two years he had been well aware of "difficulties" in the matter of Château de Feu, but a beautiful and unknown lady in black had not previously been connected with them. Somehow his father—that surprising man—had recognized and cherished the love of the wife whose faith in him had lifted him by the bootstraps out of a Scranton coal mine. Impervious to nothing else that money could buy, Old Bill would have had no investment in Paris romance. Probably the

Château de Feu had been Old Bill's last white elephant to hand down to an impoverished heir.

Certainly the title was clear. Too clear. Taxes and assessments to be paid the first of the month had left young Bill no doubt of that. And those, up to now, had been the "difficulties." How to meet the neglected taxes on the place.

Living in New York, he'd all but forgot this obscure French *château* left him by his father, as one forgets something cumbersome and gaudy tucked away for sentimental reasons in moth balls. A French *château*—he'd kept it as a gesture to Old Bill, and because Hugh, his older brother, had died under fire somewhere around there, wherever it was, during the War. They'd never found the body, but Hugh's last letter had said he was running a dressing station "of all places, in Father's foolish *château*."

He had never seen the Château de Feu; somehow hadn't wanted to. But now the day for extravagance and sentiment had passed; a *château* in France was hardly the keepsake for an American stranded in Paris with two hundred francs and a second-hand Hispano-Suiza that drank gasoline with the insatiable thirst of a broken-down Russian Duke. There were bills. His very name was characterized by Bill. Not that he'd expected to raise any money on the *château* but he'd hoped for something from the place, if only a secluded roof to think under for a while. A mysterious woman in the woodpile, however, had not been among his anticipations.

Smiling expressionlessly at Monsieur Bertrand, Bill Shepherd wondered if he hadn't imagined those words he'd heard through the door. The office of Bertrand et Frer looked too crustily respectable for any mystery. Conceivably the beauty in black might own a Château de Feu in Switzerland, and have been referring to a condition of the floors.

Bill Shepherd said, when it became apparent Monsieur Bertrand was waiting for him to speak: "As I wrote you from America, Monsieur Bertrand, it is necessary for me to sell the Château de Feu."

Monsieur Bertrand adjusted his pince-nez. If voice had color, Bill Shepherd thought, this one would be the color of sand. "Ah. I trust you had a pleasant voyage coming from America, Monsieur Shepherd?"

"Rough all the way," Bill Shepherd said cheerfully. "You see, I thought if I came over personally to see about the sale of the *château* it would save a lot of—"

"And how are things at present in the United States, Monsieur Shepherd?"

"Now about the *château*—"

"But the Depression in America, it has lifted—?"

"NOT FOR ME," Bill Shepherd declared doggedly. Monsieur Bertrand's evasive technique was entertaining, but Bill Shepherd told himself he would be even more entertained when he learned the reason for this evasion.

He faced Monsieur Bertrand squarely. "The Depression hasn't lifted for me, as the unpaid taxes on the Château de Feu may have indicated to you. I've run out of pocket money. I'm broke. I can't afford a bottle of Scotch right now, much less the upkeep on a historical French estate. I thought if you could sell the *château* for me—"

"But *monsieur!*" the dry face looked shocked. "Bertrand et Frer had no idea you were in such financial—eh—straits. A man of your position—"

"—Is usually riding the brake-rods on a freight train out of town. Instead of that, I came to Europe the southern route and stopped for a night at Monte Carlo. They say the wheel is on the level, too. I did get out with my trousers, but you can understand—"

"But your father's bonds, Monsieur Shepherd! Your father's American holdings—!"

"Burned up eight years ago. Swedish Matches and a short circuit in Mid-West Power. I can't imagine what happened to the rest—I'm only a mystery-story writer. It seems I'm left with this French property, and I can't afford to keep it. The point is, Monsieur Bertrand"—Bill Shepherd put both hands firmly on the desktop, leaning forward a little—"have you been able to find a buyer for the Château de Feu?"

Monsieur Bertrand's eyeglasses reflected surprise. He murmured, "Ah." He nodded. "Yes. But then. A buyer." He put the tips of dry fingers together, tilted back in his chair and gravely regarded a point in the ceiling. The Château de Feu was somewhere overhead among cracks in the ceiling-plaster; it was surrounded by difficulties which Monsieur Bertrand could see, and, seeing them, Monsieur Bertrand was reluctant to reveal them to his client.

"*Non,* Monsieur Shepherd, it distresses me to confess the inability of Bertrand et Frer to find as yet a prospective buyer for the Château de Feu."

"It doesn't distress you, Monsieur Bertrand, anywhere near as much as it distresses me."

"However, I wish to emphasize 'as yet.' Given more time—"

"I wish I had more time," Bill Shepherd said flatly. "The

French government's given me a month's notice. Pay up the back taxes or they'll be forced to confiscate the property. I know it's my fault for letting 'em slide at a time when I was able to pay 'em, but I haven't got the money any more, and I couldn't raise it now in a month of Sundays. I can't even meet my hotel bill at the Crillon. If I can't sell that *château* I'll lose it. Of course you advertised the property for sale?"

"The *château* and the surrounding estate, as you advised in your letter." Monsieur Bertrand shook his head. "There were a number of inquiries, but they failed to materialize."

"You made the price interesting?"

"Following your instructions, Monsieur Shepherd, we made the price positively a bargain. *Non*, it is *deplorable*." Monsieur Bertrand's shoulders lifted in sympathy. "We could find no interested prospects."

"But if you put the sale up to a good real estate operator—?"

"We have placed the matter in the hands of one of the largest, the most enterprising realty houses in France. Attend. I will show you their report." Monsieur Bertrand made a dry rustling of papers in a desk drawer; extracted a letter from a file. "However,"—pinching off his glasses and tapping the correspondence with a shiny lens—"before I give this to you, it might be well for me to prepare you—it is an unusual letter, believe me!—by reminding you of the condition of the estate in question, the *château*, Monsieur Shepherd. It has not been—how do you say? modernized."

"You mean there isn't electricity, ice cubes, a two-car garage—?"

"Perhaps; but that is not exactly"—Monsieur Bertrand

paused, frowned at the letter—"not exactly what I mean. You comprehend, *monsieur*, the location of the *château*—"

"In the country."

"In France, *oui*. But in the north of France. Several hundred miles from Paris. An afternoon's drive, I should say, north of the city of Amiens. In the Province of Picardy. *Voilà!* Monsieur Shepherd realizes there was a war—"

"My older brother was killed—"

"Indeed, I remember well your father on his last visit to Paris speaking of it. *Quel dommage.* A pity. But so. It was because of this, that your father refused thereafter to occupy the *château*. You comprehend? The *château* was somewhat damaged during the war; not utterly, I understand, but there is some ruin. And it has not since been repaired."

BILL SHEPHERD NODDED. "Of course under those circumstances a buyer wouldn't want to sink a lot of money in the place, with the back taxes and all. But there's a hundred acres in timber on the estate. The Forêt de Feu. Certainly that ought to be worth something."

Monsieur Bertrand sighed. "There are difficulties."

"More difficulties?"

Monsieur Bertrand's blink was troubled. He fastened on his eyeglasses, squinted at the paper in his hand, frowned exasperation at Bill Shepherd. *"Monsieur!* It seems this Forêt de Feu—*ma foi*—it is that which comprises the chief difficulty in the matter of selling the estate. *Monsieur* will agree with me that here is a problem the most extraordinary. This timber, *monsieur*—this forest—never in all my experience have I encountered a matter as incredible. Regard."

The office of the Agency Honneteau wished to thank Monsieur Bertrand for his kind consignment, and hoped he was as well as they were. The letter continued with the usual indirections and then:

> Our Amiens office advises us it has been impossible to sell the old Château de Feu, not only because of a prohibitive accumulation of unpaid taxes; but the estate, as you know, is situated in the Forêt de Feu, midway between the villages of Contalmaison and Thiepval, off the main road, and lying in the very heart of that region devastated by the World War, known as the Red Zone.
>
> Some of the surrounding country has remained unrehabilitated; the *château*, itself, stands in considerable disrepair; and a further barrier to disposal of this property comes in lieu of the ugly local reputation the *château* and forested *demesne* seems to have attained.
>
> Imagine the reluctance of a prospective customer when, at mere mention of the Forêt de Feu, the peasants of the district start shaking their heads and crossing themselves. Investigation discloses the most astounding rumors concerning the place—stories common to illiterate peasantry—some of which, however, seem to have foundation in several sinister occurrences recent to the forest.
>
> Bodies found in the uncleared woods have recalled the days of the Invasion, and lately, it appeals, there have been one or two unexplained deaths in the neighborhood. This may be no more than gossip; yet, perhaps as nowhere else in France, the countryside there remains still overshadowed by the last War, and under such adverse publicity an outright sale of the Château de Feu seems unlikely.

BILL SHEPHERD NARROWED a stare at the concluding paragraph. *Ugly local reputation. Sinister occurrences.* A crinkle hardened at the corners of his eyes as they flicked back over the line: *one or two unexplained deaths.* Really, that casual "one or two" was overdoing it.

This cryptic epistle on a matter of real estate read like the opening installment of *Three-Fingered Jack's Last Clue,* and made less sense. He folded the letter slowly.

"What is it all about?"

Monsieur Bertrand raised dismayed shoulders, "Truly, I know no more than the letter indicates. *Non,* I am quite baffled—"

Pushing back his chair, Bill Shepherd said with forced amiability, "Well, there's only one thing for me to do, and that's go there and find out."

Monsieur Bertrand spried to his feet. For the first time during the interview his features showed open distress. "But my dear young sir. Do you not think it would be better to wait, to inquire of the real estate agent, to make a thorough investigation of—"

"Yes on the last two; no on the waiting. There isn't time for a lot of letter writing. If something funny has been happening around there—"

"But Monsieur Shepherd! I assure you—" The other made a deprecatory gesture. "Do not take this letter too literally. French peasants are given to such talk—old wives' tales—nonsense—the back-country districts, in particular those devastated by the War, are alive with stupid—"

"That's just it," he interrupted with some heat. "After all, I own the *château,* and if it's been devalued by some sort of vicious gossip I'd like to know about it. Time I looked

up the old place, anyway." He picked up his hat in resolution. "Ten o'clock now, I ought to be able to drive out
there before dark, only a couple of hundred miles. Matter
of fact, I was going there anyway, since I can't afford to stay
at the Crillon."

Monsieur Bertrand said almost shrilly, "I advise against
it. There is only the caretaker—that one employed years
ago by your father, and he has been there ever since—
Archambaud Landru. The place will be in no condition
for you! You would arrive late at night and find the *château*
locked and dark—"

Bill Shepherd was thinking of a throaty voice behind
this mahogany door, an intriguing whisper. He said, giving
Monsieur Bertrand a steady look, "I can make it before
dark."

"Do not consider it!" A wallet was quivering in the dry
brown hands. "*Tiens!* a thousand francs to establish your
hotel credit. You shall remain in Paris; continue at the Crillon in the comfort to which an American is accustomed.
Non, but you must allow me the honor of this small hospitality. Meantime, do nothing hasty.

"I regret the impetuosity of showing you such an item:
it was merely that I wished you to comprehend the delay.
One cannot expedite business, you must realize, in a country such as this, stranded always between the ruins of the
last war and the specter of the next one.

"Stay in Paris and do not worry about the *château.*
Tomorrow—no, the day after—let us confer. Certain
authorities can be consulted on this matter. Given a little
more time, Monsieur Shepherd, I am convinced Bertrand

et Frer will be able to negotiate a more than satisfactory arrangement on the Château de Feu."

But he had not stayed in Paris, and now, driving through storming blackness in the Forêt de Feu, with that dead man in the night behind him, he wished he had taken the lawyer's advice.

Only he hadn't believed in Monsieur Bertrand. He hadn't believed in that letter from the realty agent. He had stuffed the thousand francs into his pocket, nodded pleasantly, sauntered out to his car, and started out to visit the Château de Feu.

3

THE SILENT LAND

ONCE FREE OF the city, the morning's adventure was credible. Black veiled lady—stuffed-fox lawyer—haunted *château*—penniless heir—he had written such stuff a hundred times. Bill Shepherd sighed. Any editor would have rejected Monsieur Bertrand.

He let out the big Hisso. Traffic was sparse in the yellow July heat, but the breeze at sixty-five was cool.

Rationalize it or not, old Bertrand *had* been on pins and needles. Why all the throat-clearing and hedging about a mere real estate transaction? That letter, too, with its whispery insinuations of the sinister—maybe it needed confirmation at that.

Bill Shepherd put his hand into his pocket, half expecting the letter to have been imagined. No, there was the letter, and there he was, himself, thirty kilometers out of Paris, the white road ahead. An arrow told him to take a left turn for Amiens and points north, and in the noonday doldrum a village's roofs and treetops and steeple were set in his windshield like a painting. Better stop and tank up with petrol, if he was going on with this; but before he went further he wanted another look at that letter.

He pulled over to the curb of a sleepy village square;

opened the letter skeptically. There it was, all right—that
line about bodies found in the uncleared woods and "one
or two unexplained deaths" in the neighborhood. His eye
traveled on to the sentence: *Yet, perhaps as nowhere else in
France, the countryside there remains still overshadowed by
the last War*—and then he stiffened his stare on the type-
written page.

Slanted across the paper in his hand, as if summoned
there by the words themselves, was the thin gray shadow
of a bayonet.

Bill Shepherd looked up startled, and saw standing over
his car a giant soldier.

YOU BEGAN TO pass them in the first little villages north
of Paris; you didn't notice them at first, then you did. A
public square, a monument overlooking the curb, a granite Poilu standing guard above the cobbles, or a grieving
Mother France with a dying soldier in bronze cradled in
her arms.

> *Liberte, Egalite, Fraternite*
> *Pour la France—1914–1918*
> "To those who gave their lives…
> "To the valiant soldiers who died…
> "To the sons of this village who were slain…."

Above bronze-plated death lists like the pages of telephone directories, the stone gunners died or stood at
silent attention on their pedestals; bugle's blew a sound-
less Last Post; Mother France knelt down with drooping
Phrygian cap, her face buried in sorrowful hands. You saw
these mourning figures in every town, village and cross-

roads; they intruded in a traveler's consciousness like some endless series of advertising displays; and as the highway went further northward you saw what had sculpted them there.

In a landscape of checkerboard pastures and quaint French farms, geese and indolent bicycles and lazy wains— on a road that swept smoothly toward a cobalt horizon where slow clouds grazed like flocks of washed sheep— you passed (instead of highway billboards for soft drinks, gasolines and chewing gums) the pages of history. Tablets along the roadside recording a time marched by. Signposts that measured the highwater mark, the tidal inrush and ebb of a disaster that had come and gone and left those names in bronze on the village squares.

Here The Uhlans of Von Kluck Penetrated To Their Farthest Point. To Be Stopped By The Army Of Galliéni, 4 September, 1914. (Nineteen miles from Paris—that had been close!)

At This Bridge French Cavalry Of Manoury Withstood For Five Hours Three Prussian Guard Regiments Of The German Right Wing. (Blue and gray-green horsemen grappling over a trout stream.)

In The Orchard At The Right The Second British Army Corps Under General Smith-Dorrien Made Its Headquarters After The Retreat From Compiégne. (The Old Contemptibles had come!)

On The Night of 15 September '14, General Joffre Occupied The Farmhouse On The Left And Issued Orders For The Battle Of The Marne. (The turning of the tide!)

Along that highway to Amiens the names and dates were like the lingering echoes of yesterday's half-forgotten songs. Joffre. Von Kluck. The Old Contemptibles. Fragments of the past, left strewn along the roadside in the summer weeds. Von Bissing. Sir John French. The Blue Devils. 1914-1915. Years and names unremembered in America where they thought of the War as 1918 and a song by George M. Cohan.

But the echoes you heard along that Amiens turnpike were not *Over There* and *Where Do We Go From Here,* but the *Marseillaise, the Brabançonne, It's A Long Way To Tipperary,* and *Ein Feste Burg Ist Unser Gott.*

You heard the clack of cavalry, the summer's doze startled by the first shocks of iron thunder, the tramp, tramp, tramp of hobnails coming out of the east. The little markers along the highway were like bulletins crying the alarm, telling a story of French Red-legs in desperate retreat, refugees in panic-stricken migration, Tommies from across the Channel fumbling their khaki lines on unfamiliar roads. You could picture a sullen tide of gray rolling slowly, implacably across the landscape, like a flood of smoking lava, incinerating all before it as it came.

MEMORIES FOLLOWED THAT north-bound highway across France. Of miles of bayonets falling back before miles of machine guns. Of burning grain fields and shell-chopped trees. Rivers of helmets, banging artillery trains, cavalcades of ambulance, foraging parties, charging infantry, attack and counter-attack.

The captains and the kings had departed, but the landmarks remained—a broken mill with vines overgrowing its stalled wheel, a deserted roadside inn with the sky showing through its roof, farmhouse walls splotched with plaster patches that looked like adhesive on old wounds.

You were surprised to see the Germans had come so

far; and if you'd had a brother with the Allies, you might feel a surge of sentimental pride at the crossroads where an assault of Canadian Regulars had driven the Prussians back. You might wonder what colossal gall had brought that invasion goose-stepping here; what god-like conceit had given it permission.

Then at Amiens, where Bill Shepherd stopped for lunch, the echoes loudened. There was a cathedral spire moth-eaten by shrapnel holes, and he drove across a bridge marked *The River Somme*. He hadn't heard of the Somme, or thought of it, since a letter, one of the last, from Hugh. Odd to come across it now. Like dreaming of a place you'd seen before in a dream. He paused to read about it on a tablet at the bridge-head.

> The Battle of the Somme—July–November 1916. The British Supported by the French in an Attempt to Hurl the Germans from the Fields of Picardy. Stalemate of Trench Warfare was not Broken by this Tremendous Allied Effort— The Germans Holding Their Lines—The Allies Counting A Loss Of Half A Million Men.

1916, Red-Legs and the Old Contemptibles had gone; there were new names on the roadside plaques. Sir Douglas Haig and General Rawlinson. General Micheler and General Fayolle. Today the Somme was placid, ribboning soapy green across the landscape, but as you followed its bank beyond Amiens, you saw where monster cannon had once smashed its bridges and churned its channel to a boiling torrent. The furies of that tempest had left something more than bronze tablets in the landscape beyond Amiens.

Late in the afternoon, driving slowly along a ridge-top, Bill Shepherd came upon a vista such as he had never imagined. A road sign directed him to look at the view, and he stopped the car, and climbed out, shading his eyes to stare.

Before him spread Picardy—rolling miles of tableland nested with little pottery-roofed villages and meandered by winding pasture streams. Nowhere did the landscaping rise to obstruct the view; the eye seemed to carry as far as the Belgian border.

How still it was....

In all that horizon-bound distance of earth and sky nothing stirred. He had read somewhere that the Picards called their country the Silent Land, but this hush was something more than a phenomenon caused by a configuration of land-surface. It was as if the afternoon had paused in its waning, and time with space here remained suspended in a spell. Somewhere back there near Amiens a detour had turned him off the national highway, and he might have come to the edge of a country in mirage.

The stillness around him was that of a reflection in a mirror-quiet lake. Smoke stood becalmed in an erect blue tendril above the chimney of a far-seen cottage; southward on a ridge above the marshy greens of the Somme valley a miniature train moved motionlessly and soundlessly across the picture; far westward an airplane was a gnat-speck stationary in a high distillation of azure. The quiet deepened for the murmuring of bees, and the landscape was a painting by Corot.

What struck Bill Shepherd next was the brilliant color-work of flowered poppy fields emblazoned across the nearer meadows like red flannel blankets spread out to dry in the sun. And in the panorama beyond, what seemed a curious litter—at first glance, of odd-shaped rocks and boulders left scattered across the terrain as if by some long-ago glacier—and acres of white that, patchworked in pattern across the whole topography, looked like ranging expanses of unmelted snow.

A pointer at the roadside directed his attention to a pair of field binoculars mounted on a little platform nearby— *See the Battleground of the Somme—4 fr.* There was a map for tourists, and arrows pointing out the various sectors. Bill Shepherd peered through the glasses, inserted the coins, adjusted the directional finder, and brought the lenses into focus.

Then he saw the littered objects weren't glacial boulders, but monuments—cenotaphs, monoliths, marble pylons, granite sculptures in distant perspective diminished to the size of figurines. Monuments everywhere as far as the eye could see. And the acres of white were armies of men.

4

THE MARCHING DEAD

THE TROOPS! THEY came uphill from the direction of Albert Village and swept, company after company, across the pasture lands below him. They formed on a rise behind a stone barn at his right—*Headquarters Thirteenth British Army Corps*—and marched on toward a salient posted *Sausage Valley*. In the north they advanced along a highroad, platoon formation, moving in on Aveluy and Gommecourt, sweeping up the slopes of Beaumont Hamel. Eastward their ranks stood close about La Boiselle, Ovilliers, Mametz Wood.

More troops! Occupying the far banks of the River Ancre; extending their lines across the misty farm lands beyond. Gathered in companies along the road to Pozières; holding the turnpike going to Peronne.

Uphill and downdale they traversed the fields, debauched from sleepy woods, massed along country lanes.

What names they wore, and what actions they engaged. He consulted the map which diagrammed their intricate battle positions.

There were the Black Watch and the Gordon Highlanders. The Sixth Dragoon Guards, and a battalion of the Ulster Division. The London Territorials. The Connaught

Rangers. The First South-African Infantry. The Inniskillens. The South Wales Borderers. The King's Royal Rifles. The Manchester Guard.

The British were supported by battalions of the French—Fayolle's First Army Corps—companies of Lorrainers, Zouave detachments, Colonial Cavalry, Tirailleurs, Blue Devils, troops all the way from Arras to Avignon.

Sighted through the binoculars, their formations were seen to be orderly, their ranks ruled in precise parade, their flanking obliques and advance stations in perfect military alignment. Following their battle lines, Bill Shepherd could make out their dugouts and earthworks, weedy trenches running zigzag across the meadows, slopes where great shell holes had been gouged, mine craters, patches of charred timber, barren stretches of No Man's Land where hurricanes of shellfire had left a soil of loose ore. He focused the binoculars on an abandoned village—a clutter of broken walls and mounds of gray ash—and on a ridge to the east he found the German line.

The German emplacements were strangely labeled—*The Zollern Redoubt—The Schwaben Redoubt.* Holding these heights were battalions of the Prussian Guard, Bavarians, Potsdammers, Magdeburgers. 10,000 Guards Fusiliers, 18,000 Badeners. 24,000 of the Lehr Regiment. Company after company of the German Fifth Division. A battalion of the famous Cockchafers. The crack troops of Brandenburg. Their High Command was not present, but their names were recorded on the battle-map. Ludendorf. Von Quast. Von Gallwitz. Sixt von Arnim.

On those distant slopes Bill Shepherd could make out concrete gun-pits, steel-roofed pillboxes, the brush-

screened parapets of deep fortifications. The map made
note of these fortifications extending for miles, but it was
not the magnitude of these Martian engineerings that
impressed Bill Shepherd. The limitless numbers of those
men out there—!

There were thousands massed within range of his binoculars, countless thousands out of range in the rolling meadows of Picardy beyond.

In the foreground you could make them out as platoons,
regiments, battalions—shoulder to shoulder on parade—
each one erect, face front, the uniform twin of the next. But
stepping back from a pair of high-powered field glasses,
you could not find them with the naked eye. In distance
their ranks merged into fused legions, their numbers
blurred into multitudes.

In the presence of this vast and silent host, Bill Shepherd felt hollow and queer inside. Involuntarily he took off
his hat, and as he did so there was a faint far muttering in
the east where some clouds had blundered together, and
there came to his mind a passage from *The Shropshire Lad.*

> *On the idle hill of summer,*
> *Sleepy with the sound of streams,*
> *Far I hear the steady drummer,*
> *Drumming like a noise in dreams.*

> *Far and near and low and louder,*
> *On the roads of earth go by,*
> *Dear to friends and food for powder,*
> *Soldiers marching all to die.*

But those soldiers out there were no longer marching.

The acres of white were acres of little white crosses, and a signpost in a near-by bed of poppies named the rendezvous. *The Red Zone.*

"Killed," a voice behind Bill Shepherd pronounced somberly. "Two hundred thousand of them, *monsieur.* All of them killed."

BILL SHEPHERD TURNED with a start; that sermon-toned voice might have spoken out of the air. An old peasant had approached him without making a sound.

Posed beside the car, he made a shadowy watcher in waning sunlight, bearded and weather-beaten. He was faded and bleached, and his dimmed eyes dreamed at the landscape. He might have been regarding Infinity, the shore the other side of Jordan. Bill Shepherd was a stranger, and the oldest inhabitant had paused to explain the Silent Land.

"All killed, you comprehend. All of them. All."

He spoke like the Last Survivor of a country whose population had passed away. His eyes musing, his head silver-haloed in sunshine like the hoary blossom of an autumn dandelion that might at any moment become detached and float away, the old man did not look quite mortal.

"Can you see them out there?" he quavered at Bill Shepherd. "Do you realize how many there are? *Non,* you do not, for I see you are young—you would not remember— you were not here. There are over two hundred thousand in the fields out there, *monsieur.* Over two hundred thousand—all killed."

"Do you remember them, *grandpère?*" Bill Shepherd asked. "Do you remember them, when they were here?"

He was afterward to recall how the faded eyes gave him a strange look. "When they were here?" Then, making a sweeping gesture with a bloodless, almost transparent hand, "But they are still here, *monsieur.* Still here. You can see them out there—those that never went home."

One arm outstretched, the old man wheeled and pointed like a creaky weather-vane, naming off the villages and interlaced roads, pointing out the actions fought, identifying the regiments by number and name as a general might have conned that battle-front.

"I used to be a guide," he told Bill Shepherd. "The tourists who came here in the first years after the War, I would take them over these battlefields. They would steal the little flags from the graves and scatter picnic luncheons among the memorials. Today they prefer the Paris boulevards. They have forgotten the last War, preparing for the next. But I know that country out there by every *hectare.* I was here when the Germans arrived, and I was here to see the great Battle of the Somme when the British joined with the French to drive them out."

Eyes rheumed with the mists of reminiscence, he stared off across the sleeping landscape and droned on, describing the movements of the battle. Bill Shepherd listened. Some vague urgency kept tugging at the back of his thoughts, reminding him he had come here for another reason, but the old man's voice was part of a spell which seemed to be holding him, hat in hand, with the afternoon at a standstill.

"It was Nineteen-sixteen, the First of July," the old man was droning. "For a year the Allies had been bringing up their forces from the West. For a year those Germans on the eastern heights had been digging in. There had been little battles along this front, but the flatness of Picardy smothers a bit of rifle fire, and that morning of the First there was scarcely a sound. *Bleu!* All at once the British cannon let go; for thirty miles from here to the horizon it was like an earthquake. That was no ordinary barrage, *monsieur.* The big guns spoke in one continuous roar—all day—all night—a bombardment that lasted eight days. For eight days the British poured a tempest of steel at those eastern heights where you see the German line. Woods, hills, villages on that ridge were blown to atoms. Trenches were swept away as if by a giant broom. Ah, that was a terrible bombardment that began the Battle of the Somme."

"You saw it?" Bill Shepherd wondered.

"And have been half deaf ever since," the old man nodded. "My farm was on this highroad where we stand, and I watched it from here. For eight days I watched that bombardment, and then the curtain of fire was raised and the Allied advance began. Guns. Tanks. Lorries. Men. All those hundreds of regiments you see out there came streaming across those meadows like lines of ants. Can you picture that wonderful charge, *monsieur?* Look at them out there!"

THE OLD MAN pivoted and stretched a bony finger. "Observe those columns moving east. In places it was so clear I could see the British and French officers trotting at the heads of their assault troops. They carried those little villages you see below. They took the woods with running bayonet assaults, and swept the German outposts before them. *Non,* they walked right up to that bridge where you see the German line. And then—"

The old man paused to shake his head, petting his beard with thin yellow fingers, his gaze wandering the farther slopes.

"And what then, *grandpère?*" Bill Shepherd asked.

"Mon dieu!" the old one rasped. "When the Allied charge reached that German line, that whole ridge burst into one sheet of solid flame. The slopes of this countryside are chalk, do you see?—and for a year those Boche invaders had been digging in like beavers. Those slopes they honey-combed with tunnels that go underground like coal mines. That whole ridge was an underground fortress.

"Our Maginot Line of today is nothing in comparison, for it was dug in a time of peace, and the Germans dug those tunnels under fire in our country at a time of war. They had passages fifty feet underground. Their cannon were hidden in the hillside. Out there you can still behold their famous *Wünderwerke*—like an underground Gibral-tar with deep corridors and concrete-walled galleries and cellars where the men were hidden. Ah, Fritz was snug down there, and save for those that went mad from the noise, that British barrage scarcely bothered the Boche at all.

"Eh Bien," the old man continued after a head-shake, "our guns had smashed the German trenches, but they had not crushed the fortifications in those slopes. The Boches came out of their concrete holes like a million fiends out of Hell, and can you see how those armies on the lower fields were butchered? Can you see them flung back?—attacking again?—flung back once more?

"For days that battle continued. For weeks. Picardy, *monsieur*, became an ocean of smoke and flame. The Allied armies were waves dashing day after day against that eastern ridge. The German lines were gray rocks."

A fat bumblebee buzzed past Bill Shepherd's ankles, and there was a smell faintly flavored with clover in the air, but Bill Shepherd was not aware of a summer landscape.

"The killed," the old man whispered, "piled up like autumn leaves. Do you see that hill to the northward marked by the bronze statue of a caribou?—that is where an entire regiment from Newfoundland was wiped out in three hours.

"Off there toward Auchonvillers and Montauban the bodies lay so thick you could walk across them all the way to Belgium. Thousands of British. Thousands of French. Thousands of Germans. *Le bon dieu* alone could count the slain in that massacre.

"The battle went on and on. For weeks. For months. A terrible stench smothered the air. Those meadows out there were deserts. The smoke of the guns made a fog across the sun, their flames set fire to the nights, their roaring shook this Silent Land.

"The worst fighting of all was in this sector, here, called the Red Zone, between those villages you see yonder—Contalmaison and Thiepval. Five deep the slain were lying in those woods—do you see those woods at the end of that wagon-road down there?"

CONTALMAISON; THIEPVAL! BILL SHEPHERD came back into the present with an exclamation. The Château de Feu was located half way between Contalmaison and Thiepval!

He followed the old man's pointing finger with his eye, fixed a stare on a dark patch of timber visible several miles beyond the rooftops of a distant village. Woods were noticeable in a landscape where most of the timber had been swept away—such thickets as there were did not obtrude on the prairie-like vista—he discerned that that distant acreage of greenery must be second-growth.

So that was the Forêt de Feu!

He thought of Hugh somewhere out there among those silent multitudes, and with another mental recoil he was reminded of the office of Bertrand et Frer and the cryptic letter that had brought him out here from Paris. He could not help grimacing. *Ugly local reputation! Sinister occurrences!* Well, he could understand that real estate agent's letter now. One or two unexplained deaths! More like it if that agent had said one or two hundred thousand unexplained deaths! The whole countryside of Picardy was nothing but a vast graveyard. Centered in the heart of this No Man's Land of World War cemeteries and battlefield monuments, the *château* in that unrehabilitated forest must be something like one tomb in a necropolis.

He drew a sharp breath and tugged on his hat. If he wanted to reach the place before dark, he'd better get a move on. Twilight had come stealthily, coloring the air to burgundy, hazing the farther meadows. There was a hint of rain in the stillness. Blue-black clouds had overcast the east, their upper crests red-tinted.

"*Granpère,* I've got to be going. Can I give you a lift?"

"A thousand thanks, *monsieur,* but my cottage is just over the hill. You are wondering about the traffic? But this is a holiday, *monsieur.* The countryfolk have gone to celebrate. There is a fair at Guillemont."

He could hardly explain a feeling of relief; save for this old man, he had detected no sign of life in that sweeping vista, and he was somehow glad to learn that it was a holiday which had gathered the population elsewhere.

"Then I'll be driving on." He nodded. "It's almost dark, and I'll have to hurry. Tell me, *grandpère.* That wagon-road across the meadows, there—will that take me to the Forêt de Feu? I'm on my way to the Château de Feu."

And then came the words that were to whisper through his memory as he drove through the night-black woods where the dead man lay in the poppies behind him.

"The Forêt de Feu—!" The old Frenchman had rounded, aghast, his eyes grown to lakes of fright. "But I would not go into those woods at night, *monsieur!* For a million francs—for ten million, I would not go! Because the Forêt de Feu is in the Red Zone, *monsieur*—and the dead have not died in the Red Zone. The World War is not yet over, *monsieur.* The Battle of the Somme is still going on, and the soldiers who died in the Red Zone are still fighting it, and their front line is in the Forêt de Feu!"

5

BATTLEGROUND

THERE HAD BEEN a rumble of thunder then. The light ebbed westward, and the sky in the east was dark. Bill Shepherd was aware of a sudden breeze against his face, a cool drop in the temperature. Poppies at the roadside were rustling.

"What do you mean by that, *grandpère?* The Battle of the Somme is still going on! The dead are still fighting it in the Forêt de Feu!"

Even as he spoke, then, the words had sounded ridiculous—there on that open highroad, his car parked close at hand.

"You can see those armies out there," the old man was pointing. "Armies of those killed in the Battle of the Somme. Armies of the dead, you will say. In their graves, you will say, and that battle was twenty-three years ago, and now all is quiet on the Western Front."

The old man shook his gauzy head. "But all is not so quiet on this front, *monsieur.* If you go out there among those monuments you will see the inscriptions in the stone—*These Dead Shall Never Die! C'est ça,* and that is the truth, *monsieur*—they have not died.

"Will you believe if I say those soldiers out there do not

stay in their graves? Will you believe if I say they leave their graves after dark and come to life across those battlefields? What if I tell you I have seen them, then—soldiers without arms or legs—officers torn to pieces—faceless horsemen flitting through the trees—those World War dead who rise at night to fight again. What if I tell you I have seen them, *monsieur,* still fighting the Battle of the Somme—!"

The old man was crazy, of course.

Bill murmured a kindly, "Yes, yes, *grandpère,* I'd like to hear more, but I've got to be going!" and started for his car. But the ancient gave a windy cry, and hooked him by the arm.

"*Monsieur* does not believe? *Monsieur* will not listen? But you are a stranger here, *monsieur.* You do not know the Forêt de Feu. That *château* where you are going is in the very heart of the Forêt de Feu. And those woods are in the heart of the Red Zone. The blood has never dried here in the Red Zone, I tell you. There was too much of it—too much blood!—and the dead—!"

Bill Shepherd said flatly, "Please, *grandpère,* I really haven't time to listen to your ghost stories—"

"Ghosts?" the old man cried. "Ghosts, you call them? Perhaps they are ghosts, indeed—the ghosts of the soldiers who were slain. None the less, I have seen them. It is said they come out of the poppies, monsieur—the poppies that have sprung up out of the soldiers' bones—the poppies that have in their veins the soldiers' blood! If you do not believe me, ask the inn keeper at Contalmaison. Ask the blacksmith in the valley. Ask Père Anselm, the curé in Thiepval Village—would a priest tell a lie?—*non,* but ask old Mother Landru at the very *château* where you say you are going!"

"Mother Landru?" Half way to the car. Bill Shepherd wheeled in dismay.

The old man nodded fiercely. "The soldiers leave their graves, I tell you. It is said the poppies breathe for them by day so they may rise and walk by night. I am not the only one who has seen them. Those others have seen them. And we who live here, on still nights we have heard the call of bugles—the echo of bugles where no bugles have been blown. We have heard gunfire, *monsieur*, where no guns have been since the War. We have seen the soldiers in the dark out there—the Poilus—the British Tommies—the Boches!"

SURE. A FOG-WREATHED hollow of any old battleground could be the gathering of a thousand spirits. Echo of some vagrant huntsman's horn became a ghostly taps. Thunderclaps at night made spectral artillery; swamp-lights shone as flickers in the hands of phantom signalmen; a wandering herd of cows created apparitional cavalry.

Bill Shepherd growled, "I must ask Madame Landru about these myths."

"Myths!" the old man glared. "Villagers found dead on the edge of those cursed woods out there—are they myths? A girl discovered with a bullet in her throat in that timber where the fighting was thickest—is that a myth? Is it a myth to find a child blown to pieces in a shellhole of twenty years ago?"

Something tightened in Bill Shepherd's throat. That letter from the Agency Honneteau, Carpentier et Jacques Gonjon had hinted at witchery like this. He thought aloud,

"I suppose for the next fifty years they'll keep finding the remains of refugees killed around here during the War."

"The ones of whom I speak were not killed during the War," came the wheezy voice. "But last year they were killed. And the girl this spring. And the child only last month."

"Last month?" That was too recent for comfort.

"You can see it in the papers, *monsieur*. It happened not a mile from the Forêt de Feu. Some called it murder—a child killed in a crater where no feet but hers had walked. The police came and went, after scouring the fields; they did not know the answer. But we of this countryside know. We have seen the dead soldiers; heard the midnight guns. She was killed in the battle that is still going on—by the dead who have their front line in the Forêt de Feu—"

A black wing of cloud had extended across the eastern ridge, and the dusk was darkening. Bill Shepherd could barely discern the brown ribbon of the wagon-road that crossed the meadows below and dwindled in the direction of the woods. A drop of rain splashed on his wrist, and he turned to ask the old man a question; was startled to find himself at the roadside alone.

Rounding with in-pulled breath, he saw the graybeard some distance up the road, his back bowed under the wagon-pole, moving off in the dusk. He hurried to the car and busily put up the top. Then, stowed behind the wheel, he felt better.

He sent the Hisso charging down the highway, and when he came to the intersection of the dirt road, he turned deliberately off the macadam and took the wagon-track across the open fields. Apparently the road was little used, for the ruts were weedy, the car bumped and jounced and loose stones rattled under the fenders.

It skirted the village that he judged was Contalmaison, and sloped down into a valley shrubbed with willow. The car passed several new cottages that looked, however, as if they had been deserted; clattered over a plank bridge; curved around several granite monuments, and then began passing the fields of crosses. The road dipped along over the meadows, and the little white markers went by in a blur.

There would be a cemetery, then a field of weed or poppies, a coppice of young trees, another cemetery.

Bill Shepherd tried to keep his eye on the road-ruts, but the burial plots intruded on his consciousness at every turn.

The date had stopped here—he could read it on these monuments, 1916. He had driven back into the Past, to another Time.

NINE MILES WERE gone on the dashboard meter when dark woods loomed suddenly ahead, and flanking the dirt road where it entered the woods he saw another regiment of crosses—Canadians. He slowed the car, wondering if his brother's grave could be among then. The evening queerly lightened.

There were five sharp thunder-explosions in the sky; a dash of rain struck the windshield; water fell in an opalescent cloudburst. Lightning played across the sky, and it was as if the whole landscape came into action; seen through sheets of rain all those far-flung battle lines were on the move, company after company advancing over the fields, sweeping down the slopes converging on the woods ahead.

The illusion lasted only for that recurrence of twilight; as abruptly as it had broken, the cloudburst was over; rain dissolved into a drizzle and the deluged evening blotted into night.

Bill Shepherd snapped on his headlamps as he turned the Hisso into the road through the dripping, black trees, and he had not gone a mile on that woodland road before he regretted his decision.

This forest had known a blight. Masked by the greenery of saplings and aspen, its ruin had not been discernible from a distance; now Bill Shepherd found himself in a fire-blackened wilderness, an Aceldema of dead and shattered trees, thickets of fallen timber as dismal as a Georgia swamp. The undergrowth was a jungle in which charred and leafless trunks thrust out the stubs of amputated limbs.

Felled oaks lay along the roadside like prostrate giants. Everywhere the trees were down. There was a smell of earth and leaf-mold and rotting wood, as the road wound and struggled through that desolation of mangled timber. The headlights discovered in the underbrush *an* inconceivable litter of rubbish—wagon wheels, sandbags, scraps of twisted steel and punctured sheet-iron, wire stanchions, bits of charred harness, lengths of chain, snarls of barbed wire, bent iron stakes.

In a grove of shattered pine the junk of a rusted Howitzer stood like the bones of a dinosaur.

The old man's ghost story had not seemed too fantastic on that road in the Forêt de Feu, and Bill Shepherd had been hunting for a place to turn around when he came on that peasant in the poppy bed—that dead man strangled by a murderer who had left no visible track.

6

GIRL IN THE DARK

THE DRIZZLE THINNED into mist, and the road, as he drove in panic, grew worse. Underbrush and charred trees seemed to drift in weaving cobwebs of vapor; the road was befogged; and the car-lights dimmed, their yellow rays diffused by the sluggish steam.

Deliberately he slowed the car; forced his lungs to breathe normally. That dead man back there in the poppies couldn't hurt him, and whoever had killed that peasant would have hiked for cover long ago. Was he going to let an afternoon among War memorials and a crack-potted old man play on his nerves? He steadied his fingers and lit a cigarette and drew a sedative inhale of smoke.

These woods had belonged to his father, and his mother used to come here on European holidays. This was a private road. His road. He waved the cigarette.

As for that dead man, as soon as he reached the *château* he'd telephone the nearest *gendarmerie*. Murder would out. The killer's tracks, naturally, had been obliterated by that cloudburst, and the murderer had been smart—knowing the legend of the haunted poppies, he'd laid his victim out in a poppy bed, figuring to terrify any passersby.

Bill Shepherd felt better, bluffing himself into his normal

frame of mind. The bluff became easier in proportion to the mileage between his car and that body back there. He turned on the car radio; should have thought of it before. The lighted dial brought him into the present and changed his mood. Give him a torch singer from Paris, and all the haunts would be dispelled.

But Paris was slurred, unintelligible with interference. Too much static for GBS. Holland and Belgium were off the air, and DXR Germany didn't come in. As he twiddled at the dial, the radio went dead. But he drove on, whistling tunelessly. Somehow, fiddling with the radio had given him back his confidence.

What a setting for a story all this would make. That dusty lawyer. This abandoned forest. Murdered peasant. Haunted countryside. Now if he were writing this thing, he would come pretty soon to a big limousine stuck in the mud. The plot needed a beautiful frightened girl.

Rounding a bend in the wagon-track, Bill Shepherd jammed the brakes in staring surprise.

There was the girl!

SHE STOOD IN the ruts directly in the path of his head-lamps, and her car was tilted in a ditch at the roadside. The car, an antiquated Citroën coupé, wasn't exactly a limousine, and the girl wasn't exactly beautiful or frightened; but, posed there in the mist with the night behind her and the mangled forest close around, she was certainly picturesque.

Her eyes were shiny black under the brim of a rain-soaked Leghorn hat, and Bill Shepherd saw pale determination in a tight-lipped face. She was young. A dark cape clung to her shoulders; her dress was moulded damply to her knees; her slim legs were notable, shapely in black silk.

Her shoes were ankle-deep in the mire, and there was a blunt-nosed Mauser automatic in her hand. She aimed the gun at the Hisso's windshield, and Bill Shepherd snapped off the engine as he heard her cry of command.

"Get out!" The order was given in French.

He thought, "I'll be damned!" and got out.

"Come toward me. Advance with the hands in the air."

Arms uplifted, he moved toward her.

"Stand in front of your car-lights where I can see your face."

He obeyed, nerves tingling under the aim of the gun. Yet, oddly enough, he wasn't afraid of the girl. He had a vague feeling he'd seen her before. But she wasn't the woman he had seen that morning leaving the office of old Bertrand.

"Now," she said in a level voice, her dark eyes aimed with the same disconcerting directness of the gun, "who are you?"

"Funny," he told her in English, "I've been wondering that, myself."

A fierce little V came between her brows; then her firm lips spoke slowly, handling English with a husky accent. "Do not jest with me, *monsieur*. What are you doing in these woods? I demand your identity."

"Who am I? I wish I knew. I've spent years trying to find out."

"Don't be childish, please," the girl commanded sharply. "I am in deadly earnest."

"So am I," Bill Shepherd heard himself saying. "Shepherd's the name. William Shepherd. Call me Bill."

"What are you doing here?"

"Haven't you heard of me? Your failure to recognize

my name and cry, 'Oh, where do you get your plots?' just proves how unknown I am. Well, I'm a writer. Author of *Footprints in the Dark* and *The Spider in the Easter Lily.*" He paused because mention of footprints reminded him of the poppy bed where they should have been. He pulled a breath, looking at the girl. "Anyway, that's what I used to do for a living, so save your time if you're after a generous pocketbook. She who steals my purse steals trash."

The girl said angrily, "I warn you, *monsieur,* I will shoot if—"

"It's in my right hand inner pocket, *mademoiselle,* but it isn't worth taking."

Under the dripping hatbrim her eyes went narrow. "I give you one more chance to explain who you are!"

He sighed, "Very well, I'll begin at the beginning. William Shepherd. Hundred and eighty pounds. White. American. Thirty-one. Unmarried. Does that tell you everything?"

"It does not tell me what you are doing in these woods."

"That's a long story, and I wasn't sure you'd be interested. It begins back in the States where I made my living writing stories. It's nice work if you can get it, as the saying goes, but one morning I woke up to find I was fed up with it."

He grinned at the blankness on her face, and was amused it an impulse to tell her something of the truth about himself. Talk relieved a tightness in his stomach, and the girl was becoming confused.

"Fed up means being sick of everything. To use a hackneyed term—tired of it all. A sense of personal futility, a feeling that nothing you've been up to was quite worthwhile. Do you understand?"

"I do not. Keep up the hands. Higher."

"I'll try to be lucid. My father was an unexpected genius who invented a gadget for coal mines and suddenly became an industrialist worth ten million dollars. My mother was—grand. My older brother, Hugh, signed up with the Canadians just after the *Lusitania*—believed in Democracy, good sportsmanship and Belgium's rights, and got blown to bits somewhere around here because of it."

Bill Shepherd shifted muddy feet, and eased his numbling shoulders, holding the girl's eyes with his own mocking gaze.

"That's the family tree. Good American oak. People who had faith in things and believed in what they were doing."

HE FROWNED AT the ground, then, looking up, saw the girl's grip had tightened on the pistol. He went on hastily: "As for me, I tried to write the Great American Novel, but it all turned into a lot of words. I found I'd written hundreds of such words, so many blanks on paper. The only thing left for me to write was mystery stories."

"I want to know what you are doing here," the girl panted.

"I'm trying to tell you. I wrote a lot of mystery novels, and then got fed up. I wanted to see life, you might say. If words didn't mean anything, what did? I wanted to do something that meant something—do it seriously, zestfully, importantly. Anyway—I went broke. That's why I'm here in these woods. My father left me a French *château*. My Paris lawyer told me this morning the *château* isn't even saleable. He also hinted that this forest has an evil reputation, and an old man I met this afternoon on the road told me it's full of ghosts. He didn't say the ghost would be a charming girl waiting to meet me with a Mauser pistol to ask me what business I had in my own woods. I'm on my way to the Château de Feu."

"Château de Feu!" the girl breathed, watching him.

"And since this is my own land until the government confiscates it, I'm inclined to ask what *you* are doing here?"

Grabbing out, he caught her hand on the gun-butt, twisted, flung her around against the fender of his car, pinned her body with his hip, and levered her wrist upward until the pistol-muzzle touched the underside of her chin.

"Stand quiet!" he snapped, savagely authoritative. "Stand still, or that gun will blast your pretty head off. It's your turn, now, and begin at the beginning. Who are *you?*"

In the grip of his fingers her hand seemed tiny, but it required a bit of muscle to force her wrist. Tears welling to her eyes might have called for gentlemanly deference under other circumstances. She whispered, "Gabrielle. Gabrielle Gervais."

"Good," he nodded down at her. "I like the name Gabrielle. I hope I can like the French girl who answers to it. Hadn't you better relax now, and let go of that gun before it shoots somebody. Nice girls don't carry big guns," he mocked. "Or maybe it's just an old French custom."

She panted, "Please, *m'sieur.* I—I only wanted a ride."

"They thumb them in my country."

"I was not going to shoot you, *m'sieur.*"

"You're the one I'm worrying about."

"*Monsieur,* you are hurting—"

"There!" The weapon dropped from her wrenched lingers, went *sluff* in the mud at his shoes. He stooped with a sigh, picked it up, stared at its calibre and stowed it into his side pocket. "You see this is private property, *mademoiselle*. No hunting allowed, at least from now on. Cigarette?"

She took one, staring ruefully at the mud where the gun had splashed.

Her eyes refused to look at him across the flaring match; he was only aware of dark lashes curled over hot-flushed cheeks and trembling disappointment on her mouth. She leaned back against the fender, rubbing her wrenched wrist, smoking, panting a little, blinking wet lashes.

"I told you, *m'sieur.* I—I only wanted a ride." Her chin puckered. "And I was lost, *m'sieur.* My car—you see it is off the road. In the mud. It is late at night and I—I was frightened."

Bill Shepherd grinned approval. The technique now called for an appeal to his masculine valor. Girl on lonely road in forest late at night. Lost and frightened. Didn't mean any harm with that 9-mm. automatic. Just a nice girl who had driven off the road and wanted a ride. If this ran true to form her next sentence would tell him she had no place to spend the night. This was Plot B, Angle 15-C. The follow-up on that would be an appeal to sex.

"I—I lost the main highroad to Guillemont—and I—I came through these woods on the wrong turning. In the rainstorm I went into that miserable ditch. *Oui,* I have been sitting there for an hour waiting for someone to come along. In the storm I did not dare walk off alone." She swallowed a sob. "You see the condition of my car, *m'sieur.*"

NO FRAUD ABOUT that. The Citroën was badly mired. All the king's horses would have a job hauling it out of that bog. She said wistfully, "I was so happy to hear your motor coming, *m'sieur.* But then I did not dare stop a strange car

at night. I thought—I thought if I just showed the gun—
why, the driver would not just go right by—and afterward
I could explain—"

"You could explain you had no place to go for the night."

"How did you know that, *m'sieur?*"

"Your uncle turned you out of the house—"

"My uncle? *Non, non,* my uncles were killed in the War,
m'sieur. It was my father—he—" She faced him in white
alarm. "My father did not send you after me, *m'sieur?*"

He scowled. "Not exactly. But why did Papa Gervais—
did I get the name?—turn you out? Did he say, 'Never
darken my door again?'"

"He did not turn me out," the girl said fiercely. She
stared off into the guttering boscage, pushed back a strand
of hair from her cheek, faced him with a sigh of decision.
"I suppose I must tell you, then. I was to be married this
morning. It was all arranged. The cathedral at Amiens.
The guests. The—the bridal veil. Hundreds of gifts. The
wedding breakfast—"

"Ah." It almost made him uncomfortable. "Plot B, Angle
15. The wicked Duke. Handsome, dissipated, but very rich.
You did not love him."

She looked at him sharply. Quickly rearranged an
expression of appeal. *"M'sieur* the American understands,
I see, something of the conventionalities of France. My
father is most conventional, *m'sieur.* Most. He insisted I
marry this man. *Non,* Philippe has not a title, but he is—
how do you say?—stuffy. Horses. That is Philippe. All he
ever thinks of. So it was not that I did not love Philippe—I
could not have even become used to him—it was that
Philippe did not love me. All he ever loved was horses."

"I see. A sportsman."

"*Non, m'sieur. Un boucher.* A dealer in the *Halles Centrales.* Steaks. Roasts for the butcher shops. Horse-meat, *m'sieur.*"

Bill Shepherd swallowed. "Ate his own nags, I suppose."

"So. But a man the most respectable. Terribly respectable. Rich. There is no better business in France. Only—"

He sighed for her, "There was someone else—"

"You mean—it was that I was in love with some other man?" She shook her head plaintively. *"Pas du tout!* Not that. Only I wanted some man to love me—not just marry me because it was time he married and we had known each other since childhood and my father was highly respectable." Her eyes looked up into his. "You understand?"

"Oh, sure."

"You believe?"

"Every word."

She held out a begging hand. "Then you will give me back my gun?"

"As soon as you tell me the truth."

Exasperation made her scowl. "But I have told you everything."

He said flatly, "Not quite. For instance, you said you ran away from a wedding this morning in Amiens. You drove all day and got lost. But you are only within half a day's drive of Amiens. Also your car has a license plate with a Paris number. Next, you didn't ask me for a ride when you stopped me, you demanded my name and future intentions. And lastly, do French girls running away from bridegrooms, even horsy ones, carry nine-millimeter automatics in their handbags?"

She threw down the cigarette, and faced him. Her

manner changed. Her mouth was firm again. Her eyes were defiant. She shrugged, *"Eh bien*. Take me to the police."

He shook his head, thoughtfully looking toward her car.

Alarm in her voice was real. "You are not going to leave me—"

"No. It's going to rain again. I'd hardly leave you stuck in these woods; the wolf might come along. You were going to spend the night at grandmother's house—"

"I told you I had no place to spend the night."

He decided, "I can take you with me to the Château de Feu. You can telephone a taxi from there."

"M'sieur,"—she was smoothing her dress at the hips as she picked her way through puddles for the car—*"m'sieur* is too kind."

"Not at all, *mademoiselle.*" He unlimbered in the low leather seat, kicked the gears, twisted the wheel and eased the car to a purring start. A dead man on the road. A forest accursed. A haunted house ahead. A mysterious girl. Where did the plot go from here?

7

THE FORGOTTEN OF GOD

HE COULD FEEL the girl's eyes on his profile, covertly studying, but when he switched his glance to catch her at it she was frowning at one mud-caked ankle, wriggling her foot in the shoe. The car slid in a greasy turn and splashed through wet grass, and he pulled it out of a stall just in time. Rain slashed in another cloudburst through the trees. Water trickled through leaks in the windshield cowling and spurted up between the floorboards. His elbow, negligent on the doorsill, was soaked.

He was wet and uncomfortable, and when he cranked up the window the car filled with steam and dampness and a smell of gasoline and cigarette smoke.

He was uneasy again. He drove in nervous caution, juggling the car in ruts of paste, listening to the violent rain beating the hood and roof and windshield, the splash of water coming down; straining his eyes to help the half-blinded headlights find the swamped wagon-track.

He knew he ought to be thinking fast, but he didn't quite know what he could do about anything, and for the next several minutes it wanted all his attention to keep the car floundering on its way. On a turn where the tires clawed furiously to keep going, he saw something loom up among black brushwood; something that looked like a tank left there to rot, and he would have stopped to examine it if the car wouldn't have sunk to the doors.

The road here seemed to be turning into quicksand; he raced the engine to get on. What a road this must have been during the War.

He could imagine troops moving up on a night like this. Not just one night, but night after night, night after night. Drowning in mud. Drowning in rain. Drowning under heavy packs. Drowning under terrors of shellfire. 10,000 men. 30,000 men. 100,000 men. Would he ever get those death-lists out of his mind?

He said aloud: "It makes me feel small."

The girl's voice asked, "What is that?"

He kept his eyes on the road ahead, annoyed that she was there. "You wouldn't understand." Angrily: "You're living on velvet, babe. I'm living on velvet. A whole lot of smart young people like us are living on velvet these days. When you think of all the men who died on some rotten road out here—died right here in these woods, suffering the tortures of the damned!—so that people like you and me could motor out here tonight and cut silly capers in comparative comfort—" he broke off for loss of words.

She said in a low voice, "You are a strange American, *m'sieur.*"

He said: "Not so strange that I won't wring your neck if you try to snatch that gun out of my pocket. I don't mean to scare you. Self-preservation is the first law of life. What I can't understand is what induced all these soldiers to throw their lives away as they did. What nullified their instinct for self-preservation and induced them to come out here and die in droves like herds of butchered cattle?"

"They died for France," the girl said.

He snapped, "What did the Germans die for? The British? The Americans? What? For the Kaiser? For King and Country? For Democracy? Don't you see those are just a lot of words?"

"They are ideals," the girl said quietly. "I think the thousands who gave their lives in the World War did it because they thought it would make a better world for humanity to live in."

"Who's humanity?" he gestured impatiently. "Humanity, dear lady, is you and I. Well, do we thank those fellows who bled to death out here for us? We give them two minutes of silence every year on Armistice Day—is that gratitude? But today we're falling for the same old stock words and blah. Shouting the same empty phrases. Sharpening our weapons to make the same old mistakes. I don't wonder the peasants around here think these dead are turning over in their graves."

The girl beside him murmured, "You are funny. You are not quite sure what it is, but underneath you are angry about something."

Queer girl. She had something there: he *was* angry about something. Only, now that she spoke of it, he knew. Or thought he did.

He was talking to keep his mind off that corpse with the finger-printed throat. Queer how one corpse could be more frightening than a million. Millions blurred into impersonal mathematics—like the Chinese. You could only grasp little problems, like the problem of telephon-

ing the police, and what to do with a French girl, and how
to pay your taxes.

For the rest, you just kept jockeying a nervous wheel,
watching a shiny road, breathing in a fetid compound of
gasoline and cigarette smoke.

"And here we are!" he muttered as a dim gleam of lights
developed in the mists ahead. "Welcome to the Château
de Feu!"

HE FOUND HIMSELF turning the car up a muddy driveway hedged with thick undergrowth and the tall stumps
of burnt trees. The car passed through broken gateposts
guarded by two headless stone lions, and waded in gluey
mire around a weed-grown terrace. He glimpsed the
remains of what had once been a formal garden—overturned urns and ruptured statuary and a rubbish-filled
fountain where the marble water nymph lay overthrown on
her pedestal—and then, without realizing he had reached
his destination, the car was under a shadowy porte-cochère.

He cut the engine, and climbed out. The place looked
worse than he had pictured it.

Looming dark walls overgrown with vines, rank vines
that clambered up the masonry like camouflage, weaving
their arms around cornices and ledges, eating their way
between the granite facing-blocks, climbing to the roof like
jungle-parasites, covering the windows. His eye followed
the roof-line to the silhouette of a Norman tower; he made
out dark bastions and a crumbled wing; but the building
was wrapped in ivy and night, formless as a background
in a dream, and the only light was a leak of yellow coming
through a vine-screened lower window overlooking the
drive.

Of course there was a recessed arch and a great door studded with iron bolts, and he knew there would be a knocker shaped like an iron fist clutching an iron ball. He let his flashlight play around the entry before knocking. A bicycle propped against a pillar under the porte-cochère was a surprise. He hadn't expected—and he was a little sorry to find somebody home. The bike looked new, and gave contrast to a scene of ruin and old desolation.

Listening to the echoes of the knocker, Bill Shepherd thought, "Wuthering Heights. Wuthering Heights as Edgar Allen Poe might have written it."

The girl climbed out of the car and stood in the entryway with him as he waited for an answer to the knocker. The mist changed suddenly to a sheeting downpour. Water blew in under the porte-cochère, drenching their shoes. The door took so long in opening that, when it did creak inward, Bill Shepherd was sure the man who opened it had first gone somewhere to make up in costume.

Or maybe it wasn't a man at all. Maybe it....

Bill Shepherd experienced a creep down his spine. The figure, dim in the doorframe, was too much like someone in masquerade. It was gaunt and tall and stooped, and it had a deep-furrowed sad gray face and great sad eyes that peered from under a forelock of salty gray hair. It wore a nightcap with a tassel that dangled over one ear, and a musty moth-eaten night robe that fell to the ankles. Its feet, in wooden shoes stiffed with straw, were like great clumpy hoofs, and, holding aloft a smudged oil lamp and peering out at Bill Shepherd, it was easily recognizable as a midnight version of a Walt Disney horse.

The melancholy eyes looked out at Bill Shepherd; and

the man shook his head as if to say he would like to help, but he was too poor and the house was beyond the aid of a vacuum cleaner.

Bill Shepherd mustered his French. "You are Archambaud?"

"I am Archambaud."

"Then I suppose I won't have to spend the night on this doorstep in the rain. This is Mademoiselle Gervais. I am William Shepherd, and before we go any farther, has the place got a telephone?"

But Archambaud seemed unable to answer. Elevating the oil lamp, he stared at Bill Shepherd with eyes widened to saucers; then he wheeled back from the doorway, whinnying, "Blanche! Blanche—!"

Thrusting the girl over the threshold ahead of him, Bill Shepherd pushed in through the door. He had an impression of a vast, shadow-cornered room. The traditional staircase going up into darkness at the left. The traditional fireplace smouldering against a shadowed wall. The traditional stranger warming himself by the hearth.

The traditional stranger—with pipe, knickers and wet shoes—was obviously the story-book Englishman who had lost his way. Doubtless the owner of the bicycle. Everything was running true to form. The Englishman stood up, politely raising his brows. A dog barked viciously in a back room somewhere, and the in-gust of wind and rain fluttered the lamp-flame in Archambaud's hand and brightened the hearth-coals and made shadows creep and lengthen on the walls.

And now other shadows.

A woman's figure had formed in the glooms at the head

of the staircase. This was in character, too. Dickens had written about her. Madame Defarge. Her knitting was in her hand as her felt slippers padded down the steps; in lamp light she was seen as a dowdy Amazon, six feet at least, with a combative bosom, capable jaw, faint moustache on upper lip, a head of hair like a bird's nest, and Bertrand's promised goiter—a growth that bulged from the side of her throat like a summer squash. She was waving her knitting, emitting hoarse bursts of indignant French.

"No, no, no! There is no more room for travelers. Sacred stove! Do they think this a hotel? Tell them this is not an inn, Archambaud! Tell them to go away! Are we at fault because of the eternal rain? Send them to the village! Send them—!"

Then, half way down the staircase, she saw Bill Shepherd; stopped short in her angry descent; dropped her knitting; screamed.

"Mother of heaven! The dead! The dead are calling upon us! The Forgotten of God!"

Doing an about face on the stairs, she fell deliberately over backwards, and came somersaulting down the steps, *bumpety-bump!*

8

THEY LIVE AGAIN

THE DOG IN the back room howled. A cold draught circled the room, fluttering the oil lamp in Archambaud's hand, animating the wall-shadows.

The draught crept under Bill Shepherd's collar and sneaked down his neck. He heard the French girl murmur, *"Mon dieu!"* and an exclamation, "Good Lord!" from the Englishman, and choking sounds from Archambaud; and he stared in dismay at the grotesque figure outsprawled at the foot of the stairs.

Madame Landru's mouth was open and her eyes were closed. But, judging from the muscles above her elbow and her breadth of hip and shoulder, it looked as if it would take a great deal to make Madame Landru faint.

"What did she mean?" Bill Shepherd turned on Archambaud. "What did she mean—the Forgotten of God!"

The horse-faced man seemed unable to reply. His eyes bulged at Bill Shepherd and his nostrils were spread. He was trying to swallow his Adam's apple and couldn't.

"For heaven's sake, don't stand there!" Bill Shepherd's nerves snapped in temper. "Do something! Get some brandy!" He drove the man toward a rear door with a glare. "Get some brandy and fetch some more lights. Can't a man walk into his own *château* without the servants falling in a faint?"

As the gulping caretaker put down the lamp and melted through a shadowed doorway. Bill Shepherd wheeled and stared about uncertainly. The Englishman across the room moved forward.

"You are my host, then? I—I'm afraid I may be intruding."

"Apparently I'm the intrusion." He laughed a little shakily. "I've never been here before. This place belonged to my father. These people don't know me, I—I just drove out today from Paris. Shepherd," he gave the Englishman his name. "I'm William Shepherd."

"Fielding is my name. Jeffry Fielding."

"This is Mademoiselle Gervais."

The men stood back a little woodenly, leaving the girl to succor the prostrate Madame Landru.

The girl seemed equal to the emergency after a moment's hesitation, and—rather brave of her, Bill Shepherd thought—she knelt beside the unconscious woman, smoothing her forehead and briskly patting her hands.

"Out like a light," the Englishman observed, his features expressing a politely controlled concern.

He thrust his hands in his pockets and appraised Bill Shepherd with cool gray eyes, his manner embarrassed and at the same time friendly—that of a stranger in another's household, who wanted to help, but did not wish to be in the way. "I say, if there's anything I can do—"

Bill Shepherd said, "I'm sure I don't know what set her off. Have you any idea what she meant by that sudden outcry?"

"Dashed if I have," the Englishman frowned. "She was all right when I stopped in to get out of the storm an hour ago. Not exactly cordial, but I mean to say she didn't seem on the verge of this breakdown." He apologized, "I didn't mean to be sitting around your hearth like this, Shepherd. I got soaked in that thunderstorm—overtook me in these woods, don't you know—road isn't exactly made for bicycling—thought I'd stop in a moment and dry off—"

"Make yourself at home." Bill Shepherd waved his apology. "That is," he looked around doubtfully, "if there's anything here to make yourself at home with."

He was not too sure he, himself, was going to be at home there, much less entertain guests with any sort of hospitality. The place seemed as cheerless as the dog-howls which issued from quarters somewhere in the rear.

The howls broke off into a series of sharp, painful yelps which conveyed an unpleasant impression that Archambaud was strangling the beast; and the hush that followed could only be called dismal. There was a smell of must and moldering woodwork and damp plaster; an echo-y stillness at the stairhead suggested empty hallways and closed-off rooms and unused floors above—the rustication you sensed on entering a hotel which has been boarded up for the winter and not yet been opened for the season. The roof-tiles leaked, and the atmosphere had mildewed.

MAKING A HASTY survey of his surroundings, Bill Shepherd did not know when he had seen a room as inhospitable. The high, vaulted ceiling harbored cloudy gatherings of darkness, lamplight only touching an occasional shine on the arched overhead beams.

The walls were draped with black shadows. Spare articles

The faces, like two balloons of terror, peered out.

of furniture—heavy, highbacked chairs; a huge old side-
board; a massive, thick-legged table—were engloomed.
The baronial fireplace with its handful of embers was little
comfort in a chamber that resembled the Medieval dining
hall of a monastery dedicated to severe introspection and
self-abnegation.

He made out an arched doorway beyond the stairs, and
he supposed the architecture was a blend of Gothic and
Norman. There'd be a chapel somewhere, and cobwebby
wine cellars, and flag-paved passages, and doors with iron
hinges and ancient padlocks.

Still, he had come prepared for a minimum of modern-
istic comfort; Old Bertrand, he reflected, had warned him
fairly in that respect.

But the lawyer had not prepared him for this extraordinary reception on the part of Madame Landru—he could not help regarding the prostrated woman with scowls of dismay—and neither had he expected house-guests.

He did not quite know what to do about Gabrielle Gervais—after all, the girl had held him up at the point of a loaded pistol. The Englishman was rather more welcome.

Obviously Fielding was the average Briton of the J.B. Priestly school—the kind who wandered in and out of week-end parties in books and plays—addicted to tea, tweeds and bicycles—asking no more than a fire to dry his boots and a room for the night. Mademoiselle-was a more delicate problem; and there was that corpse in the poppies, an immediate problem for a telephone.

His attention fixed on Archambaud who, having returned with another oil lamp and a bottle of brandy, was standing back in shadow, mopping his forehead with a shaky handkerchief.

The man's horsy eyes skittered sideways at Bill Shepherd; he could only gulp and shake his head at Shepherd's sharp request.

"You mean to say there isn't a phone in this place?" Bill Shepherd demanded impatiently. If he remembered anything about his father, this *château* would have been full of telephones. "It's urgent that I put through a call."

"The telephone is out of commission," was the husky answer. "We have not been able to use it, *monsieur.*"

"Why haven't you had it repaired? How long has it been out of commission?"

"The telephone, *monsieur*—it has been out of commission since Nineteen-sixteen."

NINETEEN-SIXTEEN! BILL SHEPHERD had expected

the usual storybook answer—that the line had gone dead in this evening's electric storm. Archambaud's reply came as something of a shock. That date, again! It occurred to him that the *château*, itself, had been out of commission since that date; apparently everything in Picardy dated back to 1916.

He thought, "It's as if the whole countryside has been dead since the Battle of the Somme." All the telephones had been killed, too?

A frantic little nerve at the back of his head told him he ought to make a dash for the nearest village *gendarmerie* to report the murder, but a gust of rain against the leaded-glass window at his back, and memory of the black road through the forest dampened his resolution.

Better fortify himself with some dinner first, and a glass of that cognac. By the thirsty speed with which Madame Landru was swigging it, it looked as if she might consume the entire wine cellar if he didn't speak quickly for his share.

Under the French girl's ministrations and the scorching jolts of straight brandy, madame was reviving. She sat up suddenly, grabbing at the brandy bottle. Then her eyes popped open out of sleep.

She stared blindly at Gabrielle Gervais; saw her husband; caught sight of Bill Shepherd. She pushed off the girl with a yelp; in a flurry of skirts and apron strings, whirled to her feet.

"Landru!" She caught at her husband. "Landru—in the name of God! Do something!"

His white-rimmed eyes on Bill Shepherd, Archambaud Landru crossed himself.

Bill Shepherd exploded, "What in the devil!" He

approached the couple angrily. "Just what is the meaning of this nonsense?"

The lamp-chimney rattled in Archambaud's hand. The woman's goitre shook like jelly. She pulled her husband back against the staircase. She was chattering, "It is he! He has been made whole! It is *he*—!"

The Englishman and the French girl, watching, wore expressions of bafflement. The French girl murmured to Bill Shepherd, "You are frightening this old couple out of their wits—"

IT WAS EMBARRASSING to the point of lunacy. A man walked into his father's property, and the old family servitors received him as if they thought him Banquo's ghost.

He should have written to announce his visit, of course, but announced or not, he hadn't imagined himself an object for terror. In front of strangers, this was uncalled for.

Bill Shepherd reddened in temper.

"Look here." He confronted Archambaud. "You understand English, don't you? Very well, I told you who I was. For the last twenty years I've owned this place—you two have received your wages from me."

Then it occurred to him that their wages, all other expenses of the *château* had been paid through Bertrand et Frer.

"Naturally Bertrand et Frer in Paris have been in touch with you, but this is my property—you knew my father— he hired you to stay here. Is it necessary for me to identify myself in my own *château*? I'm William Shepherd." He repeated the announcement deliberately, repressing impatience. "I drove out here today from Paris. I've come from the office of Monsieur Bertrand."

Panic faded a little from Archambaud's stare, but Madame Landru continued to regard him in abject fright.

"It is he, Landru! The Forgotten of God—!"

Bill Shepherd felt like a fool. He said harshly, "I must say I'm not used to people going into a total eclipse at first sight of me. Speak up, Archambaud! Just what does your wife mean by the 'Forgotten of God'?"

Breath sighed from the horse-faced Frenchman in an expelled whinny. He pointed toward the window at Bill Shepherd's back.

"The graves," he said in a feeble voice. "The cemeteries surrounding the forest. The graves out there in the wood, *m'sieur.* The soldiers—the soldiers who were slain in the War."

"You call them the Forgotten of God?"

Landru looked steadfastly at the floor; and his face was grave.

"The Forgotten of God are the dead ones, *oui*—the soldiers killed in the Battle of the Somme—the dead ones who do not stay in their graves. I do not say I believe these stories, but my wife is a spiritualist—she claims to have *seen.*"

Madame Landru nodded her head wildly at this, clutching her husband's arm, ogling Bill Shepherd and croaking, "It is he! It is *he—!*"

Bill Shepherd demanded thickly, "Who in heaven's name does the woman think I am?"

Archambaud's voice was low. "Your brother, *m'sieur.* Your brother, who was here in this *château* in Nineteen-sixteen. He died, *m'sieur*—we never saw him after the bombardment—the officers told us he was killed." His brown eyes looked into Bill Shepherd's sadly. "My wife thinks you are Captain Shepherd, *m'sieur*. She mistakes you for your dead brother."

The old man's lips tightened.

9

THE WAKENING CLOCK

BILL SHEPHERD COULD feel the angry flush on his cheekbones. He didn't like his brother brought into this clammy nonsense. It wasn't very complimentary to Hugh.

At the same time he was relieved to have the woman's conduct toward him explained before the French girl and the Englishman.

He said to Fielding: "My older brother was in action out here with the Canadians. Reported killed on this front, but we never knew where he was buried. Evidently the woman takes me for his ghost."

Turning on Archambaud, brusquely, "Tell your wife to stop that ridiculous bleating. If her spiritualist leanings are behind the ghost tales floating around this neighborhood, I won't thank her for it. I don't fancy her thinking up such rubbish about my brother, do you understand? And tell her to go out to her kitchen and prepare some food for these people and myself.

"You can bring my bag in from the car and put a room in order; I'm going to spend the night." He concluded with a snap: "I've had a long drive, and I'm too tired to tolerate any more foolishness."

There, that ought to establish his mortality, as well as his authority in this place.

He did not like to be officious toward domestics, and his bankrupt state of affairs scarcely permitted a high-handed attitude toward servants he could no longer afford, but something had to be done to bring the old woman to her senses.

Those bogle eyes of Madame Landru's should be able to see that a ghost wouldn't arrive by car and be carrying baggage.

Archambaud's features had returned to something like normal; he seemed eager to accept William Shepherd as human, and he delivered these admonitions to his wife.

She responded with an outburst of hoarse, untranslatable French; crossed herself vehemently; then, as though half convinced, delivered herself to fate with an uptoss of her hands, and retreated through the rear doorway, muttering.

Bill Shepherd hurried Archambaud out to the car with a glare; shrugged off his damp coat; turned to the French girl and Fielding. "If there's any brandy left in that bottle, let's have a round." He asked the girl bluntly: "Do you want to stay here tonight, or do you want to drive with me to the nearest village and stay there?"

The girl said calmly, removing her dripping hat and shaking her damp hair: "As I told you, *monsieur.* I could not stay at an inn because I do not have any money. I have no place to spend the night."

"Mademoiselle Gervais," he told the Englishman, "was lost in the forest out there and ran her car into a ditch."

"And Monsieur Shepherd," the girl said with a faint smile, "was kind enough to offer me a ride."

Fielding said pleasantly, "A bad place to be ditched." His gray eyes were impersonal, his manner unobtrusive; he nodded politely as Bill Shepherd offered the brandy. The thought annoyed Bill Shepherd—that Fielding probably believed he had brought Mademoiselle Gervais out from Paris, and that he, Fielding, was in the way.

Bill Shepherd said tartly, "Mademoiselle Gervais is from Amiens. Tomorrow I'll have Archambaud go after a team to haul out her car. Meantime, I'm afraid I can't offer either of you much hospitality.

"The place doesn't seem very cozy, but you're entitled to whatever it has to offer. Certainly there ought to be plenty of room and something to eat."

AN IN-GUST OF wind and rain brought Archambaud through the door, clumping in his wooden sabots, his back stooped to the weight of Bill Shepherd's kit-bags. He kicked the door shut with his heel; dropped the luggage, and considered Bill Shepherd mournfully.

"There are no guest rooms for company," he took up Bill Shepherd's remark. "There are no rooms in the *château* ready for occupancy, *monsieur.*"

"Then you and your wife get busy and make some ready for occupancy."

The tassel on Archambaud's nightcap wagged. "I am afraid that will be impossible, *monsieur.*"

"Impossible? There must be at least forty rooms—"

"Of which thirty are open to the sky, *monsieur.* The walls are broken in. The floors are gone. There are holes in the roof. You would not be able to sleep in them, *non!*"

"Well, how about the others. Are you trying to tell me there aren't any bedrooms in the—?"

"Ah, but no beds," was the gloomy information. "No furnishings. Nothing. Such furniture as was left, *monsieur*—it is all in deplorable condition. The beds, they were taken for the hospitals. The bedding, too, was taken. The Red Cross, you comprehend."

"Back in Nineteen-sixteen?"

"Oui. Back in Nineteen-sixteen."

Bill Shepherd looked around helplessly. No telephone. No bedrooms. No beds. Sound of rain slashing at the window loudened on his hearing.

He demanded: "There's no place you could put us up for the night?"

"There is that room occupied by my wife and myself in the servants' quarters at the back. If *monsieur* would consider—"

"Thank you, Archambaud, but I wouldn't consider it."

"Perhaps the tower, then. But it has not been opened since the War—"

"Dust and bats," Bill Shepherd said under his breath. Just the thing for a mystery yarn—a night of thunderstorm, and the old tower that had been locked up for twenty years—good for Dr. Fu Manchu, but a little too uncomfortable for an actual experience.

He decided. "You can leave those bags there by the door, Archambaud, and after dinner take them back to my car. Just now you might give your wife a hand in the kitchen. You can assure her I won't put her to any more trouble. I don't think any of us will be spending the night in the Château de Feu."

AFTER THE EQUINE Archambaud had gone, Bill Shepherd apologized to the French girl and Fielding, "I'm sorry. It seems dinner is the best I can offer, after all. I've got to go to the village after dinner, anyway, and you can drive along with me. There must be some place nearby with a comfortable inn."

Instinctively they were moving away from the staircase, crossing the room toward the faint glow of the hearth.

The room was not cold, but it was dank with the dampness of stone walls and flagstone floor; wind in the chimney had breathed on the fireplace embers to brighten them a little, and a fireplace, somehow, became the focal point of any room.

"I wish I could be a help," the Englishman sympathized. "A bicycle isn't much use on a night like this. Being a foreigner, I'm not too acquainted with this locale, but I think the nearest village is Thiepval. It seems to me there's a small *auberge* there—it's about eight kilometers north."

Gabrielle Gervais said ruefully: "I am not well acquainted with this countryside, either. That is how I became lost."

She perched herself on the edge of a chair, hitched it around to face the fire-coals, proceeded to pull her feet out of her muddy shoes and thrust her stockinged toes into the hearth-light. She looked up at Bill Shepherd. "I hope you do not mind."

"Please make yourself comfortable, *mademoiselle*."

"I know I am an inconvenience."

Thinking of the automatic he had wrested from her, he could not help an ironic smile. "Not at all, *mademoiselle*. I'm only sorry the *château* is in no condition for guests. You see," he went on to Fielding, who had drawn up a chair beside the girl, "the place hasn't been repaired since the War. I suppose I ought to explain.

"My father bought this *château* as a sort of present to my mother—castle in France—that sort of thing. They came here summers. Before I was born."

He paused to scan the room. "The novelty wore off, I suppose, and Father probably preferred Biarritz, but he kept the place to pass on to my brother, Hugh. We lived in the States here and there, and I never visited the *château*.

"Then the War came along. Of course this forest was in the middle of it. Odd coincidence, but when Hugh came across with the Canadians his regiment was thrown into the Battle of the Somme and we got a letter from him saying he was stationed here in the *château*.

"I was only nine or ten years old at the time, but I can remember my father's face when he walked in with the telegram from the Canadian Government. Hugh, of course.

"I don't think it would've been such a blow if it hadn't happened in this place. Father never got over it. After the war was over, I know he issued orders that the *château* and this forest should remain untouched so long as he lived, and he never came here again.

"We knew the *château* was in a state of ruin; I think my father wanted it left that way—the war-torn *château* and the forest—as a memorial to Hugh. The French Government objected to it, if I remember rightly; but Father had some influence, and the woods were posted against trespassers, the *château* left as it was.

"Father willed the place to me, and up to now I've never even come out here to look at it. Never thought much about it, I guess." He looked about regretfully. "The World

War never meant much to me until I drove out here today. I—I really had no idea the place would be as uninhabitable."

HE WAS AWARE that Archambaud had clumped into the room with an armload of plates, and as he stopped speaking there was a busy clatter of crockery on the table, as though the old servant did not want anyone to think he was listening.

Bill Shepherd could detect a distant aroma of boiling meat, and he hoped there would be some good wine. He'd have at least one meal in the old *château*—a farewell dinner to its memories.

Fielding broke into this thought with, "A pity you haven't seen the *château* in daytime. It's really a perfect specimen of the Norman-Gothic, and must be very old. Quite unusual in this part of France."

Bill Shepherd wondered: "You've been here in the daytime?"

"Trespassing, it seems, although I didn't see any signs. Yes, I've been out here a number of times. Usually spend my summers in this *département* of Picardy; since early June, this year, I've been living in a *pension* at Contalmaison.

"I hope you don't mind my poking about the woods like this. I've ridden about the forest a good bit on my bicycle. You see, I'm a painter."

He interrupted himself to light his pipe; his gray eyes gazing steadily at Bill Shepherd across the match-flame. He gestured the pipe toward the window. "Wonderful landscape for what I'm doing. About the only authentic war ruins left in France—the forest and this *château*."

Bill Shepherd questioned, "You're painting war ruins?"

The Englishman nodded. "Quite fascinated by the subject. Commissioned to do 'em by various officers' clubs and regimental clubs around London. The Coldstream Guards, for example. Very swank outfit, no end of tradition and all that. Like a nice painting of the Mons sector or whatnot to decorate the billiard room.

"I've done quite a number, mostly water color. Covered Verdun and the Marne and some of the old forts up near Liége, but this Château de Feu is the best war-time specimen I've run across. I say, you wouldn't object—?"

"Certainly not," Bill Shepherd assured him. "I'd like very much to see some of your work."

"I wish I could show it to you. I'm sorry I haven't my kit on hand tonight—I was only riding for my evening exercise when the storm drove me to cover."

Reminded of the night and rain, the black wagonroad through the stands of burnt timber, Bill Shepherd's thoughts returned to the peasant lying in the poppies, dead with the marks of strangulation on his throat.

Could the corpse have been there when this artist pedaled into the woods? Bicycling from Contalmaison, the Englishman must have come up the road some time ahead of the Hispano-Suiza.

But Bill Shepherd hadn't noticed the prints of any bike-tires in the mud; only the tread-marks that must have been left by the French girl's car.

He had purposely avoided any mention of the dead man to Mademoiselle Gervais—hadn't wanted to cross-examine her in that forest out there—besides, covertly studying her, he was certain she knew nothing of the murder, but was up to some game of her own.

He would question her later about that holdup stunt; as for Fielding, he would take the painter aside at first opportunity and ask the man if he had seen anything.

For all the artist's open countenance, Bill Shepherd had a feeling the Englishman was holding something in reserve. It was possible that Fielding had come here hunting a telephone, too, and in the absence of one was biding his time and holding his own council.

THERE WERE OTHER possibilities—but looking at the dark-haired French girl and the boyish-faced Englishman, for the sake of his own peace of mind, Bill Shepherd hastily rejected them.

Of course murderers never looked like murderers, but the girl couldn't have had the grip for that job, and the Englishman's clear gray eyes were hardly those of a strangler.

Bill Shepherd told himself that in this *château*, and with all those cemeteries, ghost legends and Madame Landru's goiterish spiritualism on his mind, his mystery-mongering imagination could go haywire.

Anyway, the local *gendarmes* would take charge of the thing; he'd make a run for the police immediately after dinner.

He found himself nodding absently to some remark by Gabrielle Gervais, who had engaged the Englishman with an observation on French and English art. Archambaud's sabots were clumping into the room, again. There was a rattle of dishes and a smell of meat.

The three by the fire turned.

Archambaud, tall, shadowy, horse-featured, was posed at the head of the table with a vast platter clutched in his hands. The board was set with crockery plates and pewter flagons.

Behind Archambaud, dowdy-haired, bulk-bosomed, shadowy, her eyes white-rimmed and luminescent, in her hands a great copper coffee-pot, stood his wife.

And somewhere behind Madame Landru, hidden in a recess under the stairs, an old hoarse clock began to toll. Whirrrr—*Bong!* Whirrrr—*Bong!* Whirrrr—*Bong!*

The atmosphere seemed to hold its breath, and the time-strokes dropped into this silence like a knell.

Bill Shepherd, automatically counting, ticked off the hours. The last stroke expired into a smothery hush. Ten o'clock.

"Dinner," Archambaud said thickly, "is served."

The woman behind him spoke out like an incantation.

"That clock has not struck since Nineteen-sixteen—!"

10

DINNER FOR SPECTERS

THE SHADOW-WALLED ROOM, the sound of wind and rain at dark windows, people staring in consternation at a ghostly clock that had tolled after a silence of twenty-three years—it was too much like something in a novel. Too much like something in a play.

Bill Shepherd, who knew about novels and plays, could not believe in the reality of this. A curtain should come down. It was time for the line: "To be continued."

He was surprised to hear himself demanding of the old French woman, "What do you mean, that clock hasn't struck since Nineteen-sixteen?" Just as if such an absurdity were possible!

And the old French woman was droning, as though she had been coached for the part by a stage director, "It has not kept time since Nineteen-sixteen, *monsieur.* It has not been wound. It has not been running. That clock stopped during the War."

Her jaws were jiggling, and her eyes were staring like a mesmerist's as she spoke. Her husband was pale, gulping his Adam's apple again. Shakily he put down the platter of meat, turned to stare at the alcove where the clock had bonged.

The French girl and Fielding regarded Bill Shepherd blankly, and a tickle went through his scalp because this was actually happening and not something imaginary.

He had to clear huskiness from his throat. "Madame Landru! Will you kindly stop acting as if you were holding a séance? If that clock hasn't been running since the War, it's running now, which only means somebody's wound it."

"Ah, but *non!*" Archambaud managed to speak for his wife. "What she says is true, *monsieur*. The clock was damaged by the shell-fire. It has never been repaired.

"This is the first time I have heard it since—since the day the *château* was bombarded during the Battle of the Somme. Besides, it could not have been wound, for the key has been lost ever since."

Bill Shepherd heard the French girl murmur, "*Extraordinaire!*" and a muttered, "I say!" from the Englishman.

He stifled an exclamation, and caught up an oil lamp, determined to put an end to this business. His nerves were getting the better of him when his scalp prickled at the tolling of some old clock.

But it was exactly the sort of clock to bong off at an eerie time like that—the lamplight found it in its recess under the stairs—an old grandfather clock that looked, in its shadowy retreat, like a mummy case.

Cobwebs attached it to the wall and hung down over its parchment-yellow face like hair. The mahogany cabinet was scratched and marred; out of one side several large splinters had been gouged; the whole clock was heavily coated with dust; its door stood ajar, and the pendulum chains, with their gilded corncobs, were entangled.

Impossible, that the ruined old antique could have spoken.

Bill Shepherd stepped close with the lamp to examine its face. It wasn't ticking; he couldn't believe that it had been. The minute-hand was missing. Under the dust and cobweb, he discerned the pock-marked clock-face as painted to represent a smiling countenance. The eyes were moons. There were clouds painted on the cheeks, and meters in the ears. The mouth was marked off like a calendar.

One of those old almanac clocks that chronicled the moon-phases, the hour, the day and the year.

The weather indicated was rainy, and the hour-hand stood at ten. The day was undiscernible, but the year was plain. 1916.

BILL SHEPHERD MOVED back with the lamp. He said flatly, "Certainly it hasn't been running for years. Surprising it should have struck at all, the condition it's in. Something must have touched it off—released a spring or something—probably just enough life left in it to strike.

"The time isn't right anyway," he held up his wrist watch. "Ten-forty. Which means if we want to reach some inn before midnight, we can't delay here too long."

Then, looking up, he surprised a furtive movement on the part of Madame Landru. Something had passed between herself and her husband, a low-pitched word, a gulp from Archambaud, the woman wheeling with a gasp as she caught Bill Shepherd's glance, starting back with something in her hand clutched to her bosom.

Bill Shepherd snapped, "Here, what's that? Give me that!" catching the woman's arm.

"It is nothing! *Ah, la, la*, it is nothing!"

"You're hiding something in your hand there. What is it?"

Madame Landru called upon the Mother of God to witness it was nothing at all.

"Let's have it, then!" Bill Shepherd forced the woman around to face him. "I'm sorry, *madame,* but I want to know what you've got in your hand."

It wasn't the clock-key as he had expected. As it fluttered from the woman's fingers and lighted on the flagstone floor, he saw it was a picture, a dim, yellow-edged snapshot such as might have been pasted in someone's Kodak album. Wordless, he stooped to pick it up; then he stood motionless, dumbstruck by the faded print. An army officer standing at ease before a vine-grown wall. Feet apart, swagger stick in elbow, trench helmet jaunty. The shoulders wore their captain's tabs with pride. The eyes were smiling, and the youthful face quirked with a familiar grin.

Staring blindly at the picture, Bill Shepherd sank into a chair.

Madame Landru's bleating seemed to come from a far-off corner. "*Voilà!* Do you deny it, Captain Shepherd? God save us—your own photograph. Have I not seen you with my own eyes, roaming the forest? Have mercy on our souls—is that not you—?"

THE WOMAN WAS groaning and wringing her hands, the others were staring at him, and for two cents, Bill Shepherd told himself, he could snatch up the coffee pot and bang it down over the old blowzy's head.

"No." He roused himself to declare through set teeth, "This picture isn't me! Where did you get this photograph!"

"Ah, *sacré dieu!* Was it not taken outside this very *château* the day before the bombardment in Nineteen-sixteen? Did not you yourself give it to me?"

"I did not!" Bill Shepherd brought his hand down flat on the table. "I did not give it to you, because it isn't a picture of me, and if you don't stop that moaning and crossing yourself and superstitious nonsense, I—I'll have you taken away somewhere and put under observation." His own nerves were frazzling badly, combination of shock at finding that corpse in the woods, emotion at visiting this old family estate, anger that memories of his brother should be dragged into a ghost story and subject of an old woman's brainstorms.

He checked his voice on a shout; gave Madame Landru a wrathful glare, and turned in his chair to hand the little snapshot to the Englishman.

"Fielding, that's my brother Hugh. The one I told you about, was out here with the Canadians. He was nine years older than I—I was just a kid when he enlisted—when he was killed he was only nineteen. I—I didn't realize I'd grown to look so much like him."

The artist nodded sympathetically, handing the picture to Gabrielle Gervais. He said quietly, "A very close resemblance. You might have been twins."

Gabrielle Gervais said, returning the picture, "Your brother was handsome, *monsieur.*"

"Thanks," gruffly. He tucked the picture into his wallet; stowed it in an inner pocket. "I'll take the liberty of keeping the photograph, if you don't mind," he said to Madame Landru who was watching him somberly. "I don't mean to be rude, but I don't care to have my brother's name involved with any local legends and hoodoo hocus-pocus. Just get

it through your head that I'm not some wandering specter to begin with, and there aren't any such things to end
with. Understood?"

Madame Landru's features were now wooden.

Bill Shepherd appealed to her husband, "Archambaud,
can you please serve the table?" and stood up to hold out
the chair for the French girl. He indicated the chair across
the table to Fielding, and himself sat beside Mademoiselle
Gervais.

It was not a festive dinner. The clock which had not
struck since Nineteen-sixteen, and the incident over the
photograph, were not the sort of things to quicken an
appetite. Neither was the dinner.

The bread was like brick; the legumes and vegetables in
the platter looked greasy. There was no soup course, and
Archambaud sawed and sawed on the stringy-meated
joint. As for the coffee, it might have been boiled in the
year 1916. It was as thick and black as water from the River
Styx, and tasted like it.

Bill Shepherd put down his cup with a gasp. "And can't
you hurry a little with the carving, Archambaud? It will
be midnight before we start. The driving on that forest
road is bad."

"*Oui.*" The murmur came from Madame Landru, with-
drawn in shadow. "It is very bad."

The woman was staring once more.

Bill Shepherd put down his spoon in exasperation.
"What do you mean by that?"

She said with a headshake, "Monsieur Shepherd would
not believe."

"Well, what are you trying to tell me now?"

"It is dangerous—most dangerous to drive across a battlefield."

11

THE SOUND OF BLOOD

BILL SHEPHERD DIRECTED a wry grin at Fielding. "The ghosts are walking again. I suppose there's nothing a plain, unimpressive American can do about it. Such stuff has been out of fashion in the States more or less since the Salem witch trials.

"France clings to her spooks and spirits. I got a dose of it this afternoon; old gaffer I met on the road gave me the warning. The dead in the World War cemeteries around here leave their graves after dark. The Battle of the Somme is still going on.

"They fight it every night out here in the Forêt de Feu "

Fielding's quiet smile came across, "Indeed. I've heard something like that from the inn keeper at Contalmaison."

Gabrielle Gervais said at Bill Shepherd's elbow, "Such tales are common in my country. I do not know. I am only a woman."

"I know," Madame Landru droned out. "It is because I am a woman. I have seen."

The coffee was pure acid, but it warmed up the cognac, and Bill Shepherd retorted a little more amiably, "The old gaffer on the highway said he had seen a lot of things too.

Funny how a fog at night or shadows under trees can play tricks on the imagination."

"The things I have seen were not fogs at night. They were not shadows under trees. They were soldiers," Madame Landru droned. "An infantryman without arms. A cavalryman without legs. A blind officer led by a cripple. An aviator without a face. Germans there were, and Frenchmen, and English.

"In the shreds of old uniforms, their helmets eaten with rust. From my window I have seen them, in the night's stillness I have heard their voices. They are those who were killed in the Battle of the Somme—the dead who do not stay underground—the spirits who do not rest—the Forgotten of God."

"As I told you before I do not say I believe all that," Archambaud put in gratuitously as his wife paused. "But I, myself, would think twice before venturing at night through the Forêt de Feu."

"Why do you think this ghostly front line is in these woods?"

Madame Landru intoned, "Because the bloodiest fighting of all the Battle of the Somme—the bloodiest fighting of all the War!—was in the Forêt de Feu! Around this *château* the battle raged for many weeks. First the Germans were here—I remember them when they came. The proud Uhlans. The splendid officers—those evil Boches!—in their shining boots, and glittering spiked helmets and fierce military moustaches.

"Until Nineteen-sixteen they held the *château*, forcing Archambaud and myself to work like slaves to feed and serve them. Then, in the first charge of the Somme, the

French drove them out. Ah, the poilus came through the trees with bayonets, and the Boches fled in terror before that charge—"

SHE FLUTTERED HER fingers before her face, and the wall-shadows were Boches fleeing in terror through the woods.

"But the poilus could not hold the *château.* Ah, *non!* The Germans had left machine gunners behind them, machine gunners in the upper rooms, machine gunners in the tower. The French were mowed down like wheat by a scythe.

"Again and once more they charged; once more and again the Germans drove them back. Then the English came into the fight. *Sacré nom de dieu!* the British attack swept through the woods like a tempest. The Germans abandoned the *château* in desperate retreat."

"But the English could not hold it, either," Archambaud put in. "It was a strategic place, you comprehend. It was a nice place for the officers to live in. *Eh bien,* each army that captured the woods would employ the *château* for a headquarters. The Germans did not like to leave it, and they returned, fighting like madmen to drive the British out and capture it once more."

"Time and again this *château* changed hands in the fighting," Madame Landru droned. "First one army would take it by assault, then the other. The Germans, the French, the British—all of them were here at one time or another as the battlelines shifted.

"There was once even a corps of Italian officers here. Medical officers and observers. Sixt von Arnim, the German commander-in-chief was quartered here. At one time there were even some officers of the Russian air corps."

"The *château* was most continuously under fire," Archambaud carried on. "Hand to hand fighting raged around its walls. Some days it would change hands so swiftly that I would start to serve a meal to a German officer—*tiens!*—I would look up to find a British colonel of the Guards or a French general of the Zouaves sitting there.

"Then guns would crash. Whistles would blow. Shells would scream. Madmen in gray-green uniforms with helmets like inverted coal scuttles would rush through the doors. Like this, like that, the Prussians would be back."

"They fought on the stairs," Madame Landru pointed. "The charges were terrible in the woods, but they were most terrible between these walls. They fought on the stairs, and they fought through the rooms above. They overturned the furniture and tore up the tapestries; smashed whatever had been missed by the shell-explosions, and drove their bayonets into the walls.

"The good God only knows why they did not drive their bayonets into Landru and me—we hid in the cellar for days at a time. But they drove their bayonets into each other, I can tell you. *Ah, la, la,* when the charge would be over, we would creep out and clear away the dead. It would be like a morgue, this *château.* Like a morgue!"

Shepherd avoided his guests' eyes. Not much use trying to eat.

Archambaud looked up, his carving knife stuck in the joint on the platter. "Some of them were shot. Some of them blasted. Some of them cut to pieces. You could tell the handiwork of the different troops. The Germans had bullets that would make a little hole going in, and a hole like a dog's yawn going out. They had saw-tooth bayonets that would rip a man down the middle like a slaughterhouse pig—I remember the kind-faced General Von Arnim telling his officers what good weapons those saw-teeth were.

"On the other hand, the French had needle bayonets—they would flash in and out, quick as rapiers, and leave a body leaking like a sieve. The British were better with grenades. They would rush in through that doorway, and throw! Ah, a Boche would jump when one of those bombs went off under him.

"Part of him would jump one way, and part of him would jump another. You would find the pieces all over the room, *monsieur.*"

"THEY WOULD LIE on the stairway; they would sprawl in over the windowsills." Madame Landru nodded somberly. "They would lean on the banisters and slump down in the chairs and genuflect in the chapel. In the bed chambers above I would find them—under the beds—huddled in the wardrobe closets—hanging head down through holes in the ceiling. 'Sweep them up! Scrub those floors!' the officers would order me.

"Dieu! I would sweep and scrub until my back was broken, but next morning there would be another batch. A thousand housekeepers could not have kept those rooms tidy. Rubbish everywhere. Bodies everywhere. Parts of bodies everywhere. I have found legs in the pantry. Heads in that fireplace. Eyes—"

"Never mind the details," Bill Shepherd half rose from his chair. The eyes in Madame Landru's head were enough for him just then. He realized he should have shut the woman off before she started these reminiscences, but shutting off the flow of Madame Landru's tongue seemed about as impossible as turning off the Mississippi.

"There was too much blood," she droned at him. "Too much blood. On the very flagstones of this room it lay in pools. Out there in the Forêt de Feu it lay in lakes. The mud was scarlet. The earth was soaked crimson. The very steam in the air was pink. That is why they called this the Red Zone, *monsieur*. For days, for weeks, for months the earth was soaked in blood."

"Night and day the guns thundered in that forest out there." Archambaud gestured the serving fork. "Night and day death ran riot through those trees. The roar of flames, the crash of guns seemed endless. Worst of all was the bombardment when the Canadians were here—the third week of the Battle of the Somme. My wife can tell you how the sky rained iron and fire.

"The walls shook like those of Jericho. The roofs fell in. Hour after hour the big shells crashed down on the Château de Feu. My wife and I, for three days we hid in the wine cellar. It was terrible. When at last the bombardment was over there were but five Canadian officers where there had been a score. Your poor brother—how glad we had been to see him—was no longer here. The five remaining Canadians could no longer stay. The Germans were coming back."

"There was too much blood," Madame Landru repeated, staring.

"That bombardment was the worst," Archambaud wagged his nightcap-tassel. "The guns, the death, the fires went on after that, but that bombardment during the Battle of the Somme was the worst. Everything here in the Forêt de Feu was the worst. But finally? *Enfin.*

"My wife and I crept out of the wine cellar one morning. Something was wrong. Something had happened. It was quiet, *monsieur.* It was very quiet. We crept up through the ruins and we stared. In that forest out there, there was not a sound. The *château* was deserted, no soldiers to be seen. The cannon had stopped.

"You could hear somewhere a bird chirping. Then the bird stopped. It was sudden, the silence of that morning. It was, *monsieur,* as if Picardy was dead."

"You could only fear the blood," Madam Landru droned. "The sound of blood soaking into the ground."

"**IT SEEMED LIKE** that," her husband solemnly agreed. "But it was only that the troops had been ordered elsewhere. The artillery had gone to another front. The Battle of the Somme was over."

"But the Battle of the Somme was not over." Madame Landru shook her gray head. "The soldiers who had been killed and buried—they could not die. Does not the Bible say, 'Dust to dust'?

"But in this countryside of Picardy the ground could not dry. In the Forêt de Feu there could be no dust. The earth in which those slain were buried, it had soaked up too much blood."

That was what the old gaffer on the highroad had said. The poppies of Picardy had soldiers' blood in their veins. They breathed for the dead in the daytime so that they might rise and walk by night. Bill Shepherd told himself he couldn't take much more of this. This old woman's voice had put a spell on the room; her staring was almost hypnotic.

He squared back in his chair, resentfully. "For the last time, Madame Landru, put an end to the séance. You can go to the kitchen. My guests would like a bottle of wine before they leave."

"You do not believe, then—?"

"No!"

"—that I have seen these unhappy dead—?"

"Nor heard ghostly gunfire, nor any of the rest of it." He stood up threateningly. "The wine—"

"But what of those slain, *monsieur,* in the last two years? In these very woods. Where no feet but theirs have walked. What of Farmer Castignac shot down one night when he was trapping rabbits, and no trespasser in the woods but him and his dog? What of the blacksmith's daughter found one morning with a bullet in her throat in those woods out there, and no tracks for a mile but her own?

"What of the child killed only last month—found dead in a shell-hole, *oui,* with her feet blown off—but that shell-hole one that was dug in Nineteen-sixteen?"

Yes, and what of that peasant back there in the poppies with fingerprints on his throat?

Bill Shepherd tapped the table, eyeing the woman narrowly. "If people have been murdered in these woods, it's a matter for the *gendarmerie.* High time something was done about it, it seems to me. I'm going, myself, when I get to the village. I want to talk to these local police."

He thought Archambaud gave a start; he was conscious, too, of a movement by the French girl at his side. But Madame Landru gave a laugh. Not a mirthful laugh, but a queerish, gargly laugh that seemed to be half choked by the roots of the growth on her throat—the sort of laugh a person might give in sleep.

"The police," she laughed. "As if they could put their hands on the spirits!

"Did they not search and question and pry? But whom to arrest, when someone is killed by the bullets of the dead? Can soldiers be jailed when the earth cannot keep them in their graves? With neither Heaven nor Hell to receive them, must these poor Forgotten of God report to the police? They cannot live. They cannot die.

"They can only fight on, as their officers and countries commanded, on and on through eternity. Is it murder when some earthling wanders into their battlelines?"

She was backing from the room, eyes shining, hand upraised. "The Battle of the Somme is not over, and they are out there in the forest even now. All those who died here in Nineteen-sixteen are there. All those who died in this *château*. The British. The French. The Russians and Italians. The Germans—"

12

THE DEAD WAIL AT NIGHT

THE DOG IN the back room howled. Archambaud Landru murmured something under his breath, put down his serving cutlery, and backed out after his wife.

Bill Shepherd was glad the couple were gone from the table, but their retreat left a pall on the dinner party. Wind moaned in the fireplace chimney; rain beat at the shadowy windows; the room seemed a-prowl with memories of death and destruction and sombre thoughts.

Fielding was examining some point in mid-table with a concentrated gaze; and Gabrielle Gervais sat, wordless, her eyes on nothing in the lamplight. Bill Shepherd tried to break this atmosphere by passing the platter.

Infestive wasn't the description for this meal, he reflected. Reasty. That was the word.

It was hard to make table conversation in a room where heads had rolled on the hearth and corpses had crowded the staircase. He tried to concentrate on the meat, but the joint was undercooked, too lean, the meat reddish and stringy.

He didn't blame the Englishman for laying aside his fork, excusing himself with, "Really, old man, I had a late snack this afternoon; I'm not very hungry—" and cross-

ing the room to the fireplace mantel where he had left his
tobacco pouch.

Gabrielle Gervais was regarding her plate with repug-
nance.

"Horse!" she murmured.

Bill Shepherd coughed in his napkin.

"And speaking of that," he said in a low aside to the girl,
"I'd like to hear more details concerning your butcher-shop
romance. If you'd care to really enlighten me before we set
out for the *gendarmerie* tonight—"

He had meant to pause significantly—searching her
profile with a sideways glance he was again convinced he
had seen her somewhere before this evening—but into his
pause there came an interruption.

The dog in the back room howled, *Yah-hooooooo—!*

Then the front door was shaken by a violent knocking.
Thumpety-thump-thump-thump!

Shepherd and the girl were on their feet. At the fireplace
Fielding stared. All heard the voice that begged admission
from out of the night. The cry in German—

"Darf ich 'rein kommen—!"

IT WAS WORSE than the clock. It was worse than the
woozy capers of Madame Landru. And, when Bill Shepherd's fingers managed to release the iron latch and he
yanked open the massive Gothic door, it was almost as
stunning a shock as the dead man he had seen in the
poppies.

The figure swaying on the threshold—he could almost
have believed it was dead.

The German looked it, in the rain-swirl. He was thick-
set and bald and flabby-handed and pale. His jacket was

drenched black, a shapeless garment buttoned to the throat. His britches, soaked, were torn at the seam. His boots were mud-plastered to the knees.

Spurred and booted, in those rain-sodden garments, he might have been a cavalry officer—he might have been anything. His blunt-jawed face was colorless. His bald head gleamed. His eyes stared blindly at Bill Shepherd. A raw, red bash seemed to glow on that hairless forehead.

He muttered in guttural French, "I want to come in!" and stumbled in over the doorsill in a cloud of rain.

Bill Shepherd shut the door, dumbly; dumbly regarded his visitor. The man stood dripping and panting. He lifted a slow hand and gently touched the abrasion on his forehead. He jerked his fingers away, gasping, *"Himmelherrgott."*

He stared about, dazed.

Bill Shepherd blurted involuntarily in English, "You're wounded!" He did not know why he said wounded instead of hurt.

The dazed eyes looked at him. "Wounded. *Ja!* My horse. Three hours ago—I was thrown! In the barbed wire!"

In the barbed wire! Bill Shepherd felt a cold muscle tighten around his heart. He shot a glance at the French girl and Fielding to see if they were hearing this too.

"I was riding fast. The thunderstorm. My horse threw me in the barbed wire. It ran away. For three hours I have been picking my way through that forest. Crawling among the trenches and the guns. I—*Himmelkreuz-donnerwet-ter!"* The man's eyes brightened on Bill Shepherd; his features cleared on the furious oath.

"I am a stranger here." His voice loudened, biting off the English. "Is this the way a stranger is received in France?

Is this the way you aid an injured foreigner who comes asking for help out of a storm? Can you not see I have had an accident? Or is it perhaps you stand staring and do not help me because I am a German!"

Bill Shepherd jolted out of numbness. This man was angry. He had a bad gash on the forehead, and he was about all in. An accident! Bill Shepherd reached out a steadying hand.

"Of course you're welcome. We were all a little star-tled—! Archambaud," he lifted a shout. "Archambaud, bring some of that brandy out here. Quiet that dog. And have your wife heat some hot water and bring an antiseptic. Be quick!"

The German's expression altered. He panted, "I did not mean to give offense. It was that you stared so. But forgive my ill manner. My head is not good." And as Bill Shepherd led him to a chair, "You are my host?"

"I am the present owner of this *château.*"

The man groped under his jacket; produced a sodden card.

Siegfried Kull. Essen.

Bill Shepherd solicited: "Won't you make yourself comfortable in that chair, Herr Kull. I'll have a drink for you in a minute, and we'll take a look at that bash. I am William Shepherd; and this young lady, if I may present her, is Mademoiselle Gervais; and this is Mr. Fielding. We were all more or less driven in by the storm, and—would you like me to go at once for a doctor, Herr Kull?"

"Ach, nein. I do not think the hurt is severe. I was stunned—then, clawing my way through those woods out there, it unnerved me." He patted at the abrasion

with a handkerchief, and his breathing was becoming less laboured.

Gabrielle Gervais asked in a small voice, "Perhaps you would care for some black coffee, Herr Kull."

"Coffee? I think not. I do not like French coffee." Then he offered quickly, *"Ja,* but the wine is sometimes all right. The brandy will do. Thank you very much, *mademoiselle."*

ARCHAMBAUD HAD COME in with the brandy, then stalled in mid-room to eye the newcomer. Gabrielle Gervais hurried to take the bottle and pour Herr Kull a glass.

Herr Kull drank the brandy at a swallow, then closed his eyes and rested his head against the chair-back.

He said, in his slow English, "That is better. It was not nice out there in the rain. I did not know where I was. Never have I seen a forest as dark. I would trip over things and fall down. I was glad to see a light."

Bill Shepherd thought, "The man has been badly frightened."

But what was a German from Essen doing in the Forêt de Feu? This Picardy, the country of the Somme, was not on the German border. Germany, the Rhine, was some two hundred miles to the east. The Kaiser's troops had marched a long way to get into this part of France. They had goose-stepped down through Belgium, meeting bitter resistance every mile of the march.

And that had been in 1916. This was 1939. The troops of the Kaiser had been gone for twenty-three years. They had gone back to Germany, and the World War had passed into history; Berlin now belonged to Hitler, and today's battlegrounds were in China and Spain—Europe was busy planning for the next war—today's headlines carried no news of the Forêt de Feu.

He looked at Herr Kull uneasily.

Herr Kull sighed and took the handkerchief down from his forehead.

Ja, am feeling much better. I am going to be all right. That stupid swine of a horse, it shied at a lightning flash. The next thing I knew, I was in a tangle of barbed wire and the beast was gone. I suppose it will go back to its stable. Can you tell me, am I far from the village of Thiepval?"

"You rode from Thiepval?" Bill Shepherd asked.

Ja. This afternoon. I did not realize it was so late. The sun went down suddenly, it seemed. I thought to take a shortcut through the woods, and the storm was on me. The horse broke into a gallop. I have seen this forest often, but I did not think it covered such an area. I lost my sense of direction."

The English artist volunteered, "Thiepval is about eight kilometers from here. You must have taken the wrong turning and been headed for Contalmaison, the village to the south."

"This, then, is the Château de Feu, *ja?*"

Bill Shepherd nodded and asked, "Do you ride often in these woods?"

"Until tonight I have only scouted around them."

"Scouted around them?" Curious the German should have said *scouted,* Bill Shepherd thought.

Ja, I have covered the territory more to the east and north, and around Beaumont Harnel ard Bapaume. Ordinarily I have a field map, but this evening when I set out I left it behind. It was foolish of me, for I was warned the roads were intricate and the Forêt de Feu was No Man's Land. *Herr Gott!* I could not find the regiment I was looking for."

FIELDING LOOKED UP quickly, spilling tobacco out of his pipe. Gabrielle Gervais drew a sharp little breath. Bill Shepherd said in a strained voice, "You were looking for a regiment—!"

The German grunted. "But I do not know this front very well."

It was not the moment for Madame Landru to arrive in the doorway beyond the stairs and drop a pan of hot water.

At the clang and splash, everyone turned in alarm. The woman's eyes were white-rimmed in hypnotic fixity under a blowze of hair. On the edge of the lamplight, she stood like a somnambulist. One arm was upraised before her to the level of her shoulder, the finger pointing at the German in the hearthside chair.

"They have come," she intoned into the silence impeded by her eyes. "They are back in the Château de Feu. The Germans are here—!"

It was a minute or two before Bill Shepherd could speak. The German had seemed normal enough after that first startling moment of his arrival.

Conceivably he might be a vacationer in France, a tourist who had set out on horseback for an evening's canter. But his military turn of speech—scouting the forest—looking for a regiment—didn't know this front—the words had fallen strangely in that room of memories and shadows, and Bill Shepherd could hardly blame the old frenchwoman for pointing and staring.

He said unsteadily, "Pick up that dishpan, Madame

Landru. And stop that blithering! The Germans are not here—this gentleman is alone. He has had an accident riding in the forest. Bring some more hot water and some iodine."

Herr Kull had screwed his head around to focus a squinted glance on Madame Landru. His scowl showed resentment.

"What is the matter? Am I such an object for fright? I have no doubt, the mud and brambles I have been through. Does the woman take me for an invasion? Is a German so much to be feared?"

Bill Shepherd said huskily, "You talked of looking for a regiment—spoke of this front—!"

"A regiment of Uhlans, *ja*. Is this not the front line of the Somme? The German lines extend for so many miles one becomes lost. I did not realise I had ridden into enemy territory—I mean the territory occupied by the French and the British."

Bill Shepherd wondered if his hearing was aright. He sent a sidewise glance at a night-blackened window. Rain slashed at the leaded-glass panes, and wind cried faintly under the sill; the forest beyond was engulfed in streaming ink, and the only Uhlans possible out there were dead Uhlans, the surrounding territory occupied by French and British cemeteries.

Madame Landru had picked up the dishpan; her skirts swished through the puddle as she stepped forward; she came to a halt ten feet from the German's chair, and peered at him with eyes like the lenses of binoculars.

"I KNOW THESE Boches. The general, Von Arnim, used to sit in that very chair. *Oui,* and the other German generals with their collars buttoned to the throat and their shaved heads like that. They, too, spoke of scouting the forest and of losing their regiments. This will not be the first Boche whose wound I have bathed and bandaged."

Herr Kull stiffened upright in his chair. His shoulders arched back and his chest swelled out.

Crimson welled up his throat, up his jaws, a tidal flush that mounted to his temples and reddened his hairless head.

Stiffly he reared to his feet.

"Mein Herr!" he faced at Bill Shepherd. "Am I to be insulted by this old fishwife who calls me Boche? It is not the first time I have been grossly treated by these French. Believe me, I am not used to such terms of address from menials. Apparently my card means nothing to you. Evidently!"

"There is no insult intended," Bill Shepherd said in as level a tone as he could command. "We do not mean to be rude, Herr Kull. It is just that we don't understand what— what you were doing in the Forêt de Feu."

Herr Kull was trembling in anger. He made a visible effort for control, and managed a caustic smile.

"Doubtless my English is imperfect. I have not employed that poetic language for a considerable time. I suppose I have no right, either, to object to being called a Boche, since I am an intruder here.

"If you will allow me, I will attempt to make clear who I am and how I came to be in this forest. Although my home is in Essen and my business has to do with steel—I am not unknown in my homeland, *mein Herr*—I have spent a good bit of time in this part of France. Pardon me, am I making myself clear?"

Bill Shepherd nodded woodenly.

Herr Kull said acidly, "Thank you. So I have made my headquarters in the village of Thiepval. I want to inspect the battlefields. I go among the regiments—is that all right? I try to find out who they are and where they are placed. I am looking for this certain regiment of Uhlans.

"To date I have been unable to locate their position. Are they at Bapaume? Are they on the heights near the Schwaben Redoubt? I have maps, but I cannot find them. This evening I set out in saddle to look again. Perhaps they are hidden in these woods. How I was thrown by my horse I have already told you. Do you understand?" He gestured impatiently. "I am searching among the World War cemeteries!"

Relief passed through Bill Shepherd as though his nerves had relaxed with a sigh. He thought, "Good Lord, I've been acting like a fool!"

It was Madame Landru who had keyed him up like this. That woman and her spiritualistic flubdub. And an afternoon among graveyards, and that old gaffer along the highway, and all these superstitious ghost stories, and stumbling across that dead peasant by the road.

Why, this German was only a tourist seeking out a regimental cemetery—only a business man somewhere in the middle forties, a little stoutish in a riding habit, somewhat dazed by an accident, confused at finding himself at a stranger's fireside, choleric at what he considered inhospitable treatment—a German who had come to Picardy to visit the historic battlefields.

AND THEN BILL SHEPHERD'S thoughts took an ugly tangent. That strangled peasant back there in the poppies. Could Herr Kull know anything about that?

The question became generalized. Did anybody know anything about anything? Monsieur Bertrand; the woman in black; Mlle. Gervais; the Englishman—each of them appearing to hold some vagrant key to this *château* of his. And now this German....

The German's mien was one of chaotic emotions. Hot-tempered, infuriated one minute. Obsequious, nervously apologetic the next. In contrast to Fielding, whose British reserve had only cracked to the point of spilling some tobacco, Herr Kull was a mass of temperament.

The German was once more seated in his chair. The flush had ebbed from his features. His hands were passive on his knees, and his gazed fixed somberly on the dying fire.

"Forgive me if I am overwrought," he said. "You see, I have been trying to find a grave."

The words might have been a cue for what happened then.

As if timed to the second to come in at the end of that speech there was somewhere in the night outside a rumbling crash. It wasn't thunder, and it was followed by four sharp gun-like explosions. Somewhere near the *château* there were faint shouts, yells. An engine raced and died like an airplane taking off.

Everyone stood appalled. Then Bill Shepherd lunged for the door. He caught up his coat in passing, whipped out the Mauser pistol he had taken from the girl, and rushed out into a rain-squall.

It was bad enough—mighty bad. But even as he rushed headlong into the black rain, Bill Shepherd thought this was far better than sitting listening to the horrors that had poured from the caretakers' lips, meeting the sinister challenge of this strange German whom the night had thrust through his door.

Lights glimmered in the blackness some distance up the road, and he sprinted out through the gate-posts and pounded up the wagon-track, slipping and sloughing in the mire. The road, in the direction of the light-glimmers, was walled on either side by steep banks of earth, the soil washed raw by the rain.

Mud sluiced down into the roadbed, and the ruts were like gushing streams.

Bill Shepherd splashed blindly toward the rays of light. Then, some several hundred yards from the *château* gates, he came on the scene.

The lights, slanting skyward, silhouetted black cannon wheels. The gun was directly in mid road, a field piece Bill Shepherd recognized as French 75, its wheels askew in the road-ruts, its barrel tilted at a crazy angle, aimed up the bank. The caisson was wrecked, half buried under a landslide of earth.

Bill Shepherd made out a tangle of harness; could see nothing of an artillery team.

But there was a car.

A mud-splashed motor lorry in a culvert beyond the field gun. The jagged concrete foundations of a bridge that had spanned the culvert jutted where the road ended in a yawning gap; the bridge was a mass of broken masonry at the bottom of the culvert; the motor bus, wreckage at the culvert-bottom, shot its lights up into the air.

THE DISABLED CANNON in the road, the shattered bridge, the wrecked motor bus in the culvert made a war-time scene in the rain-blur. Smoke surged up from the car, and there was a smell of burning rubber—that bridge might have been a direct hit. Bill Shepherd stood dumbfounded, hardly aware that Fielding and Gabrielle Gervais and Herr Kull and Archambaud had arrived on the scene and were there in a frightened little group at his side.

He only knew that men down there in that car were groaning.

Then a figure detached itself from the smoke-hazed wreckage and came climbing up the embankment. Bill Shepherd reached down to give the climber a hand, and hauled up to the road a man in a mud-smeared uniform—a Frenchman in military boots and blue tunic, a chevron on his sleeve, aslant on his head a rakish French *képi*. His face was wild with excitement and grease; blood trickled from one nostril, dripping through a little black moustache; he waved his arms frantically and began to shout.

"Help me get them out of the wreck! They are in that bus down there! Help me get them out—the Italian!—and the Russian—!"

And from somewhere behind Bill Shepherd, Madame Landru's voice droned through the rain.

"They are all here tonight—! All together they have returned—! The British. The French. The Russians and Italians. The Germans. All here in the Forêt de Feu—! Fighting the Battle of the Somme—!"

13

THE CANNON IN THE ROAD

AND THERE ON that mud-swamped road with the shell-torn forest surrounding, the black rain pouring down, the lights of the wrecked bus spearing up out of the gap where the bridge had collapsed—the Frenchman in uniform outlined by the car-lights, and that French 75 gun mired in mid-road—one could believe it was the Battle of Somme. Was that muffled booming in the west the sound of thunder, or was it guns? Cries, faint groans from the wreck in the culvert were spectral. Everything was spectral in the downpour.

Bill Shepherd, peering in the rain-blear, saw the scene as something in a dream.

Yet the splash in his face was real enough. The Frenchman with the little black mustache was shouting. Someone elbowed against him, shoving him against the field gun; the cannon-barrel was cold and wet against his shoulder, undeniably solid iron.

Voices blurred and came back—Madame Landru's droning—oaths in German. Faces swam up through the rain—Archambaud's horsy countenance—Fielding's British features.

He found Gabrielle Gervais clinging to his arm—the

girl had run out without a hat, and her hair was pasted to her cheek—and there was this Mauser pistol gripped in his fist, and he wasn't imagining any of it.

He heard himself crying at the uniformed Frenchman, "What happened? What happened here?"

The little man with the bloody nose was wild. "How did I know it would be washed out? How did I know the road was a wreck? Would I round a bend and expect that cannon to be blocking the road? No one told me the forest was full of artillery!"

Fielding exclaimed, "By Jove, Shepherd! I bicycled over that bridge yesterday afternoon. This cannon wasn't here—"

"Someone will pay for it," the little lorry-driver wailed. "How can I explain the loss of my transport?"

It was Gabrielle Gervais who brought Bill Shepherd to his senses. *"Mon dieu!* Cannot you do something? There are men down there in that wreck."

Somehow he found himself slipping and sliding down into the culvert. Fielding was with him. Whatever had happened in this night of crazy fantasy, the emergency was actual. The thing was like a nightmare in which reality blended with jabberwock—the background was beyond the realm of possibility, yet the thing was happening.

Here was the bridge, a pile of broken cement blocks at the culvert-bottom. Here was the wrecked bus, a shapeless heap of wheels, machinery, spare parts and scrap tin—the sort of old car one might see in a junk heap. Yet it had just fallen through the bridge; its engine was smoking; its headlamps, bent at a crazy tilt, were on; and as he stumbled toward it, Bill Shepherd discerned an old Fiat—such an antiquated, wartime bus as one saw in the flickery news reels (it came to him as a shock) reviving the scenes of 1916.

Two gray shapes struggled to extricate themselves from the wreckage. Unbelievably one was cursing in firecracker Italian.

"Aaah, Corpo di Bacco! Santa Maria! Madre de Dio—!"

Unbelievably the other poked its head out of a broken window-frame, thrust its shoulders through the bent framework and crawled out through the aperture in a jangle of broken glass. As it straightened up to a stand, brushing its arms and chest, it was swearing in Russian.

"Are you all right?" Bill Shepherd reached the gasping man.

"And no fault of the devil who crashed us through the bridge," the answer came in thickly accented English. "I have seen bad roads in Siberia. *Da!* Nothing to this. Two hours of jolting capable of breaking one's spine, then this crash to break every bone in one's body. My ankle is badly wrenched, but I think that is all. Fortunately we Russians are thick-skulled. Here—let us rescue the Italian doctor."

FIELDING HAD ALREADY gone to this second passenger's aid; Bill Shepherd gave a hand to tear loose a crumpled fender and pull open the twisted door; the Italian, coughing and sputtering, was hauled out and balanced on his feet.

His felt hat was mashed down over one ear, and in the glare of the rain-glazed headlamps he looked no more than an average civilian, disheveled, badly shaken, dancing up and down and wringing the fingers of a pinched hand—as though this were any commonplace automobile accident.

Aside from the fact that Russia was a thousand miles away, the Russian, too, was unextraordinary—a stocky

*"I have seen them march by night, m'sieur—
these dead who will not sleep."*

man in a belted waterproof coat, limping up and down
and running his fingers through tousled hair in a most
naturalistic manner.

The Italian was distressed about a case of medical instru-
ments; Fielding was looking for it; if that bus had been a
station-wagon instead of an antiquated Fiat, and if that 75
cannon hadn't been up there on the road, and if this hadn't
happened in the Forêt de Feu, it ought have been an ordinary motor crash.

Bill Shepherd found himself helping the Russian up the
culvert bank, and Fielding and the Italian followed. The
people on the road above the culvert resembled any little
accident-crowd; the uniformed Frenchman might have
been any bus-driver trying to explain.

To his surprise, Bill Shepherd heard the man call himself
a bus-driver, bemoan the loss of his vehicle and curse the
luck that had turned him into the forest on a detour.

"Sapristi! and I thought to save time. I would not listen

to the keeper of the *bistro* at Thiepval. I thought to cut off ten minutes in the run to Contalmaison, and first it is the accursed mud; now this! Will someone explain that cannon blocking the road?"

It was strange to hear the little Frenchman asking for someone else's explanation.

Strange to hear Herr Kull's gruff voice in the rain, "Your army must be having troop maneuvers, but where in the devil are the artillery horses?"

The little Frenchman waved his *képi*. "I saw the cannon as I drove around that bend over there, but I did not see any horses. Sacred pipe! I jammed on the brakes. But my car was already on the concrete bridge. If I had not slowed for the accursed gun, I might have gotten across.

"*Non,* the bridge gave way with a crash. The next thing I knew we had plunged into the culvert. Did you hear the engine race and backfire as we hit the bottom? Lucky for the rain, or that wreck would be in flames. That is a ten-foot drop down there.

"Someone should pay for that—leaving up these treacherous bridges that the German army built in Nineteen-fourteen. You can see where the rain has washed out the bank and the concrete was undermined. Now I will get the blame. It is a wonder we were not all killed."

Bill Shepherd heard himself blurting, "So you drove through the woods on a shortcut for Contalmaison. The bridge caved under your car—?" And the motor-roar had only been the wrecked engine racing; the shots had been backfires from the exhaust.

"You can see for yourself where that bridge was washed

out, *n'est-ce pas?* It looks as if the rain has caused a land-slide."

BUT THAT DID not explain this cannon mired in the road ruts. It did not explain the little French driver of the Fiat, or his Russian and Italian passengers. From the background of night came the muttered ominations of Madame Landru: "The dead have never died in the Red Zone—!" and there was that corpse Bill Shepherd had seen in the woods at eight o'clock, and nothing in the Forêt de Feu was explained.

The others were crowding around the Italian and the Russian; voices rose in a medley of French, English, German—"Are you hurt?"—"Do you feel all right?"—but Bill Shepherd's throat had become constricted; his thoughts were black cats fighting inside his head; he could only stare in unbelief at the cannon and wonder how it had come there.

People might be hallucinary, but who had ever heard of a ghostly cannon? Could a ton of iron materialize out of nothing? Even that Fiat in the culvert had been powered by gasoline—he had smelled it leaking from the broken tank. What power had dragged this field gun across the road?

The wheels were clotted with mud, as if it had come a long way through the night; but the heavy iron rims had left no track. The caisson was half-buried in the hillside. It might have charged out of the bank above the road and taken up its position there to guard the bridge. The tilted muzzle gleamed blackly in the rain.

Bill Shepherd reached out and touched the sullen metal. There it was.

He realized Fielding was at his side.

"These woods of yours are full of old artillery pieces. Some farmer must have seen this gun and thought to salvage it. Probably tried to get it out with a team, and got bogged down here in the road. Did his salvaging at night because this forest is private property."

The British were always logical. Fielding, with his coat collar up and his cap-brim lowered to shield his eyes from the downpour, was the sanest of that night's jabberwocky. He went on:

"Hadn't we better get back to the *château?* It's a bloody nuisance, Shepherd—a lot of storm-victims barging in on you, like this—that bridge going down has cut the road to Thiepval; better dry us all off, then take us in your car to Contalmaison. That's your best bet, I should say. I wouldn't fancy sitting up with the lot of us all night—I think we're getting on the nerves of your Madame Landru."

The English painter had a level head. Bill Shepherd found himself nodding his own head, which wasn't level, and everyone was moving off in the rain, mud-slogging down the road for the *château.*

Madame Landru took the lead, her coat pulled up over her hair, the others followed in a sodden group, Shepherd and Fielding bringing up the rear.

As they turned through the broken gate-posts of the *château* driveway they were like, Bill Shepherd thought, a party of shades led by a spirit medium to a séance. Or was he making this whole thing up in his mind?

As a writer he had learned to mistrust imagination; in too many instances the mental picture became more real than the actuality; was all this some caper of a brain that had been steeped too long in mystery stories?

Of course Fielding was right and some peasant had tried to drag off that cannon as a nice piece of scrap iron. Doubtless there was a reasonable answer to a Frenchman in military uniform driving a doctor from Italy and a Russian from Muscovy across the middle of Picardy in a 1916 Fiat.

And Gabrielle Gervais, who had held him up two hours ago at the point of a loaded pistol? Well, the girl must have had her reasons, although the ones she had given had sounded too improbable.

More than ever Bill pondered his part in this incredible business. No chance of being a mere spectator.

He should have first solved that strangled corpse in the poppies; that murdered peasant was at the bottom of his panic. He resolved to speak to Fielding about it as soon as they were indoors; it would be a relief to get that one dead man off his mind.

14

THE VANISHING DOG

BUT EVERYONE WAS talking at once as they crowded under the porte-cochère; the last one cut had left the door open, and they jostled in out of the wet, filling the dim-lit room with the excitement of their voices.

He had no immediate chance to speak to Fielding. The Englishman, anxious to help, was assisting the limping Russian to a chair. Gabrielle Gervais had volunteered some sharp-spoken dialect to Madame Landru that sent the old Frenchwoman muttering to the kitchen. Archambaud clumped after his wife, obviously glad to get out of the picture. As he shut the door against the rain, Bill Shepherd heard himself being introduced to the Italian by Herr Kull.

The German was saying: "Herr Shepherd, here, is the master of the *château*. I, too, suffered an accident this evening. My horse threw me in the woods. It is Herr Shepherd to whom we are indebted for this haven."

The Italian had been handing his coat and hat and a little black bag to the driver of the Fiat. He gave William Shepherd a stiff bow.

"May I present myself? I am Doctor Arnoldo. This lady," he turned expectantly toward Gabrielle Gervais, "is your wife?"

The girl spoke up quickly, "I am Mademoiselle Gervais. Monsieur Shepherd was kind enough to rescue me from a ditch where I had stalled my car earlier this evening."

Doctor Arnoldo commiserated; "So you also have suffered from the storm." He smiled formally at the girl; drew a pair of pince-nez glasses from his waistcoat, and attached them to his nose; and somehow, despite muddied trousers and mussed hair, became dapper, suave and professional.

He inspected the room coolly, his glance returning to Bill Shepherd with polite appraisal. "It was good of you to come to our rescue, *signor;* I do not like the thought of spending the night in that forest. I have heard of how it rained in this part of France, but *Madre Maria!* it was as if the road from Thiepval was under a waterfall. And what a road!"

"The main highway to Contalmaison is flooded," the Fiat-driver complained. "I was only trying to detour from a dangerous route."

Doctor Arnoldo said agreeably, "For myself, I am grateful the mishap was not worse. I entered Thiepval Village by ambulance; I am glad not to be leaving by one. Indeed, had I not taken your omnibus, I might have been killed, for I was intending to leave by plane. Naturally," he said to Bill Shepherd, "I did not care to fly on such a night."

"Naturally," Bill Shepherd said.

"I would have flown in a plane any time in preference to that bus," the Russian, who had taken a chair by the fireplace, spoke up. He grunted, bending over to unlace a muddy shoe. "Uh! I have gone up in weather much worse than this. You die more quickly by plane," he grunted.

Herr Kull interjected the question that had numbed on Bill Shepherd's tongue. "You are an aviator, *mein Herr?*"

"I have a pilot's rating," the Russian nodded, kicking off his shoe and gingerly fingering his ankle. "In such a country as this you are safer in the air than on the ground. These French fly much better than they drive. I should have had more sense than to risk my life in that Fiat."

"It was a fine car," the little French driver lamented. "It had seen a lot of service, but the motor was in excellent repair. Blame these miserable wartime roads, but do not blame my poor car—wow, I feel as if I had lost a baby. And look"—he regarded himself unhappily—"at the grease on my tunic, the mud on my *képi*. The commandant at the station will take my head off."

BILL SHEPHERD'S OWN head was woozy. His brain had stalled. He wanted to account for these people distributing themselves about the shadow-walled room—people who took off wet coats and mopped their faces and dropped into chairs as would anyone under the circumstances.

Yet just when their conduct seemed natural, the Italian spoke of entering the district by ambiance, the Russian confessed himself a pilot, the little Fiat-driver bemoaned the "wartime roads" and spoke apprehensively of "the commandant."

Bill Shepherd heard the Italian doctor saying: "The fellow worries about mud on his uniform and the loss of that rattletrap motor. Me, I will only miss tomorrow morning's train to Paris. I have given my fingers a bad pinching, too. That is what I get for coming all the way from Milano with a surgical case, an idiotic old army general with a cranial concussion.

"Not another surgeon in Italy could perform a trephining as difficult; now I will not be able to operate with these fingers"—he held them up aggrievedly—"for at least three weeks."

"Would the doctor mind examining my ankle?" the Russian looked around to ask. "I think it may be sprained."

Gabrielle Gervais said in an aside to Bill Shepherd, "I sent the old woman after more hot water and soap. I think I can help the doctor if necessary; I used to be a nurse."

The place was assuming the aspect of a Red Cross station.

Fielding had found a log in a nook by the fireplace and thrown it on the grids. Herr Kull with his raw-scratched forehead, and the little Fiat-driver with a nosebleed, moved closer to the hearth. Doctor Arnoldo knelt to inspect the Russian's ankle. And Gabrielle Gervais became a nurse.

As he started automatically toward the table to offer the brandy bottle, Bill Shepherd would not have been surprised to see ten dead infantrymen littered on the staircase and a Prussian officer bayonet-pinned to the grandfather clock.

Then he realized the Russian was addressing him.

"Sir." The lamed man turned in his chair to gesture. "I have neglected to introduce myself to you, and doubtless you think me a boorish guest. Please attribute my bad manners to this devilish sprain, and know how much I regret putting you to inconvenience. I am Myroslav Pavlovich Putinov, Professor of Metaphysics and Psychic Research from the State College at Tomsk."

Bill Shepherd swallowed. "Professor of Metaphysics and Psychic Research—Tomsk—?"

The Russian smiled. "People appear surprised when

they bear of a university in Siberia. Tomsk has one of the
biggest libraries in the world." He grunted amiably. "Really,
we Russians are sometimes quite civilized. We are not all
Cossacks by any means."

"I—I thought you were an airman."

"Because I said I was a pilot? That is only in line of duty;
in civilian life I am merely a college professor. At present
I am—how do you phrase it?—on furlough. It is psychic
research that brings me to this country."

He included the others with his glance. "I am making a
study of the psychic phenomena, the metaphysical experiences of troops at wartime. If I survive long enough,"
he regarded the Fiat-driver caustically, "I will complete a
volume on the subject. Doubtless I should have remained
in Tomsk with my books. I did not anticipate being killed
on these battlefields of France."

"Nor I," Doctor Arnoldo added. "I am sorry I left Italy to
accompany that idiotic old general in his ambulance. But
he was rich and insisted, afraid he might die on the journey. Fate takes him safely to his family at Thiepval, and I,
the surgeon, suffer the dangerous accident."

BILL SHEPHERD WANTED to sit down with relief. What
a fool your imagination made of you in the face of simple
facts! This Russian was a college professor on leave, in
France doing research work. The doctor had brought a
patient in an ambulance from Italy.

They were travelers like Herr Kull—like him, himself—
and no more ghostly than Fielding.

To the Russian and the Italian, the little Fiat-driver was
complaining sullenly, "Well, you did not have to ride in
my bus. The commandant at the bus-station told you the

Contalmaison Road was flooded. I would not have set out, but I have never before missed the schedule, and I wanted to keep the record. Always before I have come through the Forêt de Feu in safety. There is no better driver in France than Marcel Tac."

Bill wanted to laugh.

This grease-smeared little bus-driver named Marcel—in the technique of drama it was known as low comedy relief. People invariably reminded Bill Shepherd of birds or animals; the black-eyed Frenchman was a ruffled rooster, and Marcel wasn't the name you expected from a bantam.

Doctor Arnoldo was more in keeping; the man was sleek and a little like a cat; while Putinov just suited that Russian, who had hairy hands and bushy eyebrows and a thick black mop, and resembled, symbolically, a grumbling bear.

And there was Madame Landru in that doorway at the back, looking like death!

Bill Shepherd's scalp went tight again as he saw the woman was signaling him with a witchlike finger, and he hurried around the table to find out what she was staring at now.

"There is someone in the *château*," she told him in a croaking undertone. "Someone who came in while we were out. I can hear someone moving about in the room above the kitchen. And the dog is gone."

15

NONE BUT THE GHOSTS

FIIELDING CAUGHT BILL SHEPHERD'S beckoning look and joined him in the passageway. Bill Shepherd muttered, "Look here, Fielding, I may want your help for a minute. It's probably nothing, but I don't want to bother those others. The old woman thinks there's a prowler in the place."

The Englishman made a reassuring sign, and they hurried down the narrow passage to the kitchen.

Bill Shepherd was glad of Fielding's company as he entered that arch-ceiled *cuisine*. It was not the homely kitchen of American standards, a friendly workshop for cook and matronly housewife.

This kitchen was cavernous; a brick-floored chamber, dank, engloomed, its corners too far away for the feeble rays of a single oil lamp. There was a vast brick oven built into the wall, and bins for vegetables ranged alongside, and a vast array of kettles and cauldrons and iron cookpots hanging under the eaves.

Shelves of crockery sent faint gleams from an alcove; in the middle of the floor stood a massive, rough-hewn table, bumpy-surfaced like a meat cutter's table in a butchershop; there was a smell of dead fires and stale cookery.

Bill Shepherd couldn't decide whether the atmosphere, with that vast brick oven, was that of a crematorium, or—with that chopping table and those cauldrons—a torture chamber.

At any rate, it wasn't a domestic scene with Archambaud standing against the wall as though rooted in his wooden shoes, and Madame Landru posed in mid floor, saucer-eyed, her finger pointing at the ceiling.

"Listen, *messieurs*. Listen—!"

Shepherd and the Englishman listened.

"There it is. *Voilà!* Now!"

Listening, they heard overhead what sounded like a rattle of loose plaster, a faint moan, the creak of a door-hinge.

Archambaud whispered steamily, "There is a crack in the ceiling, a place where the bricks are broken, that is why we can hear."

"*Ssshhhhh,* idiot!" Madame Landru glared. "Would you have the spirits come down here after us?"

Fielding whispered, "There's a prowler on the upper floor, all right."

"And no one in the *château* except Archambaud and myself," Madame Landru breathed. "That is," she looked at Fielding, "until you and these others came."

Bill Shepherd set his teeth, "I'm going up there. Give me that lamp. Is there a stairway at the back here, or do I have to go by the front?"

Archambaud pointed at a door dimly visible at room's end. Fielding said quietly, "I've got a flashlight," and producing one from his pocket sent a small ray at the indicated door.

Bill Shepherd said to the oggle-eyed Archambaud, "Come out of that, you're going with us. You know the upstairs; I don't. I'll be right beside you with the lamp. Lead the way."

He could hear the old caretaker's teeth clicking as he opened the stair door and disclosed a steep flight of stone steps. His own teeth weren't any too courageous. He kept his right hand in his pocket on the Mauser pistol, and held the oil lamp in his left, and gave Archambaud a knee-shove to start him up the climb.

THE STAIRWAY MADE a hairpin bend, and Archambaud had to stop and cross himself before going on up. A door at the top was closed. "Shall I open it, *monsieur?*"

"Does it open into a corridor?"

"Into a bed chamber," Madame Landru's voice floated up from the rear. "It has not been occupied since Nineteen-sixteen. But perhaps its former occupants have returned. A colonel of the Prussian Guard and two French officers of the *Chasseurs Alpines* were killed by shellfire while sleeping in there."

Bill Shepherd muttered, "Damn!" under his breath, and opened the door with a kick.

Dust swirling at him out of darkness was ghostly, and black shades fled across the room as he entered, racing to escape the yellow lamp. He stood across the threshold, swearing. But whatever had prowled in that chamber was gone. The shades were only shadows and the wraiths were puffs of white plaster-dust.

A door at the front of the room hung ajar on a broken hinge, and the footpad must have made an exit that way.

But the room looked as if it had not been entered for

years. The windows were boarded over, and a gap in the ceiling was covered with heavy timbers. Glass and chunks of broken masonry were strewn across the floor; one corner was stacked with odd pieces of furniture and trash; bed-springs stood upright against a windowsill; under the gap in the ceiling there had been a landslide of plaster, and every thing in the room was gauzed over with cobweb or coated with a thick, gray-white powder.

"False alarm?" Fielding's voice behind Shepherd was cheerful.

"Nothing here," Bill Shepherd elevated the lamp. He gave a winded laugh. "No footprints in the plaster or hand-marks on that door, but—there's something for you. Look there by the door. Dog-tracks!"

"Sure enough." The Englishman spotted them under the white circle of his flashlight. "You can see where the animal came in from the hall, trotted around the room. Look, he sat down at this stair door; then went out by the front way. George! That moan was a dog-whine. And when he went out he moved that broken door on its hinge."

Bill Shepherd handed the lamp to Archambaud. "Nothing but your hound. He came upstairs while we were out on the road, and tried to get down the back way. Why the devil didn't you know it was your beast?"

"Theophile does not often leave the kitchen," Archambaud murmured.

"Theophile! Is that the name of your dog?"

"And a splendid watch-dog he is," came Madame Land-ru's drone. She was framed with her goitre at the top of the back stairs, finger pointing into the gloomed room. "Dogs can see what we do not; dogs can tell with a seventh sense.

Theophile would not have come from below had he not known someone was here. The dog scents a track that we do not see. There are those in the Forêt de Feu who do not leave visible tracks."

It jarred on Bill Shepherd's nerves. There had been no wheel-ruts left by the cannon in the road; no murderer's footprint near that dead man in the poppies. He opened his mouth to tell the old woman to close hers; then shut his teeth with a snap.

In some far wing of the *château* the dog was howling.

Yah–wooooooo—!

THE HOWL ECHOED eerily through the *château's* mildewy upper stillness, a long-drawn ululation that sounded as if it had traveled through many galleried rooms and corridors, across high balconies and down successive flights of winding stairs before it arrived, faint and weak, in that bed chamber over the kitchen.

As Bill Shepherd listened, the howl was repeated. Then a third time, more prolonged. He recognized it now as an urgent baying. He had heard hounds bay like that in the pine woods in Maine when they had some animal treed.

He flung at Archambaud: "Where's that dog?"

The man's hobby-horse eyes bulged in fright. "It sounds as if he was somewhere in the tower wing. *Parbleu!*"

"I'm going to find out. Lead the way with that lamp! Get a move on!"

White dust smoked up under their shoes as they crossed the devastated room; the hinge screamed dismally as Bill Shepherd pulled open the door; a gust of stale air breathed into his face as he stepped out into a corridor.

Lamplight wiggled its way down the corridor to reveal

a balcony at the far end, and white-toed dog tracks led them on. Their shadows ran along the wall with them as they advanced down the passage, and the dog—the sound seemed to come from a mile away—was baying like the hound of the Baskervilles.

Emerging from the corridor, they came to a wide mezzanine; the lamp-gleams picked out a marble balustrade at the head of a broad staircase, and Bill Shepherd knew they were on a balcony overlooking a great hall.

The caverned dark in front of him was like night in a closed museum; Archambaud's sabots, clacking on a floor of tile, raised answering echoes, and his hoarse voice interrupted a silence that might have been long unbroken by human speech.

"Be careful here. There are gaps in the floor. The balcony is littered with obstructions. This," he groaned, peering around at the darkness, "was the main hall of the *château*. Ah, what could anyone want in here now? There have been no visitors since the Invasion."

"None but the ghosts," came Madame Landru's droning undertone. "I have heard them in here before. They use this hall for their headquarters, even as the living generals gathered here to map their battle-plans. They are in here tonight—the Forgotten of God!"

If ghostly generals gathered anywhere to map their battle-plans, this hall, Bill Shepherd told himself, was certainly the place for such a conference.

Fielding was switching his flashlight across the balcony, and the white ray, spearing through blackness, journeyed across a desolation of havoc, ravagement and ruin. Fire and earthquake had been here.

The balcony at a distant end was caved and twisted like an old wooden dock. There were gaps in the balustrade where the marble bannisters had been smashed as though by a vandal's sledge. The ray followed the railing to a wall that was fire-smudged and pitted; dropped hastily to the floor below, and circled off across mounds of wreckage.

Tiles were scattered everywhere like shot clay pigeons; everywhere there were piles of broken plasters, junk-heaps of smashed furniture, dumps of trash and rubble and kindling.

From wall to wall the great room was scattered and strewn—carpets torn up and thrown aside; mahogany tables overturned; chairs and divans piled together; a great grand piano with its legs in the air; in the center of the floor a vast hummock of bangles and glass that had once been a pendent chandelier.

Mold and rust had added their smell to corruption. A line of tall windows at the side had been boarded over, and a great breach in the front wall patched with lumber, but rain and weather had leaked in; water ran in rivulets down the scarred walls, there was a vast puddle at the foot of the staircase, and here and there the ceiling was dripping.

Fielding said, "Whew!" The flashlight ray had stopped on a figure that was standing at the curve of the staircase. A knight in armor leaning on his mace! The visored helmet was bowed in contemplation; the mailed fingers were folded on the axe-head. He might have come there from seven hundred years ago to view the demolition of modern war. In the Middle Ages he had never seen anything like the destruction he beheld below.

Bill Shepherd pulled a sharp breath at sight of this

watcher. But Archambaud said huskily, "That is only a suit of armor. It was worn by the *Grand Seigneur*, the Charles of Picardy who was here the first *châtelain*. Ah, this was a fine hall before it was destroyed. If you could have seen it before this *délabrement*—!"

It was no moment to pause over toppled grandeur and ravished magnificence. Bill Shepherd rasped, "That dog—! Get on!" But he couldn't help a stomach-twist of emotion as he followed the old caretaker to a corridor at the end of the balcony—an emotion of horror at the wreckage.

TAPESTRIES TORN TO rags, statuary pulverized, flooring ripped up, things trampled and half-burned and smashed to kindling and dismantled—what a mad, inhuman fury must have once raged unchecked through here. The devastation was senseless. What end had been gained by gouging those holes in the wall? What cause had been served by tearing a plumbing-pipe out of the plaster, mutilating a teak-wood cabinet, hurling a settee into a marble fireplace, shattering a great jardiniere?

The havoc had not been confined to this hall.

Insane furies had swept through the rooms beyond. Archambaud led the way down the corridor to a library where the ceiling had crashed in, and books, dumped from their shelves, were smothered under the avalanche of rubbish that had been furnishings in the room above.

The lamp and flashlight made strange and senseless discoveries. A four-poster bed and a commode in the library. Volumes of Rousseau, Montaigne, Molière, Hugo, Baudelaire strewn down the hall. The library table up-ended in the drawing room, and a bathtub exposed nudely in the midst of a clutter of gilt-legged chairs.

The drawing room had a ceiling, but it lacked a sidewall; and they walked in and went through the gap to get into the room beyond because the corridor was blocked up with sandbags. This room had been a parlor.

The furniture had been removed, but the pictures had been left on the wall, pretty ladies in big hats smiling from gilt frames, and charming landscapes and garden scenes. There was a black hole in the ceiling, and a shovel in the middle of the floor; on the carpet someone had been mixing cement.

They climbed a stairway to the floor above and found their heads exposed to rain. Here the rooms were gutted, the outer walls shot through with jagged holes that let in the downpour and the night. There was a succession of empty bedchambers; then surprisingly a room choked with saddles, harness and riding equipment, useless and fire-charred; more empty rooms. Another stairway brought them to the *château's* top floor.

They proceeded carefully, for in many rooms here the floor had caved. The rooms were like jungles full of broken brick, collapsed timber and masonry. Doors were burst and walls and windows gone.

Bill Shepherd would never forget one room where the limb of a tree reached in through the window like a great black arm, and they had to claw their way to get through the branches and foliage.

Trees growing in through windows—beds in the library—bathtubs in drawing rooms—chimney bricks at the bottom of a flight of stairs—the *château* had the atmosphere of one of the mad poems of Baudelaire, whose volumes littered that lower corridor. One could believe a horde of apes had run with axes through the halls, rampant. They had chopped and battered and breached the walls, and they had been followed by swarms of monkeys with torches who touched fire to whatever the apes had missed.

Bill Shepherd had seen such glimpses of wanton destruction in news reels of Shanghai and Madrid. He had heard of the freakish tricks of shellfire, and he had been prepared to see considerable ruin. But ruin furred over with mold and decay was more disheartening than the wreckage in the news.

The *château* was worse than the forest where the saplings had grown as camouflage. Its wounds had been neglected and gangrene had set in. It was like those ghosts old Madame Landru was mumbling about—neither buried nor reconstructed, a haunt from Nineteen-sixteen carrying on with the Battle of the Somme.

"Get on with it!" he gave Archambaud a nudge. At every doorway and corridor-bend the horse-eyed Frenchman had balked; it had taken some driving to get him up that last flight of steps.

"Theophile!" Archambaud panted. "He has stopped."

16

A HERO IS DEAD

IN THE TRIP through these halls of destruction, occupied by darkness and demolishment and spiders and rats, Bill Shepherd had almost forgotten the dog howls leading him on. Now he was aware the hound had gone silent.

"There goes his track," Fielding spotted the toe-marks with his flashlight. "Be careful, Shepherd. The floor here is shaky. You can't trust shell-shocked buildings like these. A jar, and you might drop through three floors to the cellar."

Shell-shocked. That was a good description of these ruins. The floor up here was as shaky and treacherous as scaffolding. Many of the rooms were open to the sky, their black walls starkly silhouetted against the night.

The rain had temporarily quit, and you could look up and see green-black clouds surging across a watery moon. In places the roof was a skeletal framework, and there were areas where the slating remained undamaged.

These mansards and undermined floorings were perilous. The dog-tracks wove about through the wreckage, and the men, following, picked their way cautiously through tangles of collapsed timbering and across fire-eaten floors.

Madame Landru brought up the rear, mumbling sombre memories of air raids and bombardments. They clambered over piles of slate and residue and climbed between broken chimneys and roofless gables. Archambaud seemed to know where the going was secure—the dog had chosen a sure-footed route—and they came at last to an enclosed chamber where the ceiling was buttressed up with massive stone arches and the walls had not been breached.

The dog-tracks trotted about the room and clustered at the back wall, as if the beast had walked in circles there. Archambaud lifted the lamp, peering anxiously. Fielding let his flashlight play about the corners. The dog and whatever he might have hunted there were nowhere in sight. Only an empty chamber full of night wind and shadows and dog-tracks.

"See," Madame Landru whispered. "The dog has followed someone we have been unable to see. He comes up here to this room underneath the tower, and howls."

Bill Shepherd looked around. "This room is under the tower?"

The old woman nodded, pointing up. "The Norman tower. It rises above us, another fifty feet. Alone of this quarter of the *château* it withstood the terrible shelling."

"And the dog comes up here and howls?"

Madame Landru nodded, "A number of times before. Archambaud and I have come up from the kitchen to find out why. We have never seen the intruder, but the dog has seen him—the dog knows where he has gone. Always the dog sits in front of that wall and bays his soul out."

"He is not here now," Archambaud peered nervously. "Theophile—!" he raised a quavering call. "Where are you, Theophile—?"

Fielding said quietly, "Your Theophile went out through

that side passage over there. Probably he chases big rats or rodents from the forest or something up here. At any rate, it looks as if he's gone back to the kitchen."

"So," Archambaud looked hopeful. *"Oui,* there is a stairway down to the ground floor at the end of that passage. It is choked up with rubbish and in some places the steps are gone, but a dog would be able perhaps to use it. Very likely. Doubtless it was that he was chasing rats."

"Comedian!" Madame Landru gave her husband a glare. "There are dog tracks left by his feet which have walked in plaster dust. If it was a rat he pursued, there would also be rat tracks."

Fielding suggested, "A bat, then. He might chase up here after bats he has hounded from the rooms below. There's a big one, right now, on that wall up there."

HE SPOTTED THE nocturnal creature with a circle of white light from his pocket-torch—a large bat high up on the backwall, its devil-wings spread, like a great black butterfly. Startled by the light, the creature detached itself from the wall like an animated shadow; came flying across the room in a series of eccentric dives.

Madame Landru shrieked, throwing her coat over her hair, and Bill Shepherd struck at the whizzing thing as it circled his face. Squeaking and fluttering, it shot out through a portal and vanished into blackness beyond.

"You should not have done that," Madame Landru gasped. "There will be a death in the family if you strike a bat. Besides, you do not know. They say these bats are the mascots of the dead—the messengers in the armies of the slain—the carrier-pigeons in the battles of the Forgotten of God. Perhaps he was waiting there on that back wall for a message. A message," she pointed, "from the one whom the dog followed tonight—the one who went through that tower door."

Bill Shepherd couldn't see any tower door. The old woman's finger indicated the rear wall. The wall was blank.

Archambaud said huskily, "My wife means the door that was there, *monsieur*. One entered the tower through a door in that wall, and a circular flight of steps ascends to the room high in the turret. The door is sealed up with plaster, Monsieur Shepherd. It was your father's order that the tower be closed, the door sealed over."

Stepping forward, Bill Shepherd could make out a spread of gray plaster across the older stonework. He said in an uncomprehending tone, "My father gave orders the door was to be sealed?"

"I did it myself," Archambaud nodded. "I can show you your father's letter of instruction. It is only a thin covering of plaster that can be easily broken through if you wish to open the door and enter the tower. The turret remains in a remarkably undamaged condition. A thousand shellings failed to make a direct hit. This is the old part of the *château*, and the tower walls and foundations are very strong. *Enfin*, your father wished the tower closed."

Bill Shepherd stared at the wall where the door had been sealed. "Why?"

"They say it was in the tower that your brother died, *monsieur*."

"Hugh—?" Instinctively Bill Shepherd made a backward step from the wall.

Archambaud's face lengthened mournfully behind the lamp. "I did not see it. My wife did not see it. It was the day when the bombardment was at its worst. You would not blame us for hiding in the deepest wine cellar?"

Bill Shepherd gestured impatiently. "What about my brother?"

**"CAPTAIN SHEPHERD, *MONSIEUR,* was a fine officer—one the most brave. Myself, I thought the War was over when he arrived at the *château* with a company of Canadians. My wife and me, he treated us as old friends.

"We brought out the best champagne, such a few bottles as we had been able to hide from the German thieves, and we prepared those Canadians and your good brother a magnificent meal. *Ah-la-la,* the next day the German guns began their counter barrage.

"Blanche and I retired to the cellars, but even there the thunder was like the Day of Judgment. For three days the blasting lasted, and it was in that bombardment that your brother was reported missing."

The old caretaker sighed and shook his head. "My wife and I never saw him again. There were so many bodies, you comprehend—but you imagine now it was in those rooms which you have just seen. For hours the Red Cross and ambulance men sorted and dug and hunted. Several officers said they had seen Captain Shepherd hit. It was established he had been struck in the leg and carried into that library you saw. But the ceiling crashed there, and the wounded were taken to another room.

"An officer in that quarter said Captain Shepherd had a shattered arm. A rush of Prussian Guards charged the *château* at one hour when the shelling was lifted, and it was impossible for the Canadians to escape to the rooms below.

"They said your brother with others of the badly

wounded was carried finally up to this tower which was withstanding the shells. But airplanes came over with gas bombs. In the confusion of a gas attack the Red Cross men were ordered from the tower. Then there was heat from the burning rooms, and much dust and smoke. Afterward—?"

Archambaud stopped speaking with lifted shoulders.

"They said he died in the tower," Madame Landru muttered. "There was a stretcher-bearer who said he had left Captain Shepherd dead in the tower. But the bodies that were brought down, you could not recognize them. The heat and gas—!"

"They were all carried quickly away," Archambaud remembered. "The ambulances came and went with the wounded in constant traffic. The dead went away in truck-loads, hour after hour. The Canadians charged back in. There were other bombardments—other counter-attacks. There was no time to pay respects to the dead in that first month of the Battle of the Somme."

Bill Shepherd turned away from the sealed wall with a heaviness in his heart. There was no time to pay respects to the dead now.

Too many had lost their lives in this charnel house to admit any feeling of personal bereavement. In the years since the War, Hugh's personality and character had faded in memory like a boyhood myth—this plastered-up wall and shell-torn ruin, and even the photograph of Hugh, had failed to revive a sense of close relationship.

Bill Shepherd could feel his father's presence in this wreckage more strongly than that of his brother. Hugh had been here and gone in one breath of cataclysm, but

Old Bill's heart had been buried here—entombed in grief behind that sealed wall.

"Let's get out of here," Bill Shepherd rounded and spoke harshly. "There's no prowler here; that dog was only chasing bats. Come on, we've got to get back below with the others."

His mood was a mixture of relief, chagrin, *malaise*. Relief that no lurking footpad had been found. Chagrin at having chased off at the summons of a dog-howl. Uneasy because the evidence of death had filled his mind with formless dreads.

IT WASN'T THE old woman's mumbling—that was picayune idiocy, to be ignored. He knew Madame Landru was mentally unbalanced; and he didn't wonder, considering the War experiences she had been through and the years she had spent afterward steeped with her husband in the dismal atmosphere of these unreconstructed walls.

The couple had been here for twenty-three years, and one night in these ruins was enough to have you haunted. The ruins themselves were a consequence of madness.

As the party picked its way cautiously down to the floors below, Bill Shepherd went angry and cold in turn at the aspect of human violence.

Shellfire hadn't destroyed these walls. Men had destroyed them. Neither apes nor monkeys had burned and battered these rooms—men had gutted them, deliberately and fiendishly, training their giant engines of destruction on this mark, giving the orders to fire and smash, working with all the science at their command to blast apart what they had built.

All over Picardy this blasting and smashing had gone on;

the Forêt de Feu was another evidence of man's handiwork; the Red Zone cemeteries a final achievement of insanity. One conceived in this *château* a picture of mankind gone stark berserk; hordes of maniacs hurling themselves at each other's throats; a whole world degenerated to demonism.

It was enough to make you look sideways at your neighbor; if he had run amuck yesterday and plunged into a revelry of homicide, what assurance had you that he wouldn't turn berserk here tonight?

Bill Shepherd caught himself glancing at Fielding; checked himself sharply. No time for this sort of philosophizing. No place to start an analysis of War. Think of this *château* as an historic ruin, not an evidence of mankind's cruel vandalism. See the War cemeteries as lawns set with beautiful white crosses—forget the thousands of corpses moldering under them. That murdered peasant in the poppies was the important problem. No, the important problem was the murderer—

They were passing the library, and a rat dashing out of a nest of torn books and racing between Bill Shepherd's ankles cut his line of thought. He sprang sideways, startled by the scurry.

Fielding said, "Take it easy, old man."

He paused to handkerchief from his forehead a rush of prespiration. "Sorry, Fielding, you must think my behavior damned odd." He put a confidential hand on the Englishman's arm. "My nerves are all wearing through my skin. I saw something on the road, driving out here tonight. I think I'd better tell you—"

"Was it a dead man?" Fielding asked.

17

VICTIMS OF THE RESTLESS DEAD

MADAME LANDRU AND her husband were a few feet ahead; Bill Shepherd dropped his tone out of their hearing on a tense-whispered. "How did you know?"

"Mademoiselle Gervais told me."

"Mademoiselle Gervais!"

Fielding nodded, meeting Bill Shepherd's consternation with level gray eyes. He said in a low voice, "The French girl saw him, Shepherd. A dead peasant lying by the road. In a patch of poppies. He wore a blue smock and wooden shoes, if it's the same one you—"

"Of course! The girl must have driven into the forest an hour or so ahead of me. I saw the prints of her tires in the mud. And she saw the peasant too." He narrowed his eyes. "Why didn't she tell me? How did she happen to tell you?"

"I suppose she didn't tell you for the same reason that you didn't tell her." Fielding assumed. "You didn't know she'd seen him, and you didn't want to alarm her, isn't that it?

"Well, her story is that she passed this dead man in her car. Too frightened to stop, of course. In her panic, she drove on at top speed and ran herself into a ditch. She told me all this a little awhile ago when we were running down the road to that bus accident "

"She didn't say a word about it to me, Fielding."

"When you drove up behind her in the forest there, she'd been sitting in her ditched car too scared to budge. She saw your lights coming, and she pulled out a pistol her uncle or somebody had happened to leave in her car. Natural thing, I suppose—forest at night—stranger approaching—rainstorm and all that."

"But why didn't she tell me she'd seen—?"

"You frightened her. She says she asked you who you were, and you went rambling off in a strange way about the literary profession and life in general. I take it she thought you were—eh—a bit balmy."

Bill Shepherd declared in a savage undertone, "I was kidding her. I thought it was a stickup. I was trying to talk her off her guard."

"So I assumed when she told me about it. A European wouldn't understand American kidding. The girl says you grabbed her gun. I guess she wanted me to know you were armed with a pistol. Anyway, that's the story she gave me when we followed you out to that bridge. She wanted my advice about you.

"I must say, I was a little taken back; I'd rather imagined you and the girl were—pardon the presumption—old friends. I told her I thought you were right as rain, and that you belonged here—we're all strangers more or less in the same boat, and that I'd speak to you about the dead man."

"Did she explain how she happened to be in the Forêt de Feu?"

Fielding shook his head. "Wasn't time, and I didn't ask

her. We'd come up to the accident scene by then. But I'd been going to speak to you about that dead man, Shepherd. After the girl's story, I'd conjectured that perhaps you hadn't seen the body. But that was your reason for wanting a telephone as soon as you came into the *château* tonight, what?"

They were crossing the wrecked mezzanine of the main hall. Archambaud and his wife were moving in advance; and Bill Shepherd slowed to a lag, whispering to Fielding the circumstances surrounding the dead peasant. He concluded grimly, "The man had been dead about an hour, and he died from violence, Fielding. Fingernails dug in his throat, and the marks of a choking clutch on his neck. Murder."

Fielding gave him a straight look. "I was afraid you were going to say that. The description tallies. Shepherd, I saw that man this afternoon."

Bill Shepherd's feet stalled. "Where?"

"IN THE FOREST. I should say it was around half past five o'clock. I was on my bicycle. As I told you, I'd come into the forest for a bit of exercise. I couldn't say where it was exactly—there are a lot of paths in the woods—I'd judge it was a mile or so north of the wagon road. This fellow in the blue smock was in a clump of bushes."

"What was he doing?"

"I couldn't see very well. The sky was a bit overcast—do you remember, there was an odd sort of gloaming? But I think the chap was digging."

"Digging?" Bill Shepherd echoed.

"At least he was bent over in an industrious kind of way. Couldn't quite make out what he was up to in the underbrush—he might have been picking berries—but I had the impression he was working with a shovel. Only caught a glimpse of him.

"When he saw me, he gave me a startled look, dropped something in the brush and scuttled away. Struck me as all very furtive. I didn't seen anyone else around. The storm was making, and I took the nearest bypath for the *château*."

Bill Shepherd thought, "So that's why I didn't see bicycle tracks on the wagon road." He said in a low voice, "Well, the peasant was murdered, Fielding. There's something going on in this forest. Other murders. You heard the old woman."

"And talk in the village," Fielding nodded. They were rounding into the corridor leading to the back bed chamber where the dog had first been heard. The Landrus were shuffling well in the lead.

Fielding's voice lowered confidentially. "If you don't mind my saying so, Shepherd, this forest of yours is a dashed gloomy property. All sorts of rumors about it, but I do understand there've been recent casualties around and the police can't seem to figure them out.

"I don't like to put my finger in your business, so to speak—this is your *château* the domain, and I've been trespassing myself—but has it occurred to you that your caretakers might know more about this than they've cared to divulge?"

He glanced at the couple entering the bed chamber ahead; and Bill Shepherd growled. "It hasn't only occurred to me, but when we get down to the kitchen, I'm having a word with the Landrus. Maybe the old woman's batty, and maybe"—he broke off with a gesture, but he finished the sentence in his mind—"maybe there's method in her madness."

Maybe a lot of things.

He hadn't forgotten old Bertrand's skittish conduct that morning, or the lady in black who had swooped out of the lawyer's door. He hadn't forgotten the value of this property. He wasn't forgetting, either, that Fielding was a stranger for all his open-handed conduct, that all these people were strangers. You couldn't help mistrust in your fellow man after a tour through a *château* that gave evidence to mankind's savagery, and with murder still afoot in the potter's field, all neighbors became suspect.

He said, "Stand by, will you, Fielding? While I question this pair. Then we'll drive out and take a look at that body on the road."

THE LANDRUS, HOWEVER, could shed no light on the matter. If anything, their answers obscured it in deeper shade. Madame Landru did most of the talking. Bluntly ordered to tell what she knew of this latest and all previous murders, the old Frenchwoman lapsed into a mediumistic trance more glassy-eyed and fuzzy-haired than before.

"I said keep to facts." Bill Shepherd rejected her immediate references to the spirit world. "Did you know this peasant I've described, or didn't you?"

"Ah." The old woman's eyes glazed over in thought. She hooked a finger over her nose, thinking. "But I seem to recall such a neighbor, *monsieur*. A farmer who had a cabbage patch on the edge of the forest where now there is a Canadian cemetery. But I have not seen him in a long time."

"How long is that?"

"I have not seen him in twenty-three years, *monsieur*. He was shot and killed by the Germans in Nineteen-sixteen."

"This man was killed out there in the forest tonight," Bill Shepherd reminded sternly. "He was murdered not four miles from this *château*, and he was strangled to death. You—" He switched the question to Archambaud. "Do you recollect ever having seen the man?"

The gaunt caretaker edged backward against the shadowy brick oven, like a horse backing up in a stall. His eyes roamed the kitchen and settled finally into a nervous stare on his hoof-like wooden shoes.

"I do not recollect such a man, Monsieur Shepherd. I knew the farmer my wife refers to, but as she says, he was killed in Nineteen-sixteen. He was taken as a spy by the Germans, and they—"

"This man was murdered tonight, not twenty-three years ago. If you don't know who it was, say so "

Archambaud said so. He added that there were few neighbors living in the immediate vicinity of the Forêt de Feu, as the farmlands surrounding the woods were now cemeteries. He and his wife seldom left the *château*.

Perhaps once a month they went to Contalmaison or Thiepval after grocery supplies, but they did not spend much time in either village. They had no friends; new villagers had moved in since the War; many of the refugees driven out by the Germans had never come back; it was seldom that anyone came near the *château*.

"They know about the undead soldiers," Madame Landru droned in. "They fear the Forgotten of God. The peasant you found by the road tonight but proves what I have told you. The armies of the slain are in the forest. Their sentries must have killed him."

Bill Shepherd's jaw hardened.

You couldn't argue over ghosts with an old woman who was probably demented. Archambaud's mentality seemed little better. He found his glance going to Archambaud's hands—long-wristed, big-knuckled peasant's hands, no doubt capable of wringing someone's neck—but there had been previous murders in the forest—if this couple had had anything to do with them, it seemed incredible the police would not have found it out.

"Never mind the spirit legend, Madame Landru. What about the people killed around here in the last two or three years? You named a farmer and a blacksmith's daughter and a child."

"That is true. *Absolument.* The old Farmer Castignac, he had come with his dog one night after rabbits. A poacher, *oui,* setting traps out there in the forest. He was not of much account, a rascal. In the valley this side of Thiepval Village where he lived, he was known as an atheist, he did not believe in spirits, saints or demons, and he laughed at the stories about the Forgotten of God, even as he laughed at the legends of the church.

"Perhaps the undead soldiers in the forest heard him—perhaps he was killed by a stray bullet in the unseen battle—I do not know. *Enfin,* he was shot dead.

"It was not a night like this, but one of no moon, very dark, very quiet. Landru and I were here in the kitchen. We heard the rifle. We ran out. Theophile went with us, and found the body. Off there in the woods, perhaps ten minutes from the *château,* there is an old German cemetery, a front-line graveyard that has never been transplanted. Farmer Castignac was there. The bullet was in the sack of his head. *Oui*, that was three years ago."

"What did the police do?"

THEY CAME. THEY went. They did this thing and that. They said it was murder. But by what hand? From where? Farmer Castignac had no friends; at the same time, no enemies. He had only a dog and some traps, both there beside the body. The woods were surrounded and scoured. No killer with a rifle was found. No tracks.

"Landru and I were questioned—as if I could aim a rifle with this accursed growth on my neck!—as if Landru were a sharpshooter who could hit a man in the black of night! No assassin was ever apprehended by the police. Naturally!"

Archambaud mumbled, "There was one queer thing about it, Monsieur Shepherd. The police established the bullet was from a German Mannlicher rifle. No one in the countryside today possesses such a gun."

"Have you a rifle, Archambaud?"

The answer was a vigorous headshake. *"Non, monsieur.* I had a small carbine at the time, for shooting rats. The police who investigated took my carbine away."

"What police investigated?"

"The Lieutenant Jaloux, from the *gendarmerie* at Contalmaison," Madame Landru growled out the answer. "That good-for-nothing! A typical *agent* of police, cock of the walk with his curled mustachios and bullying manners. He said I was crazy when I told him the Battle of the Somme was still going on, and that Farmer Castignac had been killed by the living dead. *Alors*, it was he who investigated the death of the blacksmith's daughter five months later.

I think that time he laughed from the other side of the mouth."

The blacksmith's daughter, as described by Madame Landru, had been a beautiful, but not dutiful, girl. Gaspard, her father, was the best horse-shoer in this district, and he had not deserved this tragedy.

Daughter Paulette had not stayed at home every evening as a respectable French girl should. No, she had preferred to stroll of an evening with the boys, even in winter. Her father had forbidden these strolls, but she took them anyway—this December night she had strolled too far.

As a matter of record, she had been riding in a cutter. With the son of the Mayor of Contalmaison. For reasons best known to Blacksmiths' daughters who go sleigh-riding with the sons of mayors, the girl had decided to walk home. She got out near the Forêt de Feu, and despite the efforts of the mayor's son to get her back into the sleigh— he had made a considerable effort, judging from the scuffle-tracks left in the snow—the girl had determined to walk.

The boy's alibi had been unimpeachable. He had climbed back into the cutter and driven straight home. His tracks didn't follow the girl's on her lonely walk. No tracks followed the girl's. She had started through the snowy woods alone. There was a bright moon, but no one saw what happened or heard any shot.

The body might not have been soon discovered, had not Lieutenant Jaloux and one of his men happened up the highway in a police car. They saw where a sleigh had stopped and feet had scuffled at the roadside. They saw a girl's tracks go into the woods alone.

They thought, "What is that which is that?" and hurried after, on foot. What did they find? They found Paulette the blacksmith's daughter lying dying in the snow with a bullet in her neck. They cried, *"Ah-la-la,* Paulette—who shot you?"

She whispered, "I did not seen anyone!" and that was all. She died as they rushed her to the hospital.

They came back with police from three villages and looked for tracks. They did not find any track beside the girl's. They searched the woods for a mile around. There were no tracks in the snow. There should have been tracks within several hundred feet of the body, because the girl had been struck by a pistol bullet. There were no tracks anywhere.

That was when the police lieutenant began to laugh from the other side of his mouth.

"Eh, bien." Madame Landru's eyes were somber. "There were those who said the case was hushed up because of the son of the mayor. There was a newspaper man up from Paris who said Lieutenant Jaloux could have chased and shot the girl himself. The *lieutenant* challenged him to a duel, and the newspaperman apologized because the *lieutenant* had a War-record as an expert marksman.

"Others claimed it was suicide, but could not explain why the girl did not have a pistol in her hand. Then? Then the inquest was dumbfounded. The bullet in the girl's neck was from a Webley-Fosbery pistol, such a pistol as the British officers carried in the War. But this was in Ninteen-thirty-seven. And this was the second death."

"And you said the third was a child?" Bill Shepherd probed.

"**LAST MONTH. A** little girl. She had wandered away from her cottage in Thiepval Village. Everyone was already looking for her. They came to the *château* to ask if we had seen her. That night, too, there came up a thunderstorm.

"In the dark here were many crashes and much lightning. After the storm passed they found the child in an old shell-crater on the edge of the woods. Lightning, they said. But lightning could not have mangled the little body like that. She had been in an explosion—I know, for I had seen many like her—there were many children killed by the bombs thrown during the War.

"I tried to tell the people it was a hand grenade. That the explosions in the sky were not all thunder. That the little girl had been killed in the present Battle of the Somme."

The veil was over Madame Landru's eyes; her voice settled into a rune, an incantation.

"I have seen the dead soldiers walking—the midnight riders through the trees—the blind and gassed and maimed who have risen from their graves to fight. The police want foot-tracks, but the undead dead leave no footprints.

"The night Farmer Castignac was killed I saw the legless Uhlan go galloping down the road out there in the darkness. The night the blacksmith's daughter was killed I saw the armless French infantryman and the crippled Italian adjutant hurry past the kitchen window. And the night the little girl was killed I saw the blind Canadian officer on his crutches, led by the Russian airman who has no face.

"They were here when those others were killed, and they are here with the dead peasant tonight. The British and French—the Russians—the Italians—the Germans—"

That was enough. The old woman's murder mysteries

needed no spectral embellishments. Bill Shepherd waved her silent to terminate the interview, and said to Archambaud, "Brandy. Hot coffee. Take care of those people out there."

Rounding on his heel, he linked his arm through the Englishman's, and when they were in the passage between kitchen and the dining *salon,* he asked, "Fielding, what do you think?"

"I think the old woman's a dash unhinged, you know."

"I mean about those either unexplained deaths. Farmer Castignac sniped through the head, and the murdered blacksmith's daughter and the little girl, and the police never finding any clues."

"Substantially they're the same tales I've heard noised around the village. Do you know the French people? Rational as cash registers on the surface; and underneath, a flare for the supernatural all wool and a yard wide."

"You'd think the police—"

"Remember, they're provincial police. Your Paris *gendarmerie* is as smart as the London Metropolitan and as tough as New York's Finest, but Contalmaison is a small town. Can't you see this Lieutenant Jaloux with his medals and mustachios? The local priest probably hears more at Saturday's confessionals than Jaloux could learn in a year of cross-questioning and examinations."

Bill Shepherd snapped, "He must be a dumb one."

"I wouldn't say that," Fielding spoke slowly. "Possibly he's been smart.

"Take the shooting of farmer Castignac. The man was a poacher, an atheist, obviously a worthless character. French attitude would be, what did it matter? Probably saved the police a job. They'd poke around in the bushes a while, and give a couple of shrugs. Maybe some good citizen out hunting mistook Castignac for a wolf—they have 'em in the backwoods sometimes. Let the case go at that. The village atheist, you see, would have no political implications."

"Whereas the blacksmith's daughter, playing around with the mayor's boy, would."

FIELDING SMILED FAINTLY, "I'm only conjecturing. And of course from an Englishman's point of view. But I've been around this French countryside a bit, and I've even passed a few words with the mayor. Fat as pompousness, itself, with a red sash around his middle and a top hat on national holidays. Just the type to tell the police chief to keep his son's name out of the papers. Old Mustache-cup Jaloux knows his business. Such things have even happened in large cities, not necessarily French. Remember, Shepherd, I'm only guessing the same as you are."

And doing some pretty logical guessing, Bill Shepherd thought with a faint twinge of envy. He, Shepherd, was supposed to the mystery expert. Funny, wasn't it?

He'd written dozens of these who-killed-who yarns; yet confronted with mystery in fact, he was failing to rationalize. Maybe he'd spent too much time on involved, imaginary puzzles to be able to solve simple realities.

Fielding was saying in his quiet way, "The child is something else again. My guess would be lightning, though, from the story.

"There's a lot of old iron and trash in the forest and steel and barbed wire imbedded in the ground. Lightning plays queer tricks sometimes. Lieutenant Jaloux probably found

himself on the spot about the child, and if the local peasantry want to believe in ghosts, I doubt if the police would
work too hard to dispel the haunts.

"But they'll jump when they hear about this strangled
peasant, I fancy. Another unsolved murder might cost the
lieutenant his job."

They had paused in the passage for this consultation.
Bill Shepherd said, moving forward, "Not that it matters
in comparison to human life, but these murders and spook
yarns have probably cost me the *château*. I'll bounce this
Lieutenant Jaloux out of bed on his ashcan, anyway. Come
on, Fielding."

He strode in grim resolution. "We're driving to Contalmaison to wake up the cops, and we'll have a look at that
body on the way. Since I've got to transfer the others to an
inn, and my roadster can only take three at a time, it might
be a good idea to go first with this Italian doctor. He can
make a professional report on the dead man."

18

FINGERPRINTS OF DEATH

THE WIDE, ARCH-CEILINGED room with the little group of people gathered about the fireplace looked almost cozy after a visit to the other apartments, *salons* and halls of the Château de Feu. At least this wing of the ruin was habitable.

Bill Shepherd asked Fielding if he would mind speaking to the doctor, and as the Englishman took Doctor Arnoldo aside, Bill Shepherd called, "Mademoiselle Gervais, would you mind stepping over here a minute?"

The French girl rose from a chair beside the Russian, and came across the room with questioning eyes.

She asked in a low voice. "Is something wrong, Monsieur Shepherd?"

"You know as much about it as I do," he said quietly. "Fielding told me you saw the dead man."

She said with a little shiver, *"Oui,* I saw him. It was exactly as I told Monsieur Fielding. I did not speak of it to you because—"

"I can understand. But I wish you'd tell me why you were driving through the forest in the first place."

"I told you, *monsieur.* The wedding was to have been this morning, and—"

He sighed, "All right, Mademoiselle Gervais. Now Fielding and I are taking the Italian doctor for a look at that body down the road. I'll drive them on to Contalmaison and come back with the police. Is there"—he gave her a level look—"any reason why you might not want to stay here until I get back? Would you like me to return to you your gun?"

"No, I do not mind staying. I—I would like you to have the pistol if you are going to stop out there in the forest."

Did the girl mean that? The expression of dark-eyed concern? She was certainly not hard to look at—brunette hair smoothed back and a freshening touch of lipstick, and—and there was that impression of having seen her somewhere—a remote familiarity.

"You'll be all right then?" he smiled. His glance went across the room. "Not afraid of ghosts?"

"Of ghosts, yes. Of people, no. They are only lost travelers like myself, indebted to you for your very kind hospitality."

Bill Shepherd felt that he had been brusque and muddleheaded and not at all hospitable.

He saw Doctor Arnoldo and Fielding at the front door, shouldering into their wet coats, and he called to the others at the fireplace, "Professor Putinov—Herr Kull—Monsieur"—(what was the little bus-driver's name?)—"Monsieur Tac. I'm driving over to the nearest village, and I'll be back for you inside half an hour. Archambaud is bringing you coffee and cognac, and will serve you in any way possible. Please make yourselves as comfortable as you can. *À bientôt.*" He pressed the French girl's arm. "I won't be long."

HE DIDN'T LIKE to leave her, and he was a little surprised that it should matter. Just the natural masculine protective instinct, of course, hardly necessary when he had left her in the company of three men.

But he didn't care much for Herr Kull on short acquaintance. The Russian and the little French man he did not know. It seemed a little tough to leave anyone to the woozy séances of Madame Landru and the fumblings of her husband.

As he tooled the lumbering Hispano-Suiza down the driveway past the shell-smashed garden and out to the road, he couldn't help admitting that he, himself, was relieved to get out of the *château*.

But Gabrielle Gervais would be all right. Girls these days knew how to look out for themselves. She hadn't been any clinging vine when she had that gun. And she'd been a nurse, which meant she was pretty competent.

He fixed his attention to keeping the car on the mud-swamped road. Fielding, at his elbow, was telling the Italian doctor about the murdered peasant. The doctor exclaimed, "Murder? *Porca Maria!*" but made no further comment than, "Strangling is a rare form of homicide, is it not? I will be interested to see a case."

They drove the next mile in silence, their eyes concentrated on the muck-rutted roadbends.

Twice the heavy car slithered and slewed into a stall, and it was all Bill Shepherd could do to keep from bogging down. The rear wheels spun as though in gray paste; puddle-water splashed up into the windshield; he had to kick the transmission into low gear to give the tires traction.

The moon was obscured under cloud; the sky was grumbling again; the forest was pitchy black. Bill Shepherd looked at his wrist dial. Ten after twelve.

If he'd been writing this as a story, something should have happened at the stroke of midnight. The plot had missed an angle. He wished this had been fiction instead of fact; he didn't hanker to see that throttled peasant again. Five hours ago when he'd spied that body and come careening up this road—it seemed like five years.

They passed the French girl's Citroën coupé tilted in the roadside ditch.

Bill Shepherd nudged Fielding. "There's her car."

A little further on the Englishman said, "Funny thing, Shepherd. All evening I've had a feeling I've seen Miss Gervais somewhere before."

Bill Shepherd was a little startled. "That's odd. So have I."

"Do you know where?"

"No, I don't."

"Why"—Fielding smiled—"I've just been able to place her. Resemblances are strange things, aren't they? You think someone's face is somehow familiar, then it turns out they look like some other person you've seen in the past. Miss Gervais looks strikingly like Nurse Cavell."

"Nurse Cavell—?"

"Edith Cavell. You know. Famous nurse shot by the Germans as a spy during the War. Raised no end of anger against the Prussians. Of course Nurse Cavell was English and this girl is French—it's her profile, I guess, and the way she carries her chin. Just something in the expression."

Fielding added, groping into a pocket for his pipe, "Of course I never saw Edith Cavell to begin with. But I saw her picture on all the recruiting posters, and there's a statue of her in front of the National Portrait Gallery in London. You've doubtless seen pictures of her too; got 'em in the back of your memory. The French girl's expression could be her double."

IN THE PAUSE that followed, Bill Shepherd tried to remember if he had ever seen a picture of Edith Cavell. No, she hadn't been on the American recruiting posters. He could recall one of Uncle Sam pointing a finger straight at you, and another of a doughboy in spotless uniform on the parapet of a trench waving a flag. *Do Your Bit! Save The World For Democracy!* All that had been in '17. Edith Cavell was earlier. She belonged to this middle period of the War. There couldn't have been much flag-waving here in this Red Zone.

Doctor Arnoldo's voice spoke through these thoughts with, "I guess that is your murdered peasant ahead."

Bill Shepherd brought the car to a halt beside the poppy-grown knoll. The body was lying as he had left it.

The Englishman and the Italian walked around it, exclaiming, and Bill Shepherd looked off at the night-hung thickets; he had seen the body before. Fielding snapped on his flashlight, and the Italian doctor knelt to the examination. The Englishman went through the dead man's pockets, as Bill Shepherd had done, and brought out the handful of coins and the St. Christopher medal.

Then Fielding moved to Bill Shepherd's side. His expression was puzzled. "George, Shepherd, here's a queer thing!"

Bill Shepherd asked, "What's that?"

"Look at these franc-pieces. All the money in that dead man's pocket is dated before and up to Nineteen-sixteen.

Most of these coins are dated Nineteen-sixteen exactly, and they're an issue that hasn't been in circulation since the War."

"Those coins all date back to Ninteen-sixteen?"

"So does the silver medal. It's a kind they commonly sold to French *poilus* to keep them from harm."

Doctor Arnoldo's voice cut in with, "I have finished my examination, gentlemen." He had straightened to his feet and was aiming the flashlight down at the dead man's face. The doctor was pale.

Bill Shepherd asked huskily, "What did you find?"

"The marks on this peasant's throat are those of his own fingers. The skin is under the nails where he dug them into himself; from the thumb-prints it is apparent that he caught himself by the throat with his own hands. He clutched and tore at his own throat, that is evident. He was choking to death and in great pain."

Bill Shepherd glared. "You mean he choked himself to death?"

The Italian doctor shook his head. "Of course I cannot be positive. But from the bluish tinge to his skin—the blisters in his nostrils, palate and tongue—the condition of his throat membranes—I would say this man had died from poison gas."

19

YELLOW CROSS

GAS! BILL SHEPHERD could feel the jolt travel down to his heels. He glared unbelievingly at the Italian doctor.

"You mean the kind of poison gas used in chemical warfare?"

Doctor Arnoldo looked about uneasily. His nose glasses were professional, but they could not diagnose the forest that stood around them like a pitchy wall, the dense clumps of sapling, charred timber and boscage brought into stark relief by the car-lights.

He said in a serious tone to Bill Shepherd, "Yes, *signor*. Although it may be phosgene or chloropicrin gas, it looks to me like mustard. I could not be certain without making an autopsy. But the cyanic discoloration of the corpse—the burning in nose and throat—I saw many similar cases on the Austrian Front." His bewildered glance fixed on the dead man. "Yes, I am sure that is mustard gas. The kind the Germans first used in the World War—the gas they called Yellow Cross."

But that had been back in the days of the Invasion, and this was 1939. There were no gas bombs spraying their lethal chemicals over these long-abandoned woods; no Prussians in the trappings of Mars beyond those shattered

pines; no belching guns and tempests of steel and lines
of charging men; no dugouts to be raided, sectors taken,
fronts to be won.

Yet once more the night was uncanny with the hint
of echoes from a struggle long gone by. The dead man's
pocket money dated 1916! Suffocation from poison gas!
Death had come back out of history in a shroud of yellow
fumes. It was there in the dripping, black forest, invisible
and malign.

The doctor looked ready to make a dash for cover. Fielding's face had gone bleak in anxiety—for once the calm
Englishman was not ready with a logical answer—and Bill
Shepherd, standing stunned, could feel his skin prickling.
Thunder crackled in the sky as the breeze veered damply;
there was a flutter of lightning behind jaggedly silhouetted
treetops; one looked about instinctively for a bomb-proof
shelter.

Bill Shepherd asked huskily, "How long would you say
the man has been dead, Doctor Arnoldo?"

"I should say five or six hours, signor."

"That's right," Bill Shepherd agreed. He felt a little sick.
"Fielding, here, glimpsed this peasant in the woods around
five-thirty yesterday afternoon. The thunderstorm broke
at sundown just as I drove into the forest. Mademoiselle
Gervais was a half hour ahead of me on the road; she saw
the dead man then. He must have been—been gassed some
time between half past five, when Fielding saw him alive,
and—and nightfall."

Doctor Arnoldo murmured, "Yes, I should say he died
some time in the evening. I am a little bewildered. Death
by gas is not so immediate unless one is unaware of its

presence and inhales a considerable quantity. Some of the German gases are almost odorless; others have a not unpleasant smell. If a man did not at first detect it, he might inhale the deadly fumes and be overcome before he realized it.

"It looks to me as if this man suddenly found himself strangling. He began to run. But the poison was working in his lungs. He had breathed deeply of the fumes. But *Madre Maria!*" the doctor appealed. "Mustard gas is thrown in shells. Is there a war going on? Who would start a gas attack in these woods here? Were there bombs exploding last evening?"

Fielding was staring at the dead man. He declared, "I didn't hear any bombs. Those Yellow Cross shells made a big bang, too. Look here, Doctor. How—how long does gas blanket the vicinity when a shell does explode?"

The Italian was sniffing nervously. "One shell would not cover a large area. If there was a breeze it would soon be dissipated. But gas shells are thrown in a barrage. There would be little danger from one shell exploded five hours ago when this man died."

"But there was no explosion," Fielding shook his head. "When I glimpsed this peasant in the bushes last evening the forest was as quiet as those cemeteries surrounding it. In the east there was some thunder, but a shell-burst would have gone off like the crack of doom. The storm came slam-bang just at sundown, but this man must've been dead on the roadside by then."

As he spoke, he was jingling the coins he had taken from the dead man's smock—the money dated 1916. Suddenly he stopped jingling the coins; frowned at the pieces spread

*With a crash of broken
glass, Shepherd fell
into the room.*

in his palm. "By Jove! Shepherd, I've got an idea. It might explain this money—and how this duffer got killed by mustard gas."

Bill Shepherd wanted an explanation. "What do you make of it, Fielding?"

"Well, the beggar was up to something there in the woods. I told you it looked as if he was digging. But it might have been something worse. I couldn't say until I saw what he'd been up to. Look." He pointed at the path coming down through the trees to the road. "The place I spotted the fellow can't be far from here—quarter mile from the road, I'd say. What do you say we trace his foot-prints back to the place where I saw him; go there and have a look-see."

THE ENGLISHMAN AIMED his flashlight at the path going into the forest, and Bill Shepherd had no hearty inclination to follow that woodsy trail. He said, "As soon as possible we ought to get to the police!"

But he nodded toward the path—he would go. It wouldn't do to show the feather before strangers who wanted to help him. In a way, this forest was his own show; besides, he had little faith in the local *Gendarmerie* and the policework of Lieutenant Jaloux. That provincial constable had apparently bungled the Law in more cases than one, and there were things happening in the Forêt de Feu that Bill Shepherd wanted solved.

Reluctant as he was to leave the comforting lights of his car, he fell in step behind Fielding; the Italian doctor came at his heels; and the three started up the trail, Indian-file.

The path wound and climbed, tortuous in the under-brush. Lights of the parked car vanished as the path made a turn, and the night closed in behind them. Fielding's pocket-torch, guiding the way, was a small glimmer in that blackness. Bramble and laurel hedged the footpath; second-growth saplings and charred pines stood up on either side like a black wall; the darkness ahead of the flash-light was impenetrable, and the sky like a canopy of coal. Everything dripped and drained. Wet foliage glistened when touched by the ray of the flashlight as it poked and thrust in the undergrowth, hunting the path.

The path was overgrown with myrtle and woodbine, choked with weeds and thistles and forestcreeper. In places it was flooded and obscure. But the dead peasant's wooden shoes had left deep imprints in the mud and leaf-mould, the tracks had remained clear despite the rainstorm. They could see where he had come galloping along the twisty lane, imprints in the weeds where he had fallen down.

They followed the trail in silence, wary of roots and briar. Occasional flares of electricity would dribble across the sky; the woods would be unnaturally revealed in a pale green witchfire; thunder would rumble down an aerial staircase, then the forest, blacked-out, would be still.

They came to great, fire-eaten logs which lay like factory chimneys across the path and had to be climbed. Huge, uprooted stumps grabbed at them with gnarled tentacles. The path led into a thicket of blasted chestnuts, great trees bare of bark and foliage, their limbs amputated, their trunks stark as giant telephone poles and split to the heart as though by giant axes. Vines and toadstools could not hide the scars left by flying steel and flame. There was a tremendous oak lying dead, torn out of the ground as though it had been a turnip. A pine-trunk burned to a crisp. A shattered elm, broken at the middle, its top limbs bowed to earth in a mound of ashes.

Fielding made a sudden stop. "Take care, here. Mind the barbed wire."

Underbrush concealed the snarls of rusty cables strung with claws and fishhooks. It writhed in tangles alongside the path and netted through the bushes everywhere. Fiendish stuff to get caught in. Bill Shepherd hooked his coat sleeve; ripped it to the elbow.

"Look," the Italian doctor exclaimed. "A German helmet."

FIELDING'S FLASHLIGHT HAD picked it out at the trailside. One of those coalscuttle helmets, dented, brown with rust; someone had left it perched on a stray fencepost. Bill Shepherd looked at it sidewise. There were four round holes punched through the dome, like punctures in an old tin can.

Here, farther up the path, the forest floor was scattered with all manner of trash—wagon wheels, scraps of sheet-iron, gasoline tins, moss-covered mounds of junked machinery. The flashlight picked out a howitzer swamped under vines; nearby, in a nest of petrified cement bags, a rusted machine gun; and not far from that, half-buried in the ground, an airplane engine. The path took a bend, and a brilliant display of lightning overhead revealed a deep trench that zigzagged through the forest like an abandoned canal. The path crossed the trench by a bridge of shaky duck-boards, and followed the parapet for a number of yards. Fielding directed the torch-ray into the trench. The trench walls were weed-grown, caved in places, breached where the parapet had crumbled; here and there the trench was filled with rubble or choked with underbrush. But twenty-three years had not obliterated the earthworks, and even the dugouts remained.

Most of the dugouts were caved or flooded—the trench-bottom was a channel of rainwater—but the flashlight discovered one dugout in a good state of preservation. The door was like the entrance to a coal mine, shored up with heavy timbering. One could see the steps going down, and the light-ray glimpsed the earth backwall of the room below. The firing step near the dugout remained intact—niches where observers stood watch with periscopes, ladders where the men had gone over the top.

The parapet was strewn with litter. A rotted, hobnailed boot. Bits of charred leather and harness. Meat tins. Mouldering cartridge belts. Canteens pierced like sprinkling cans. An empty knapsack. A dish-shaped steel helmet, its crown torn open. A pair of broken binoculars. The charred butt—Bill Shepherd picked it up—of a rifle.

Fielding aimed the flashlight at a sign above the dugout door. The weather-beaten lettering was dimly legible.

CUTHBERT'S HOTEL.

LADIES NOT ADMITTED.

Fielding said in a hushed tone, "British trench. Cuthbert was the nickname out here for Tommy Atkins."

Surely Cuthbert was not here now. Not in this long-abandoned trench strewn with rusted equipment and debris. The dugout door was like the entry to a tomb. There was a smell of earth and rotting lumber and wet plant life at night. Cuthbert was gone. He had packed up his troubles in his old kitbag and gone back to England, or back to those cemeteries behind the line. Unless....

Bill Shepherd found himself staring at a wraith in the dugout door. It writhed up out of the aperture and floated out into the trench—a spook of white mist that nodded its head as it evaporated. Bill Shepherd started violently.

Doctor Arnoldo said in a strained voice, "It is not gas. It is only fog from the rain. Were it gas, you would not see those rats down there."

There were three of them at the top of the dugout steps. At the aim of the flashlight they raced out into the trench in a figure-eight maneuver, and vanished back into the black dugout mouth like evil thoughts.

Bill Shepherd had not been thinking of gas. The door of

that underground retreat gave him a creep. He turned on Fielding, "Come on. Let's get a move on."

"This way," Fielding said.

20

TRENCHES OF THE GHOSTS

THE PATH BENT sharply to the left and the trench wandered off in the night, and Bill Shepherd was glad to see it go. If you had an imagination you could visualize dead soldiers crouching under those crumbled parapets, awaiting a ghostly zero hour. Those disabled howitzers and scrapped machine guns in weedy nests might well be waiting phantom gun-crews, legless Germans, crippled French and British, infantrymen without arms and aviators without faces.

He dispelled the visions of Madam Landru with an oath, but the face of that peasant back there on the road, dead of mustard gas, was not so easily dispelled. How could the man have met death by poison gas on a night twenty years after the Armistice? How came his pocket money to be dated 1916? Fielding seemed to have an idea; perhaps in painting pictures of these war-ruined woods, the English artist had seen something the imagination of a mystery-story writer couldn't see.

The path was meandering through a burned-over glen. This trail in the forest, Bill Shepherd thought, was like the path through the desolation and wreckage of the upper floors of the *château*. These woods too, undermined with shell-holes and bomb-craters, blocked with burnt timber, strewn with trash and the rusted spare parts of war machines, had known the wanton fury of human vandalism. Here, too, the raging hordes had chopped and smashed and overturned; they had wielded the torch. Bill Shepherd looked at the felled trees in dread; couldn't conceive the violence that had leveled a stand of pine, shattered a pair of twin oaks to hills of matchwood.

They skirted a crater as deep as an excavation at Pompeii. Fielding aimed his flashlight into the yawning pit, murmuring, "Must've been a mine." Tons of explosive must have been used to blast out that cavity. It was wide as the mouth of a dead volcano, and the pond at the bottom resembled a quarry lake. A play of lightning overhead flooded the crater with a pale green light, and the men saw, half way down the crater-side, a demolished armor-plated engine that looked like a prehistoric animal that had crawled down there to die. That wreck had been an armored car.

Some distance farther on the path they passed something that, horizontal in the weeds, resembled a giant, fifty-foot sewer pipe. Fielding said laconically, "Big Bertha." How that monster gun-barrel had come to be mislaid there, Bill Shepherd couldn't imagine. The pride of the Krupp Works with ivy wreaths on the breech and a swallow's nest in the muzzle! Big Bertha was dead—all these engines in the weeds were dead—the Forêt de Feu was like a cemetery of war material.

But a peasant had been killed here tonight by mustard gas—a French peasant with coins dated 1916 in his pocket. Bill Shepherd gripped the Mauser pistol in his own pocket, and kept his eye on the beam of Fielding's flashlight, anxious to see.

"We can't be far from the place." Fielding paused. "There's the side path where I came up on my bicycle. Look for the hull of a burned Zeppelin in a thicket near the path. I remember halting to look at it, and thinking it must've been a pretty big crash. It isn't far from here, and a little way beyond that there's the clump of bushes where I saw the peasant digging."

They proceeded slowly; then the flashlight discovered the fire-blackened mass of crumpled aluminum at the pathside.

"This is the place, all right," Fielding said a moment later. "See where the man came charging out of the bushes? Look. There's a rag of his smock where he tore it on the thorns. He must've come out of the brush running hell for leather."

INADVERTENTLY THE THREE halted, eyeing the screen of brush for some malignant sign. The flashlight ray went probing. Elderberries, scrub oak, golden rod. Wet foliage gleaming out of darkness. Of the death that had ambushed the peasant there, the undergrowth betrayed no evidence.

Doctor Arnoldo said dubiously, "We had better hurry up, my friends, the rain is going to return any minute."

"I saw him right back in there." Fielding jabbed at the scrub with the flashlight ray. "He scuttled off behind those elderberries. He must've returned to whatever he was doing. He was lively enough then."

Bill Shepherd said doggedly, "Come on."

As he stepped from the footpath into knee-high weeds, he kicked something. He said, "Hold the flashlight!" to

Fielding, and stooping, fished from the weeds an old trench gun. He eyed the weapon curiously. It had the barrel of a large pistol and the shoulder butt of a sub machine-gun. The butt was wormy, the barrel clogged with earth, the trigger rusty.

"Parabellum," Fielding said. "Belgian make. Good pistol in its day."

Shepherd dropped the rusted weapon, and pushed on into the brush. The ground was swampy; the bush foliage showered drops of rainwater. Clawing their way through the shrubs, they came to an open space where the undergrowth had been cleared. They halted apprehensively while the white beam of Fielding's pocket-torch explored the clearing.

"He was working in here," Fielding said. "There, by Jove!"

The white circle of light came to a stop. Centered in the flashlight's focus was a spade—a rusted intrenching tool such as soldiers carried in their marching equipment. The grip had rotted from the hickory handle, but the shaft looked stout and there was fresh earth on the scoop. Someone—evidently the peasant—had been digging with the cast-off spade.

The light circle focused on a mound of fresh sods, then swerved to the left and dipped into an excavation. Not a large excavation, but a rectangular trench, some six feet long and three feet wide, dug hip-deep in the center of the clearing.

Fielding stepped to the edge of the digging and looked down. His mouth twisted in disappointment.

"Damn! It's partly filled with rainwater."

"Porca!" Doctor Arnold was peering at the rectangular hole. "It looks as if the fellow had been digging a grave."

Bill Shepherd's neck-nape prickled. A grave. That was what it had looked like at first glance. As if that peasant had had a premonition, and come out here to dig his own. Then, with that thought, there came a disturbing memory. Herr Kull, the German, who had come to the *château* in the van of the storm-victims; he had been out here in the forest looking for a grave. Could there be some connection between this brush-screened pit and the German's quest?

"Too much water in the bottom," Fielding was shaking his head. "I'd like to know how deep that grave is. It can't be much more than four feet down."

"He was digging a grave, then," Bill Shepherd muttered.

Fielding nodded cryptically. "If you asked me, I'd say his own. Wasn't for that rainwater at the bottom, I think we'd know what—"

There was a startled exclamation from Doctor Arnoldo, who had suddenly wheeled and pointed into the brush. "Attend! I hear something moving in those bushes over there."

They listened, nerves tense, eyes vigilant.

Thunder rumbled in the night.

Damp breeze rustled the foliage.

Then, in the underbrush across the clearing, Bill Shepherd heard a stealthy movement as of someone pushing through the tangled shrub. A dead stick snapped. Fielding shot his light at the bushes. "Who's there?" The challenge was answered by a scurry, a crackling of twigs and branches, a rushing through the undergrowth as the prowler bolted off.

BILL SHEPHERD CRIED, "He's getting away!" and charged across the clearing like an explosion. His nerves had wanted action. Something he could do. Something he could grab on to. Ever since entering this forest he had waited, repressed, tight-nerved, anticipating some move from some human part of the night's fantasy. Ghosts there had been in plenty—Madam Landru's eyes—murder mysteries—a man killed by poison gas. Fielding had speculated logically, but his logic had only been conjecture, and Bill Shepherd had been waiting for a gesture from whatever corporeal hand might be behind this malevolence.

He dashed for the bushes where the prowler had rushed away, shouting, "Head him off! Don't let him escape!"

Fielding and the Italian cut into the brush behind him, running elbow to elbow. Bill Shepherd plowed blindly through the tangle, following a sound of crashing in the twigs as though someone were running zigzag. The fugitive was not a dozen yards ahead, tangenting off through a thicket of saplings which were brought for a split second into view by a blaze of lightning.

Bill Shepherd yelled at the Englishman and the doctor to take the other side of the thicket, and had a flicker-glimpse of them skirting the copse of young trees. Thunder boomed over the forest tops, and the foliage flattened to a gust of wind. Fielding's flashlight twinkled off and disappeared, and Bill Shepherd tore at invisible briars, fighting to follow the sounds of the escaping trespasser. Pausing to listen, he could hear the Englishman and the Italian floundering in the brush some distance away, but the noises in the thicket ahead had stopped.

There was a sudden, dazzling illumination of lightning, and a deafening volley of thunder. A squall of water swept down over the trees. Sapling thicket and forest were engulfed. For another dozen yards, Bill Shepherd fought his way through the blotted-out undergrowth and swirling rain, then came to a panting stop. The cloudburst was over. Lightning blazed five or six times in rapid aerial displays; there were three tremendous bursts of thunder; then a silence of draining water and leaves dripping.

A shaft of pale moonlight came filtering down through the sapling tops. Bill Shepherd looked up; saw the moon riding over a tumbling sea of black clouds. The forest came to view in this lunar exposure, wan and unreal, like a woodland viewed through smoky green glass. Bill Shepherd listened to the water-soaked stillness, vigilant for action. No sound at hand save the guttering of twigs and vines. The prowler must have escaped.

He bent his glance to the undergrowth on the other side of the thicket.

"Fielding!" he called finally. "Are you there?"

No answer.

He stiffened, tensely alert. "Fielding! Doctor Arnoldo! Are you all right?"

No sound save the drip and leak of wet loaves.

"Hey, there! Fielding! Arnoldo! What's the matter? Where've you gone?"

The drip and leak of wet leaves, and a mutter of thunder retreating down the sky.

Bill Shepherd exclaimed aloud, "My God, they can't be far—I saw them not three minutes ago in that brush patch over there!"

But they weren't in that brush patch now, for it wasn't

sixty feet away; he could see it clearly through the moon-washed saplings, and the bushes were not quite shoulder-high, and if those men were there he would see their heads. They weren't in the brush patch and they weren't in the sapling copse and they weren't in that clearing back there by the path. They couldn't have gone beyond the reach of his shout, and if they hadn't why didn't they answer?

"Fielding! Doctor Arnoldo! Haaay, Arnoldo! Fielding!"

Not even an echo.

He stood quite still listening to a new sound in the forest nocturne-—the ticking of his own heart. He realized his hand was aching in his pocket, but that was from its clench on the Mauser pistol. He drew the weapon from his pocket; shouted again; waited.

THEN, MOVING CAUTIOUSLY, his eyes going from side to side, he skirted the sapling grove and breasted into the brush where the two men had been last seen. There was about half an acre of this scrub and elderberry, fenced by a stand of charred pines that stood like black masts in the moonlight. They couldn't have thrashed across half an acre of briar and gone into those pines, for their charge had kept pace with Bill Shepherd's and they had been on his flank when he entered the sapling thicket. But he started for the timber, because there was the only cover within possible running distance of the briar patch where the two men could have disappeared. He didn't reach the pines.

Barbed wire. It blocked entrance to the pines like a wall. Snarled and tangled, concealed in the undergrowth, it made an unclimbable hedge of steel thorns—a rusty snare of savage hooks—a man-trap capable of enmeshing a regiment, had one tried to get through.

Bill Shepherd followed the wire for quite a distance before he realized the implication. Fielding and the Italian doctor could not have charged on into the pines. Neither could the prowler he had chased into the sapling thicket. Somewhere in that half acre of low underbrush and that little covey of saplings—in a moment as brief as a squall of rain and six thunderclaps—the Englishman, the Italian, and the prowler, too, had disappeared.

He charged in criss-cross attacks through the brush patch, beating at the foliage with his pistol barrel. He rushed about in the copse of saplings. He knew, then, that they must have retreated to the footpath beyond the clearing; but the cloudburst had muddied the path, and in the mud there should have been tracks. When he crossed the clearing where the peasant had been digging a grave, and reached the footpath and saw no fresh footprints in the mud, Bill Shepherd yelled and ran.

He reached the car just as the moon was foundering once more and the thunder was coming back across the sky. He didn't stop to look at the dead man stiff in the poppy bed. Leaping into the Hispano-Suiza, he snapped on the switch and brought his foot down on the starter.

The engine went *grrrrrr* and the headlamps dimmed.

He worked the spark-lever and the gas-pump, frantically priming.

The engine coughed, growled, and the headlamps almost went out.

He rammed the starter to the floor. The engine turned over once, slowly, then went dead. Bill Shepherd groaned. That damned cloudburst! Water in the battery; magneto and ignition probably flooded. He knew nothing about automobile engines—secondhand Hispano-Suizas in particular—and he would not have been in the fettle to tinker with this one had he been a garage mechanic.

He splashed around in the mud and cranked wildly, his arm empowered by the knowledge that a glassy-eyed dead man at the roadside was looking on. But the engine, too, had been choked; the headlights dimmed like dying eyes, then petered out.

The moon was going. Bill Shepherd released the crank and stood back panting, shooting scared glances into the blackening roadside thickets. Swearing helped, but it wouldn't start the car. He fought once more to revive the engine. No go. Stooped over, cranking, he couldn't watch the forest, and this forest where peasants could die from poison gas and men disappeared at a flash of lightning had to be watched.

21

COMPANY OF GRAVES

HE WATCHED IT, crouching against the car, pistol gripped in hand, eyes darting this way and that. Mustn't give way to panic. Mustn't lose his head. Either something had happened to Fielding and that Italian—they'd been over-powered, held silent at gun-point, at bay in some bush clump where he hadn't seen them—or he'd missed a calculation, and they'd made off into the timber. Or for reasons of their own they'd ducked out of sight, played squat-tag in the underbrush, remained hidden. But he'd thrashed every quarter of that field. They couldn't have gone through the barbed wire. Couldn't have reached the footpath without leaving tracks.

No time for the droning voice of Madam Landru to speak out of memory in his ear. "There are those in the Forêt de Feu who do not leave visible tracks."

No time to recall the unsolved deaths of a little girl found in a shell-hole, and a blacksmith's daughter murdered by an unseen killer, and a poacher sniped by a marksman in the black of night. Those assassins had been as trackless as the cannon which blocked the road to Thiepval, as the mustard gas which had strangled that peasant in the poppies.

"I can't crouch here doing nothing like a fool!"

His snarl was brave enough in his hearing, but he couldn't stiffen his hand. It was shaking of its own accord—he could feel it at his side—fluttering like something that had become detached from his person and didn't belong to him. His knees, too, seemed infected with these tremors. He had to get going before his legs contracted this cowardly vertigo.

The Contalmaison *Gendarmerie?* Eight miles at least. Down this wretched wagon road and round-about in that landscape of cemeteries. He considered the dash, craftily. Craftily, because he wanted to avoid the voice of conscience that told him he wasn't going to do it. Don't be a fool, Shepherd. Get the police. Only sensible thing to do. Race to that town and rouse the countryside. Make the dash for Contalmaison—the quickest way to get out of this Forêt de Feu.

His feet were ready and urgent. He wanted to go. Why the devil did his mind go back to that *château*—that sepulchral ruin in the midst of desolation—that shadow-haunted room presided over by Madame Landru and Archambaud—that fireside peopled by alien visitors; the Russian savant, the German tourist, the roosterish little bus-driver, the dark-eyed French girl. Damn it, he couldn't leave the girl in that nightmare! He had to go back and get her out of there. Gabrielle Gervais....

Already he was running. It was, he told himself, his damned American weakness for heroics. Typical Yankee stuff—pulling someone else's chestnuts out of the fire. Hadn't his brother come over here doing the same thing? The whole A.E.F. a year later, for that matter. But you couldn't do anything about it if you were born that way.

Plunge in after somebody you didn't even know—no matter if they'd stuck you up five hours before with a pistol. Rush in where angels would fear to tread; but get the girl out of possible jeopardy, whether you trusted her or not. Women and children first—whether it was La Belle France or one Gabrielle Gervais.

He ran in spurts. Dashing for fifty yards. Pausing to look around. Dashing another fifty yards. He kept his finger alive on the trigger, and he held to the middle road ruts. The *château* was not four miles, and if he plugged along without mishap he could make it in about thirty minutes. The mud was gluey, and the road seemed to make a lot of bends and windings—longer than when he had traversed it in a car. The forest came closer, and the underbrush was darker, the shadows more black and fantastic for the pale revelations of the moon.

The physical effort of running relaxed his nerves a little; the fear which enveloped his skin was countered by his single purpose to outstrip any baneful evil which might be closing in around the girl. He had not forgotten that he had deprived her of her gun, and that she had later declined its return, anticipating his need for a weapon. Nice guy he'd have been to bolt off and leave her unarmed. The sooner he saw her out of these woods, the better. Funny—her bearing a resemblance to Edith Cavell.

His thoughts centered on the girl as he ran, but the nerve-ends under his skin were centered on the forest. A bush rustled by the breeze, and he skittered sideways. A looming tree shadow startled him. A white wraith creeping through a thicket made him whip about with leveled gun. Only mist raised by the warm rain.

THE MOONLIGHT WANED so subtly, the forest was blacked out before he realized it. The storm was coming back. Flares in the sky; loudening thunder rolls; quickening wind. He lengthened his stride, running doggedly, following the faint-glistening streaks of water in the road ruts. Lightning ran across the night, and the forest jumped in and out of view; and then, after one brilliant electrical flare, he could no longer make out the roadway. Thunder clapped violently overhead, releasing an inky downpour. Bill Shepherd waited for another sky flare; marked the road in that instant's illumination; put his head between his shoulders and plunged on.

He came to the girl's ditched automobile, and judged the *château* at another mile. He ran on blindly, hoping this cloudburst would pass as the previous rain squalls had. But the rain settled into a steady downpour, as if the capricious weather had at last made up its mind. The lightning was only occasional. In this black, sheeting bath, he missed the road.

He had made a side turning somewhere in the darkness; misjudged the corridor of a bylane for the roadway. He rounded and ran back, hunting the wagon ruts. No, he hadn't come that far in this direction; the wagon road lay just over there.

It wasn't over there. Blue light flared through the rain, and he was on some footpath deep in the forest. He might have been on it for five minutes——maybe fifteen. He wheeled and ran in the direction he had followed first; some cross-path must have led into this from the road. He couldn't find it. Darting and turning in the streaming black, he addled his sense of direction. He swerved and ran head-

long, one elbow in front of him to fend off the underbrush,
following the hedge along the path. He was lost.

Then he did not know how long he ran.

He was blinded, drenched, dazed, hounded by fear.
Roots tripped him, and he charged into clumps of thorn.
Brush switched at his knees, and invisible branches clawed
at his face. Dense walls of undergrowth kept him on the
path. At one brilliant glare of lightning he found himself
in a narrow gully; some moments later he was running
through a fire-scorched elm grove.

He stumbled on, reeling and floundering in the blackness; the path had to go somewhere, and his legs had to
run. He couldn't think of that girl in the *château*, now—
couldn't think of the disappearance of the Italian doctor
and Fielding—couldn't think, in this forest of death, about
anything.

He ran like a drunken man, not knowing where he was
going, his mind bleared, vision gone, all his will power
consumed in the effort to energize his legs.

Then he saw a light. A fixed beam, faint yellow in the
pouring night far ahead. The invisible path seemed to be
going in that direction; Bill Shepherd wrenched himself
out of panic, wiped rain from his eyes, stiffened himself
with an oath, and had a goal to make for.

IT WAS NEARER than he had expected. Not five hundred
yards ahead. The yellow gleams widened to a shine; the
shine was a lighted window. The Château de Feu! A blaze
of blue lightning over the tree tops silhouetted the Norman
tower, the mansard roofs. Hardly a pistol shot away, and
for all he had known, he might have been lost in the other
end of the forest.

He swore; waited for another lightning flare to show the path; then charged forward, his eye on the yellow window. The path bent suddenly, without warning in the dark, and he plunged through the hedge of underbrush, tripped on some unseen obstacle and sprawled violently in a bed of moss. He sat up cursing, clutching a twisted ankle. His next thought was for the window, and he looked for it frantically; caught sight of it—a reassuring beacon—off to the right. Not two hundred yards away, and he couldn't miss the *château*, now, even if he blundered from the path which was taking him there.

He paused a moment, considering the lighted window. He hadn't had time to think out a course of action. Wouldn't do to barge in like a panicky fool and scare the wits out of the girl. He'd scout that window first and see if everything was all right.

If it was—and somehow the window light was reassuring—he'd take the girl aside and tell her his car had stalled, the others had set out for town on foot, something like that. Then he'd take Herr Kull, Professor Putinov and the bus-driver aside and tell them what had happened. They'd better know all the details, be advised about that menace of poison gas.

Maybe they could form a mutual guard over the *château* for the rest of the night; maybe they could go down the road together and extricate the girl's car from the ditch. Yes, he'd have to tell the Russian, the little Frenchman and the German.

Sprawling headlong, he had lost the girl's gun, and he fumbled in the wet moss, groping for it. He couldn't find it at hand; the window light did not reach the brush where he had fallen. He swerved about on his hands and knees, pawing the moss. Then his blind fingers grasped something—the thing he had tripped over. It was wet and smooth and jutted up out of the ground, a thing of wood.

He ran his hand up the side—a big stake. A stake with a cross-bar at the top. A cross-bar! Bill Shepherd pulled a breath and jerked his hand away. A cross! He had plunged through a bush and tripped over a big wooden cross.

He sprang to his feet. He was standing on a grave. A ladder of aerial fire flared and flickered across the sky, and the scene was revealed in a flood of incandescence—a little graveyard recessed in a nest of bushes—a dozen mossy mounds and a little company of crosses. The crosses were gray and weather-beaten, leaning at a dozen different angles, their names hardly legible on the time-stained wood. Bill Shepherd felt his neck-hairs stiffen. Could this be the German front-line cemetery Madam Landru had referred to? This little company of neglected graves, the spot where the poacher had been slain?

He groped in a sodden pocket to find his cigarette lighter. Cupped between his palms, the little flare was only a glimmer in the rain. But it was sufficient light, held close, to reveal the lettering on the cross Bill Shepherd had stumbled over. He bent to read the name.

Bill Shepherd dropped the lighter and fell back with a choked cry.

He forgot the pistol he had lost in the moss.

He forgot his intention to be wary in approaching the *château.*

Rushing across the grave-mounds, he flung himself

into the underbrush; tore a path through the boscage on a straight line for the lighted window.

WHEN HE CAME up under the sill, he was as thrashed, thorn-scratched and muddied as though he had clawed his way through a No Man's Land of barbed wire. But he did not feel the nettles clotting his trousers, the slashes on his cheek and hands. His nerves were as numb as though his circulation had stopped; his hands were cold, without feeling.

He gripped the thick stone sill, reared his head to a level with the casement, and peered through the leaded-glass panes. Then it was as if his heart stopped beating.

They were there. Around the hearth where they had been grouped when he had last seen them together. A bright log burned and cast their shadows across the long room, and they were silhouetted in a circle, their postures relaxed, the men talking and smoking, the girl with a glass of cognac on her knee. But they were blurred silhouettes as seen through the rain-glazed window; the firelight was diffused around them; their figures were mistily outlined as though each gave off an aura of steam.

Gabrielle Gervais, who had held him up on the forest road last evening.

Herr Kull, the German from Essen, who had been thrown by his horse in the woods and had come to the *château's* door with a bleeding head.

Putinov, the Russian savant, here on research from Siberia.

Marcel Tac, who had crashed through the bridge his antique French Fiat.

Doctor Arnoldo, who had come from Italy with an ambulance!

And Fielding, the English painter, who had been there at the fireplace when Bill Shepherd had seen him for the first time!

They were all there!

No one of them had fully explained his presence. All had come to that hearth under cloudy, mysterious circumstance. Bill Shepherd could hear Madam Landru's words go tolling through his mind. "The Battle of the Somme is still going on. The dead have never died in the Forêt de Feu. They are all here tonight. All together they have returned. The British. The French. The Russians and Italians. The Germans—"

Could those people before that fireplace be the folk of the old mystic's legend?

The name on that grave-cross in the forest had been *Siegfried Kull!*

Could all those people be dead?

22

THE WARRIORS

IT WAS NOT hard to believe of those steamy, unaccountable figures in that shadowy room where a clock had struck out of a silence since 1916. That fireside where heads had rolled made a good meeting place for a gathering of vagrant immortals. In that gutted *château* with its burned-out halls and demolished chambers the spirits of the dead would be at home.

Could they be the representatives of a host of such nocturnal wanderers—that girl who chanced to look like Edith Cavell, that shaggy-headed Russian with the bandaged shin, Herr Kull with the dark abrasion on his forehead, the little French bus-driver with his lorry out of the past, the Englishman and the Italian who could vanish together in a thicket in the heart of the forest and reappear at a hearthside like this?

Bill Shepherd stared through the window with the rain running down his numbed face.

Voices murmured beyond the glass. That German whose name was on a grave-cross was gesturing, talking emphatically.

"—the Germans will win. We will not be stopped by the Allied Line. You will see. The French cannot hold out much longer. Russia will crumble. Great Britain will be unable to cope with our air force."

The little Frenchman was leaning forward fiercely. "They will not pass! Remember that, Herr Kull! We stopped you at the Marne. You will never come so close to Paris again."

The Russian was laughing with his head thrown back. The Russian, who was, as well as a college professor, an airman. "So you think my great country will crumble, you Germans? Ho ho, do not make a mistake! Russia has appeared to crumble before. She has always been going to disintegrate. Hindenburg gave us a surprise, but it will not happen again. Always, knocked down, the bear stands up stronger than before."

The little bus-driver lifted a fist. "France does not need this help from Russia. We know how to handle the Boche."

Herr Kull was half out of his chair. His voice came loudly, "I tell you now, little runt, were we not interned in this *château* by the storm—were it not that that American might arrive—"

Gabrielle Gervais was speaking. "You men are acting like fools...."

Her voice faded out behind a burst of rain on the panes before Bill Shepherd's face; she was gesturing vehemently, the others were talking all at once. Hardly aware of what he was doing, Bill Shepherd pulled himself up into the window casement; pressed his face against the streaming glass. He heard the words "Kaiser," "Hindenburg," "Lloyd George," "Belgium." Voices muffled, elided together. The steamy figures gesticulated excitedly. Hands waved in altercation. Ghosts arguing the cause of a bygone Armageddon?

It was like listening to voices of dissension from the spirit world. Those shadow-people in the firelight were the stuff of dreams. Cock-crow, and they would all go away. The disputatious murmur grew louder in Bill Shepherd's ear like the babel of delirium. He knew this was hallucinary. He had hit his head somewhere. The voices were wind and rain on the window panes before his face, and the people were an illusion of firelight and mental unbalance.

The discordant voices seemed to rise. The girl who looked like Edith Cavell was scolding the Fiat driver in French. The shadowy Englishman joined the dispute. An exclamation in Italian. The Russian was on his feet, his misty profile wrenched in anger. The German's bald head bobbed furiously, his features contorted as in rage. Shadows merged in struggle, spun across the hearth and reeled out into mid room. The German and the Russian, faces transfigured in wrath, locked together, wrestling.

Chairs went back and wall shadows jumped. It looked like a blow. The German flew about on his heels, went backward toward the staircase in a drunken totter, passed out of Bill Shepherd's vision. There was a sodden crash. The Russian in mid room stood breathing heavily, wiping his hands on his chest. Silhouettes behind him were posed as figures in tableau. Then, deep-toned out of the picture, the alcove clock began to strike.

Explosion!

BILL SHEPHERD HAD never intended to join that scene. But he had pressed against the window without thinking. Old panes gave beneath his weight, lead caulking broke, he fell in through the casement in a great burst of smashing glass. It seemed to him he was there on the floor a long time on his hands and knees, transfixed, speechless, his posture frozen, powerless to move. The clock went on bonging, and little jingles of glass continued to fall from the jagged sill.

Then Gabrielle Gervais was beside him. The little bus-driver. Doctor Arnoldo. And Fielding and the Russian were helping him to his feet. He could only stand wordless, paralyzed. Fielding was brushing his coat, brushing off fragments of broken glass.

"Are you all right, old man? Good Lord! you gave us a shock."

Bill Shepherd whispered, "I gave *you* a shock!"

"We thought you'd gone to Contalmaison."

Bill Shepherd began, "You thought I—?" and gagged.

"Corpo di Bacco!" Doctor Arnoldo's lean features relaxed. "We forget, Signor Fielding. Our friend, Shepherd, does not understand how—"

"Of course!" Fielding cried. "Stupid of me, Shepherd. Naturally you're as surprised to see us here as we are to see you. You stayed out there in that damned forest looking for us, what? I had an idea you'd see what had happened, and dash off to Contalmaison for help."

Bill Shepherd passed a hand across his forehead, staring.

"Didn't you see the dugout?" Fielding cried. "Didn't you see the cave-in? Lord, of course you wouldn't, the entrance was hidden in the bushes and camouflaged with vines! The doctor and I fell right into the bloody thing. It was there on the other side of that sapling thicket—I might've known you wouldn't see it—cunningly hidden as it was by the sappers who dug it during the War."

Doctor Arnoldo exclaimed, "It was screened over like an

elephant trap! We fell right down through the vines. There we were seven feet underground. A subterranean tunnel, and that accursed beast we were chasing was running in the dark ahead of us."

"We couldn't see what it was," Fielding said. "It dived into that brush screen ahead of us, and led us into that pitfall. We ran after it down the tunnel. Shouted for you to follow us, but I suppose you didn't hear our yells for the thunder. My God, what a piece of engineering that tunnel is! Concrete walls and ceiling. Drainage pipes and ventilation flues like the London Underground. Must've been dug by the Germans before the Allied drive. Perfect subway for troops. Two miles under the forest and brought us straight to the *château.*"

"We were here in ten minutes," the Italian doctor pointed out. "When we arrived at the *château* I was astonished."

"We ran like hell," Fielding grinned. "Do you know where the tunnel comes up, Shepherd? Right under your Norman tower! I've an idea this Somme Front in Picardy is honeycombed with a lot of old German minings that have never been discovered since the War. They dug in like termites around here.

"Anyway, we came to a flight of steps and ended up in a stairway under the tower. Sure, we climbed up three floors through a lot of trash and ended in that room on the top floor of the *château* where we saw the big bat. That's where we caught the dog."

Bill Shepherd whispered, "Dog?"

"IN THE DARKNESS of the tunnel we didn't know what it was. But that's the prowler that scared us there in the woods. Remember, Archambaud said there was a stairway down from the top floor where we heard the beast howling? It must've gone down to the tunnel and chased out into the forest where it frightened us. Then we chased it back into the tunnel. Archambaud says he did not know about the tunnel because he never dared try that back stairway. But he says the German engineers did a lot of work around the *château*. Anyway, that was the prowler. Madam Landru's hound."

Fielding grinned ruefully. "The confounded beast was more frightened than we were. Spoiled my opportunity to investigate that peasant's grave. We could've bailed out the rainwater, and learned the answer, but I think I can tell you what he'd been up to. Those dated coins are the answer, Shepherd. The man was a ghoul."

"A ghoul," Bill Shepherd echoed huskily.

"Digging up old graves, see? There's quite a number of them in the forest—I've noticed them in the thickets. Germans mostly. Never transplanted into the memorial plots. Probably forgotten. Unknown soldiers. That peasant had nice pickings. Come out and dig up these unknown graves and rob the bodies of whatever silver or trinkets he could find. That explains the date on his miserable coins.

"The gas is easy. Spading down there in that hole he'd been digging, he probably drove the scoop through the rusted case of a gas shell, a shell that had buried itself in the earth and failed to explode. Hadn't been water in the hole, we'd have seen it. But that's what doubtless gassed him in that grave."

A thick voice spoke into Bill Shepherd's hearing. "Did you say, *mein herr,* there were graves?"

Herr Kull was approaching, dull-eyed, pale, his stare on Fielding, his walk slow and heavy-footed, like a dreary menace.

The Englishman and the others turned quickly to this speaker, as if they had forgotten his presence in the room. Fielding said quietly, "Yes, Herr Kull, I have seen in the vicinity of this *château* a number of German graves. There is a small plot of them not far from here in the forest."

The room wheeled and blurred on Bill Shepherd's vision, and the German stretched out of focus like a reflection in a convex mirror.

"*Ja,*" the guttural voice was saying. "I have spent years looking. From Verdun to Amiens I have searched. Every summer I come from Germany and look. But there are too many of them—there is no record—all I know is that he was killed in the Battle of the Somme." The mottled face nodded dully. "That is how I came to be riding in the forest last evening. I am looking for the grave of my only son. He has the same name as mine—Siegfried Kull."

"I saw it," Bill Shepherd whispered. "I saw it out there in the forest tonight, Herr Kull."

The room was steadying, coming back into focus. Feeling was draining back into his hands. He could hear reality in these voices; taste blood from a cut in his lip; smell wood-smoke from the fire and a musk of wet wool—his own coat-sleeves—cloth drying out in the warmth and beginning to steam.

Gabrielle Gervais was looking up at him, her eyes filled with feminine concern. "But are *you* all right, Monsieur Shepherd? Your lip—" she reached up with a handkerchief.

"*Mon Dieu!* you frightened me terribly. Plunging through the window like that—"

"I was standing in the casement," he said in a flatted tone. The others were looking at him—Doctor Arnoldo with a sympathetic frown—Fielding in anxiety—Tac, the little bus-driver, in bewilderment—the Russian, Putinov, interested, uncomprehending.

"I was standing in the window casement. I didn't go to Contalmaison. My car was stalled. I lost myself on the road trying to come back to the *château*. When I looked through the window, I—I saw you all in here. I climbed up into the casement to hear better. I thought—I thought I heard you quarreling."

"It was my fault," the little Fiat driver declared. "I took offence at a remark about my car. They said—these two passengers I brought tonight from Thiepval—that my Fiat was a rickety rattletrap, that it should not be allowed on the roads, that it was like France to keep a lot of old busses in duty that should have been discarded during the World War."

"The fault was mine," Professor Putinov growled. "I lost my temper. The subject of this absurd motor-bus took us into a discussion of European politics. A Russian can never discuss politics and keep his head. You would think I, who am supposed to be a psychologist and a student of man's mentality, would keep his head during any topic. To Herr Kull I wish to apologize."

Doctor Arnoldo said placatingly, "All the way up from Italy, bringing that old French general to his home by ambulance, we discussed the European situation. Always such discussions are futile."

The German moved his head from side to side, his expression shame faced. "I am the one who lost the temper. When the talk turned to Germany's war-guilt. Always I am hot-tempered on the subject, and my head tonight is not good from the bump when my horse unsaddled me. I apologize to you, Professor Putinov. *Ach, Gott,* did you hear that old clock go off when I slammed into it and gave it a jolt?"

Fielding put a hand on Bill Shepherd's arm, "I'm afraid we should all apologize to you, old man. Dinning around your fireside like this. We got talking about the Kaiser, and then Fascism, Munich and Communism, and there's always a row when you get arguing over the next war—"

And they'd been arguing over the *next* war!

Bill Shepherd walked over to the staircase, and sat down heavily, and began to laugh.

23

MUSIC AT MIDNIGHT

BILL SHEPHERD FELT sick and foolish. He had made it all up in his mind. Turned a pleasant British water-colorist into a flitting haunt—an olive-skinned Italian physician into a Doctor Caligari—a Russian, a bus-driver, and a girl had become, in the pale cast of his thought, the characters of a ten-twenty-thirty.

Seeing them now gathered about the fire, in this mellow light, they were only people—tired people, lost travelers as the girl had said.

Putinov, the Russian, was talking companionably to Herr Kull; Fielding, having busied himself in aiding Archambaud at boarding over the broken window, was now sitting with glass and pipe, his eyes closed, enjoying the fire's warmth; Arnoldo had left the room, to, as he said, bluntly, "locate the W.C."; little Tac was scrubbing mud from the sleeve of his bus-driver's uniform with something from a small bottle which the doctor had given to him. Gabrielle Gervais, at Shepherd's side, stretched and yawned.

Impossible as it seemed, the room was almost cozy and domestic, provided of course, that you did not remember its situation in this shell-torn *château*. With Madame Landru and her husband and dog retired to their sleeping quarters in a room off the kitchen, even the *château* did not seem as haunting as it had before.

Bill Shepherd, rousing from reflections in which he had scoffed at himself for his mystery-story imagination, found himself listening to Professor Putinov. The Russian from Tomsk talked well and amusingly. Although his manner toward his listeners was a little like that of a classroom savant patronizing students with large words. Bill Shepherd caught references to Freud, Kraft-Ebing, Saly-Saselle, Leibnitz, Podmore, Lambert and Heidbreder. And accented equivalents for "metaphysics," "extra-sensory impressions," "mass hallucination," "psychic trauma," "poltergeist activities."

"The French," Putinov was saying, "are perfect subjects for mass hallucination. Our little bus-driver could tell you that he has seen many things in company with the villagers of Thiepval on nights when there was no moon and a German or a Russian, for example, could see nothing. The stories with which Madame Landru entertained us a few moments ago are typical. This back country in France is alive with such stories. For example, lycanthropy. But myself, I'm not interested in werewolves. It is the legends of the War that I am here to study."

"The legends of the War?" Herr Kull asked gruffly. He was trying to be amiable. He could not exactly warm toward the Russian, who had struck him a blow in the heat of argument, and his smile was a little like a sneer, but one realized that in smiling at all the bald-headed German meant to forgive his hasty-fisted companion.

"Yes," Putinov nodded, "the legends of the French Army

and peasantry. The French have a sense of humor, very amusing. For example, there was the classic legend of the Cossacks at the Marne—the myth, incidentally, that filtered through the German advance and frightened Von Kluck into an unnecessary retreat from Paris. Of course everyone knows there were no Russian troops anywhere near the Marne.

"But the hallucinations persisted. The *poilus* insisted they had seen the Russian cavalry with their great fur hats and equally great fur beards. Ha! That was funny. The Cossacks had not even passed the Vistula. But the French were so heartened by this mass illusion that it turned the tide of battle, and Russia, if I may say so, won the War even as the Soviet army today is likely to win our imminent next European embroglio."

"The Soviets seem very confident of their power," Herr Kull said shortly.

Professor Putinov retreated hastily from the point. "There was also an interesting legend that the Scotch troops in their pretty skirts had arrived in Belgium. One of the most entertaining of these myths was that about the Virgin of Albert—"

Doctor Arnoldo, who had returned to the room, said, lifting his eyebrows, "The Virgin of Albert?"

"I TOLD YOU the French had a sense of humor." The hairy professor chuckled. "So. The Virgin of Albert. Of course she was in a niche over a church door. The church had been shelled during the first German advance in which they burned the town. Although the walls were cracked and crumbling, the roof fallen in, the altar destroyed, the Virgin in her niche remained. Most precariously she remained.

Hanging out over the street by a strand of wire—a big, wooden image, smiling down on those who passed below.

"The story was that she would fall the day the War ended. Ask anybody in the town of Albert and they will tell you that she fell plunging on exactly the day the Germans surrendered. Is that not a pretty myth? Ah. Who but the French could believe such a tale?

"Me, I found out an even more amusing ending. Quite a Russian touch. In falling, exactly at her specified date, the good image crashed down on the head of the local hero who was returning, covered with medals, from four years in the trenches defending his country at Verdun where he had not received a scratch. With true irony the pretty image bashed this hero's head in."

Marcel Tac protested angrily, "He is making fun of us! He has been making fun of us all evening. These godless Russians believe in nothing! I do not like to hear this man making fun of the French *mystique.*"

Professor Putinov laughed. "It is useless to protest against science, my little friend. I understand the French *mystique.*" The Russian included the others with a grin. "It is a beautiful balance of religious mysticism and warlike patriotic fervor. France nicely combines her soldiers and her saints. They go to war, if you will forgive me, like many Christian nations, certain that God is in a general's uniform directing their troops. Joan of Arc is a classic example."

"I will not listen to this foreigner belittle the Maid of Orleans!" The little bus-driver's eyes blazed. "He would jeer at *le bon Dieu.* Mademoiselle," Tac turned to Gabrielle Gervais, "you should not listen to this infamous talk."

Gabrielle Gervais said in a low voice, "It is all right, *mon ami.* You must remember that people in other countries have other ideas."

Professor Putinov grunted. "I do not mean to harm anyone's feelings. If forty million Frenchmen wish to believe that God is on their General Staff, I would be the last man in times like these to hope it is not true. I have an idea the French Army at the Maginot Line may need Divine leadership."

Marcel Tac said hotly, "The French army will take care of the situation." He puffed his chest. "I am in the first reserve. Daily I await my call. I would not be afraid to be first to go. My father was in the last war. My uncles. I am ready to defend my country. *Non,* I want to be the first in the line. I do not remember the last war, but I will have my share of the next one, you may be sure."

Bill Shepherd regarded this martial outburst with an averted smile of cynicism. It was a touchy subject—this next war. A little too touchy for tired people at three o'clock in the morning. Herr Kull's features reflected resentment again.

The German muttered, "Perhaps this little private will not be so anxious to go when *Der Tag* arrives. I would go myself if I was not too old. My son was in the war; I have always been proud to have given my only son."

BILL SHEPHERD THOUGHT the conversation had taken a dreary turn. These Europeans were unaccountable. Fifteen minutes ago he had walked with the bald-headed German to the grey little cemetery in the underbrush where Herr Kull had shed fatherly tears over the mossy mound of his son. Bill Shepherd had wondered then how anyone could be proud of such an obscure ending for a son. There was no heroic record on the cross. Only a name. It had seemed to mean a lot to Herr Kull, merely to know that his son had been buried.

Muttering to himself, the German rose and stalked from the room. Conversation lagged. Everyone yawned, and, uncomfortable in damp clothes, they shifted in their chairs. Certainly there was nothing phantom-like in these faces harsh-lined with fatigue. The specters had gone.

There was no more mystery here than that pause in the conversation which superstitious people believed invariably arrived at the quarter hour. Of course Gabrielle Gervais had still to be accounted for. Shepherd found himself watching the girl speculatively. He liked her quiet demeanor and the dark gleams of firelight in her hair. Stubborn chin. Self-reliance about the mouth. An un-selfconsciousness that he approved. He hitched closer in his chair.

He said in a lowered voice, "Not thinking about your romance with the horse-eater, were you?" He grinned.

She frowned, "You are still suspicious of me?"

He said, "I'm always suspicious of women, particularly nice looking ones. But I wanted to thank you for the loan of your pistol. I'm sorry I lost it out there in the woods."

She said, shrugging, "That is all right. My uncle will not miss it. He has a house full of guns. He is a collector in Paris."

"That's how your coupé comes to have a Paris license?"

"*Oui*, that is how."

He couldn't help admiring her tenacity. This runaway bride yarn—Plot 33—was her story and she stuck to it. He gave up a languid effort at indirect cross-examination— suddenly in the fire's warmth he was drowsy—and lounged back in his chair, listening to the drift of conversation. Herr Kull had rejoined the group, and the talk which had been skirting the edge of power politics was resumed.

The old argument.

Bill Shepherd didn't get into it. He knew nothing about such abstractions as Communism, Fascism, and Munich. He could only have voiced prejudices. Little Tac had spoken a provocative word on the Czech steal, and Fielding was defending Britain's policies. But the Englishman's comments were reserved.

And he spoke quietly.

"Art," he was saying, "is my only real interest. War is no longer an art. The fine tactics of cavalry and infantry maneuvers have gone forever. It has become a problem in economics. There is nothing artistic about a boycott or an embargo."

Gabrielle Gervais asked dryly, "Was there ever anything artistic, Monsieur Fielding, about a lot of men killing and wounding each other?"

Doctor Arnoldo interjected a suave, "But there are many artistic wounds, *mademoiselle*. Wars are not without certain compensations to humankind. Consider, in the last war, the development of plastic surgery. Many new techniques were evolved in the wartime hospitals. For example, the improved methods of trephining and giving blood transfusions. I doubt if surgery would have advanced to its present stage had there not been wars."

The girl's eyes were caustic. "You doctors. You talk as if surgery was the end and not the means. *Eh bien*," her smile went down at the corners, "to a surgeon we are all no more than guinea pigs. Pain does not enter the equation, one would think."

THE ITALIAN SMILED loftily. "Perhaps pain is but a way of testing character. Or a restraint on human recklessness."

He looked at Bill Shepherd, amused, asking confirmation. "For my own part, I believe there is too much emphasis in the medical profession on opiates and anaesthetics. The man who endures pain builds character. Regard Mussolini, who was wounded badly in the trenches. Adolph Hitler. Even Stalin. These are men who endured hardships almost Spartan."

Bill Shepherd was too tired for philosophic controversy. The room was humid. Drugged by the fire's warmth and fatigue, Bill Shepherd dozed.

His head, nodding, gave an upward jerk. Was that a face at that window? A dream? He could have sworn he had glimpsed a face peering through the watery pane—right there at that window beyond Herr Kull. Nothing there now. His overworked imagination had been at it again. Half asleep, he had glimpsed the German's reflection on that dark square of glass.

He nodded sleepily, pretending attention to some comment from Professor Putinov. Voices and room retreated once more from his consciousness. He caught himself slumping in the chair; pulled himself upright. Then suddenly he was stark awake. Shocked to attention in his chair. That sound was no dream.

Organ music! Bellowing into the room, fortissimo! The pealing martial strains of *The Watch On the Rhine!*

Everyone rose to his feet astounded by the music which rolled into the fire-lit room like harmonic thunder. The

German national anthem was followed by the *Marseillaise*. Patriotic little Marcel Tac stiffened to salute. As he did so, the music marched into the national hymn of Italy. Doctor Arnoldo said faintly, "That must be coming from Rome." But then they were listening to the booming, measured chords of the Russian national anthem. The astonishing concert ended with the Miltonic strains of *God Save the King.*

In the silence that abruptly followed, the party at the fireplace stared at Bill Shepherd, at one another in unbelief.

Bill Shepherd exclaimed, "A radio! I didn't know there was one in the *château.*"

Fielding blurted, "But where would a program be coming from at this time of the morning?"

There was a diversion in the passageway to the kitchen. Clatter of wooden shoes coming at a gallop. Shadows posed on the room's threshold. Madame Landru and Archambaud—the caretaker with his mouth open like a robbed purse; the old woman's eyes glowing out of the dimness like bicycle lamps.

Bill Shepherd cried, "Was that radio in your room, Madame Landru?" and was choked off by the expression on her face.

Madame Landru's voice droned into his hearing like a knell.

"There is no radio in the *Château de Feu!*"

24

VIGIL LIGHT

THEY STARED AT Madam Landru in a pall of silence. The hush that had enveloped the *château* after that last booming pæan of pipe-organ music was ghastly. Thunder rumbling over the broken roofs only emphasized the inner stillness.

Then Bill Shepherd said hoarsely: "You say that wasn't a radio in your rooms back there? There's no radio in the place?"

"Jove, Shepherd!" Fielding added. "They wouldn't broadcast that Russian national anthem, anyway!"

"There is no radio," Madame Landru droned. "That organ you heard, *messieurs*, is here in the *château*."

Archambaud made a clutch at his wife's elbow. "Name of God!" he said hoarsely. "The organ in the chapel!" He broke off, choking. His eyes were bulging with fear under the salty sheaf of his forelock; his dobbin's face was lead gray.

Madame Landru was nodding, staring straight ahead of her in a trance of mystery. "*Oui,* that was the organ in the chapel. The chapel that we have not entered in twenty-three years. The organ that we have not heard since 1916."

"But who was playing it just now?" Bill Shepherd cried. "Where is this chapel, old woman! Who put on that organ concert?" It couldn't have been the wind, or the dog. Or remote control from anyone in the room, or an illusion on his hearing—these others had heard it, too. "Where is it, and who was playing on it—*you?*"

"Not I! The chapel is at the far end of the ruined wing— on the ground floor. I was in the kitchen with Archambaud. Did you think he or I could play music on a pipe-organ? *Non,* that was an instrument for a master—an organ your father had installed from an ancient monastery. The last time I heard it played was when a German general was here."

"He had been a musician at Salzburg," Archambaud whispered. "I remember! *Sacré Bleu!* he was drunk and went to the chapel to play a military march. He was killed on the organ-bench by a sniper who spied him from the forest."

"Perhaps it was he we heard just now," Madame Landru droned. "Returned from the past to finish his interrupted concert. One of the un-dead dead who roam the Forêt de Feu. One of the Forgotten of God!"

Bill Shepherd couldn't take that. Not after the puzzles of midnight had been solved so patly. This was no time for the ghosts to come back; he couldn't let his reason go once more askew. There was an answer to this organ music as there'd been an answer to everything else. A jar couldn't start a pipe-organ as it had started a long-silenced clock: someone had entered the chapel and deliberately played the thing—someone flesh and blood, with human hands.

The little group by the fireplace were looking at him in dumbfoundment; Bill Shepherd walked to the big table and, firm-handed, picked up a lamp. He was in no mood for any more spectral visitations and mediumistic capers.

"Archambaud! Get going! You're taking me to the chapel!"

The horse-faced caretaker was having difficulty with his legs. His knees had contracted the ague, and he seemed afraid to let go of his wife's support for fear of falling down.

Bill Shepherd snapped, "You too, Madame Landru! Quit the act! Somebody played that organ, and it wasn't any spook. We're going to end these stunts around here right now."

He had hoped, even expected, that the crazy old woman might own up to having started a Victrola—that she would explain how some loud-speaker attachment, or amplifiers installed in the *château* during the War, had magnified the sound. Or the insane creature had sneaked to the chapel and played the organ, herself—a madcap lunacy inspired by the haunts in her brain.

Instead, staring like a somnambulist, she freed herself of her husband's clutch and paddled off down the kitchen passage. They followed her in an uneasy party, instinctively bunched together, Bill Shepherd shoving the reluctant Archambaud in front of him, the others bringing such lamps and candles as they could lay their hands on.

HALFWAY DOWN THE passage, the old woman opened a door—Bill Shepherd had not noticed it there—and led them into the windy glooms of the great main hall. There were exclamations from the others who had not seen this vast chamber before, muted murmurs of surprise at the shadow-veiled scene of old destruction.

Bill Shepherd hurried the old woman with a word, and they crossed the trash-littered floor, skirted the broken staircase where the suit of armor stood in its somber

In that nightmare scene Shepherd struggled with the cripple.

solitude, and passed through a portal under the sagging mezzanine.

There was a long, empty corridor where the cobwebs hung like Spanish moss and their footsteps sank in carpets of stale dust. In sharp suspicion, seeing no tracks in this gray sediment, Bill Shepherd wondered if the woozy-eyed old slattern was purposely taking them the long way around. The *château* was as complicated with corridors, passages and halls as a rabbit warren. They took a side passage, and hurried through rooms as bare and fusty as abandoned catacombs. Conceivably, if she were trying to scare them, Madame Landru would lead them on this tour. Again she was mumbling about the phantoms of the forest who left no visible track.

"Phantoms hell!" Bill Shepherd thought, angering.

Hallowe'en was over. The only phantoms in this wretched manse were the lady with the goitre and her imbecilic husband. Undoubtedly there was a direct connecting passage between this chapel and the kitchen, and the tracks would be Archambaud's wooden shoes or the old woman's cat-footed slippers.

"The chapel," her voice droned back. "There it is. That door ahead."

The party jolted to a halt in the narrow corridor. The doorway ahead was dimly seen as a Gothic arch framing a churchlike interior, the chancel rail of a shrine visible in a blue dimness such as might have been cast through a stained-glass window. Bill Shepherd saw this blue shine came from the altar of the shrine. The subdued blue haze was crepuscular.

Archambaud gasped, "Somebody has lit a vigil light. There has not been a candle in that shrine since your father visited the *château* before the War—*Sacré Dieu!*"

Bill Shepherd thought it was a nice effect. Whoever was staging this flummery knew the tricks of theatrical lighting. He wasn't fooled. He'd been behind the scenery tonight; this setup was an anticlimax.

He snapped, "No you don't, Madame Landru. I'll go first!" Elbowing her aside as she started forward. He didn't want to give her a chance to stir up the dust with her skirts or whisk away any betraying sign. Advancing to the dim-lit door with swift, unhesitating strides, he thrust the lamp through the shadowy portal and stepped across the threshold.

Then he stood quite still.

The others came up behind him; the whole party jelled.

In the hush of blue dimness, the chapel interior was as empty, as still, as a crypt. The little vigil light on the altar burned steadily in its cup of blue glass, lighting the empty niche above it. The saints were gone; the chapel was bare of furnishing; only slivers of glass remained in the casement of the Gothic window which was boarded over. But the organ was there, dominating the backwall with its wing-spread of pipes, like a creature of fantasy enthroned there in the shadows, the arms of its mahogany console on its knees, its tiers of yellow teeth dully gleaming, its pinions reaching to the ceiling. It was draped with cobwebs, and ghostly. Gilt had peeled on the pipes; the woodwork was tarnished; mice had nested in the music rack; the organ-stops and keys had warped crookedly.

But someone had been on the organ-bench playing. Someone who had torn the gauze of cobweb from the manuals, swept the thick gray dust from the keys, kicked the rat's nest out of the foot bellows. Someone who had left a track!

There was a door at the back of the chapel. The track came in, went to the shrine at the sidewall, then to the organ console, then out through the door the way it had come. It was plainly stamped in the heavy carpet of dust. To Bill Shepherd it was worse than if there had been no track at all. It was a very clear footprint. Made by a left shoe!

"The man who played that organ had only one leg!"

The cry had barely blurted from his lips when from the room overhead there came a muffled crash. The ceiling trembled, and some flakes of plaster came down. There was a dragging sound, and then—all in the chapel heard it—the sound of someone moving off, *stamp, stamp, stamp.*

25

SKELETONS, ATTENTION

FACES AT THE chapel's threshold were blue-complected in the light. Aghast, they listened to that one-legged stamper go crutching away.

Gabrielle Gervais sobbed, "Who's that?"

One of the men behind her groaned, "The organist!"

Madame Landru droned, "The Forgotten of God! The Forgotten of God!"

Distant in the kitchen, the dog began to howl. Bill Shepherd spun about, snarling. "Keep your shirts on! This is a trick! Someone's trying to scare me out of here, and I won't scare! Madame Landru knows who it is!"

Madame Landru made the sign of the cross on her goitre. "I do know, *c'est ça!* On my faith! As God is my witness, I have seen this maimed spirit in the forest. It is one of those killed in the Battle of the Somme. One of the dead who—"

Bill Shepherd cut her off furiously, "He's making for the east wing! Don't let him get away! I'll take this back passageway. The rest of you get back to the main hall. Fielding! Take Putinov, and head him off at the marble staircase!"

But Fielding and the Russian had already gone. The Ital-

ian doctor, Herr Kull and Marcel Tac were retreating with
Archambaud down the corridor. Bill Shepherd, racing for
the little door at the chapel's rear, found Gabrielle Gervais
at his side.

"Go back! Stay with the crowd!"

"Non! I'm coming with you!"

They left Madame Landru, grimalkin-eyed, in a swirl of
dust. Charging through the chapel's back exit, Bill Shepherd saw a short hallway, steps ascending into darkness at
its end. A one-footed track went up the steps. He swerved,
handing the girl the oil lamp.

"Keep behind me! Mind your footing! There'll be holes
in the floors and all sorts of rubbish up there. That fellow
may be armed."

He paused to snatch up a big spindle of wood, a bannister spindle smashed out of the stair-rail. Hefting this
adequate club, he mounted the narrow staircase three steps
at a time, halting at the top to cough his lungs free of dust,
wipe spiderweb from his eyes and wait for the lamp. A girl
in this damned hide-and-seek was a nuisance. He didn't
want her with him; couldn't leave her behind. Whatever
was the motive of this organ-playing stunt, it was something more than a practical joke—someone nuts or up to
skulduggery—and this four-story ruin was a dangerous
place to play hare and hounds.

"Watch out for the flooring, and stick close," he advised
snappishly. "I don't mind telling you, if I get my hands on
this organist there may be a scrap."

She murmured, "Please be careful."

He grunted, gripping the bannister spindle. Someone
ought to get their head knocked off for trying to scare

a lot of storm-marooned people at half-past three A.M. He'd been through too much hazing tonight to take this organ-playing stunt in good humor.

"There's the track. Looks like he stumbled over that heap of plaster and fell down here. Must've been up here listening when we rushed into the chapel. Come on!"

The lamplight wavered on ahead of them, showing the way. The one-footed track went through a series of empty bed chambers, out into a rubbish-heaped hall, then hopped up a flight of broken stairs to the third floor. Bill Shepherd had hoped it would go down instead of up. Voices were calling, feet were running somewhere on the floor below in the direction of the main hall, a faint hue and cry in the *château's* catacombed stillness. Bill Shepherd saw where the one-legged man had circled back, frightened by the chase below, stopped to judge the location of his pursuers, then gone up the stairs hippity-hop.

Motioning to the girl, Bill Shepherd mounted into the third-floor darkness. In the blackness at the stair-top, he listened. *Stamp, stamp, stamp.* There it was fading off in the dark to the right, a number of rooms away—the hump-thump of a man on crutches—a sound immortalized for nightmare terrors by Robert Louis Stevenson's grisly Long John Silver. Bill Shepherd's calloused nerves were not shaken by it now.

He shouted down the stairwell, "Hey, Fielding! Up here, everybody! He's up here on the third floor!"

THE FAINT STAMPING sounds quickened in flight. Seizing Gabrielle Gervais by the wrist, Bill Shepherd yanked her after him, raced down the wreckage-strewn corridor in hot pursuit. Through the rooms where the ceilings had fallen and the walls were shot full of holes. Around the trash piles of smashed furniture. In and out through the heaps of tile and débris and bathroom fixtures and uprooted plumbing and crashed chandeliers.

It seemed a long time ago he had passed through these ruins, pursuing the howls of Theophile, the dog. He had been unnerved by them then; he wasn't afraid now.

He snapped at the girl, "Steady that lamp! Don't be afraid here! This floor's all right! I've been over it before!"

Whoever that bird on crutches was, he was moving fast and knew this flooring, too. The one-legged footprints were spaced about four feet apart. You could see inter-jected marks where the ferrules of the crutches had dug in. The crutches avoided pitfalls, and the footprint hopped nimbly over gaps in the floor. The one-legged man knew the *château.*

If he was a man with one leg. Bill Shepherd didn't voice this thought to the girl. He'd been tricked once too many tonight, and he wasn't going to fall again. The idea could be quicker than the eye. He wouldn't lose his innate agnos-ticism this time. Things were not what they sometimes seemed. He had written a murder story one time about a killer who left crutch-prints and the track of a single shoe. Scotland Yard and the readers had been baffled. But the killer had had his right leg hitched up under his greatcoat, and when he got back to Limehouse he threw away the crutches and walked off like any biped.

"If I nail him," Bill Shepherd panted, "duck, and yell your head off."

Gabrielle Gervais whispered breathlessly, "Who can it be?"

Bill Shepherd didn't bother with that. Time to wonder at the showdown. He had his own ideas about some of this night's hocus-pocus now. This organ-playing was too stagy. Madame Landru's jitters too jittery. And another angle—before that organ-blast, everyone by the fire had made a brief exit, at one time or another, from the room. Easy enough to meet someone who might be waiting for you in the passage. Who? Bill Shepherd, wanting to find out, towed the girl so swiftly that she stumbled. Luckily he caught the oil lamp. As he ran on, he was certain of one thing. The fellow ahead of them wasn't any wraith.

They could hear the footstep pounding up a stair.

Bill Shepherd set his jaw. That top floor was a hazardous place. He told the girl, "He's trying to reach that stairway at the end of the wing. The one that goes down to that tunnel Fielding and Arnoldo discovered—the tunnel under the forest!"

"*Mon Dieu,*" the girl gasped.

"We've got to stop him. I don't want to mix it under there!"

They raced past the room where the great black arm of a tree reached in through the window; Bill Shepherd fairly yanked the girl's arm loose on the stair-flight. The track hopped off through the maze of the shell-smashed mansards, and Bill Shepherd had to follow more slowly for these undermined attics were as perilous as scaffolding. Rain swept in through great gaps in the roof, turning the plaster-mounds to slippery cement and threatening the lamp. A boom of thunder brought down a shower of slates. The girl stifled a cry of fear, dodging the slates and trying to shelter the hissing lamp-chimney with her elbow.

Bill Shepherd muttered, "You shouldn't have come."

"*Non, non.*" She shook her head. "I was afraid for the light. Are you going on? Then I am with you."

He found a second to privately admire her gameness. Her lips were white, and her eyes were scared to death, but she didn't hang back. They clawed through the jungles of fallen roof timber, climbed the bricks of shattered gables and wormed between the pyramids of broken lumber where the foot track hippity-hopped. They came out into an enclosed attic-like room full of night and wind, a quarter of the mansard where the roof and gables had held and the floor remained secure.

Bill Shepherd did not remember this end of the wing. The brick facings of a great, flat chimney squared up in the center of the chamber; in the darkness under the eaves beyond he could see nothing. He could see no footprint crossing the floor. He signaled the girl to listen. Only the downpour of the rain; gusts of wind. No other sound.

Bill Shepherd hunted the floor with uneasy eyes. Loss of tracks and the dark-eaved silence warned him of ambush. He gripped the heavy spindle in his fist, calling, "Come on out of there! I know you're back there!" peering at the darkness under corner eaves.

He said from the side of his mouth to the girl, "He's pulled himself under the eaves somewhere, careful to hide his footprint." Squeezing her arm with his left hand, he edged her into the room, watching the corners, vigilant, wary. Under his breath, "When we get there, stand with your back against that chimney. Keep the lamp high. If he makes a dash from any corner, I'll get him. I'm going to scout there at the back."

He placed her against the chimney bricks; stepped away from her, ready to spring. What was that sound? Somewhere, barely audible on his hearing, there was in the room a queer, asthmatic whistling, as of someone wheezing through clenched teeth. He had not heard it at first. Now, as his hearing sharpened, it became more apparent. It wasn't like human breathing. More like the thin, elfin *wheee* of a whistle on a peanut wagon.

A quick-moving floor-shadow warned him. Head down, he spun.

Only in time to see the handle of a crutch as it lashed out from behind the brick chimney, shattered the oil lamp in the girl's upraised hand and smashed the attic into pitch darkness.

"DUCK! DUCK!" HE cried at the girl. He sprang at the chimney blindly in the dark. The girl's stifled scream was smothered under a sound of scuffling. The queer wry whistling loudened in Bill Shepherd's ears. He was afraid to strike out for fear of hitting the girl; couldn't seem to locate her in the blackness.

He never quite knew what happened. Something cracked against his forehead like a flying broomstick; flung backward by the blow, he lost balance, sprawled under the eaves. Sounds faded, and he lay stunned. Through a haze of numbness he sensed a fierce struggle going on in the dark; tried to shout to the girl to run. The queerish whistling added to the confusion of his dazed senses; then be thought he could hear a voice in guttural German, a low sob from the girl, the sound of her dragging feet and the muffled one-legged stamp of the unseen assailant departing from the room.

He strove three times to reach his feet before he accomplished his balance. He knew they were running, and he groped across the floor in drunken pursuit. Somehow his hands remembered his pocket lighter and he lit the small flare and stumbled around the chimney toward a corridor of shadows at the back.

Then, without realizing how he had come there, he discovered himself in the chamber under the tower. Footsteps seemed to be fading overhead. Elevating the tiny light, he made out the back wall where Fielding had seen the bat. The sealed wall had been broken through. Large chunks of plaster were scattered before the aperture which looked as if it had been breached by a pick-ax. Dust rolled smokily from this yawning portal and the light gleams picked out an inner stair.

Shepherd had no time for astonishment. Lowering his shoulders he charged into the tower; went up the stairway in headlong chase after the sounds of climbing feet and the eerie thump of crutches. His head was clearing; the pain of the blow sharpened his senses. Rage at this antagonist who had struck him from the dark had burned through the first shock of fear; he wanted only to get his hands on the man and rescue the girl.

Sounds on the stairway above him had quit. With no thought of caution for himself, he charged up at the waiting darkness. Stumbling across the last step he sprawled on the stone floor. He picked himself up, panting, grabbing blindly into the blackness. He was at the top of the tower, he knew. The air was stale and smelled of bats. Then green lightning flooded through a barred window; he saw himself in a circular stone-walled room. The room was empty!

Thunder seemed to be crashing about his head. Lightning flared again into his face. He rushed to the window, gripped the mossy sill, thrust his head through the rusty bars and looked down. A bright play of aerial electricity revealed a sheer fifty-foot drop to the ground below, no handholds where a climber might have descended. The he saw something else.

In the forest below a file of small figures were running. He made out the Russian, Putinov, the little bus-driver, Doctor Arnoldo and Fielding.

He shouted, "Help! Fielding! Up here! Up here in the tower!"

Fielding looked up once, then dived into the trees after the others. Thunder blacked out that momentary glimpse, and whether the Englishman heard him or whether his cry was drowned in the rain, Bill Shepherd could not tell. He turned and glared about the tower room, cupping the lighter in his palms, straining to see by the futile gleam.

No door apparent save the one at the stair-top. The single window barred. The dust-carpet on the floor had been swirled by hurrying feet; gave no clue to the egress of his assailant and the abducted girl. Where could they have gone? They might have been absorbed by the shadows swimming under the high conical ceiling.

Peering up, he stumbled over something sodden, heavy. A body—! No, a canvas bag. A soldier's kitbag left there in the spider-webbing and dust. He bent with the lighter. The bag was weather-beaten, stained; some infantryman of 1916 might have stowed his duffle up here for safe keeping. Initials dimly printed on the canvas. *S.H.* Or—he tensened in a crouch—reading upside-down, *H.S.* He exhaled, "Hugh's—?" But there was no time to speculate over an old canvas bag.

HE BEGAN TO explore the walls. His groping hand tore loose curtains of cobweb; encountered a nest of wires. A dusty switchboard! A shelf of electrical apparatus and dead batteries! The tangle of forgotten wireless equipment? This long-sealed turret had once been a wireless station? He had no opportunity to wonder.

Clawing through the snarl of lifeless wires, his fingers must have touched some hidden mechanism; to his astonishment the switchboard on the wall swung inward, and, losing balance, he was nearly precipitated down a black ladder of stairs. A secret exit!

Without pausing, he stepped through the trap, started in pitch darkness down a circular stair flight secreted in the tower wall. Where could it lead? The *château* seemed as honyecombed with escapes as the Tower of London.

In black ambush below, that organist might be waiting. A broken step might plunge him three stories down to the ground. But Bill Shepherd rushed on down through the darkness, unhesitating.

He fell the last dozen steps, tumbling, caroming off unseen walls, landing in a smothery cloud of soot at the bottom. A dungeon? A wine-cellar? He glared into blackness, cursing silently, clenching empty hands. Loss of his cigarette-lighter was a disaster that he had no time to repair. In his precipitant descent, he had gained in the chase and as he picked himself up, in what seemed to be a passage, he thought he could hear sounds of running ahead of him.

He shouted into the blackness, "Gabrielle! Gabrielle!"

There was no answer. Hands in front of him to fend any obstacle, he pursued the sound of fleeing footsteps, banging into sharp turns, bruising his elbows and shoulders against smooth concrete walls.

He did not know how far he ran in this unlighted corridor. He was aware, suddenly, of a freshening of the air, then wind in his face, and the steady drumming of rain. Rounding a turn, he plunged out through a screen of underbrush, found the storm in his face. A blaze of lightning silhouetted trees against the sky; he was in a winding trench that zigzagged head of him and burrowed off through thickets and underbrush.

He followed the trench, splashing through deep channels of water; came to his dismay to a fork where a shallow communication ditch joined this larger earthwork. In the swirling rain and dark, lit only by blue flares overhead, he was unable to discern any track. He ran on blindly keeping to the deeper trench.

Could this be the old trench he had seen earlier that evening when he, Fielding, and the Italian doctor had followed a dead man's trail to a ghoul's grave? He didn't know. He shouted Fielding's name, shouted to the girl, receiving no answering echo.

Slowing to a walk, he moved on helplessly. Could not tell how far he was from the *château,* but he knew that he must be in the forest well beyond the little German burying ground. Then he stopped in quick alarm. There was a figure at the trench-turn directly ahead.

He could only see the dim outline, a man standing motionless in the black rain. He recoiled in a crouch, grabbed into the unseen weeds around him, hunting a weapon or missile. His fingers closed on something—the broken hilt of a rusty sword. Inching forward, lifting his feet stealthily from the mud, he advanced on the motionless figure. Lightning flared across the sky, witch-blue in the sheeting rain; trench and forest leaped into view, and he saw the man.

A SCOTCHMAN! A Guard of the Black Watch posted at the bend of the trench. His posture was slovenly; his uniform hung to his knees in blowing rags; his rifle leaned against the trench wall beside him; in that flare of lightning Bill Shepherd saw the sentry's face was turned toward him fixed in a grin. A Lady from Hell to scare any German raider all the way back to Berlin. One of the dead of the Red Zone, indeed. In uniform and upright, posted on sleepless guard, a human skeleton.

Bill Shepherd went by this bogle at a leap, and the Scotchman collapsed with a little clinkle of bones. Bill Shepherd did not stop to aid him to his feet, but went rushing down the trench in a cloud of water and mud. The trench turned abruptly; he was halted again. Not by any skeletal guard this time. By a light.

It streamed like swamp-fire from the wall of the trench ahead—lamplight shining through a dugout door. He crept along the muddy wall, clutching the broken sword. There was no sound from the dugout; the muddy mouth was curtained with rags of canvas and the light came palely through this moth-eater drape of camouflage. He crawled up on the crumbled firing step, put his eyes to a rent in the moldy canvas.

The dugout scene was a stage-set from *Journey's End,* revived for one night in the Forêt de Feu. The players were not there, but the scenery awaited the overture. Candles guttered on a table fashioned of planks and wooden boxes. There were bunks piled with tousled bedding; tunics, underwear, khaki britches, cartridge belts, even a gas mask hung shabbily from a row of hooks along the wall. Fire-coals smouldered in the stove made of a black tar-barrel; the air was dank with smoke and a smell that might have been compounded of tobacco, wet grass, and stale socks. Bill Shepherd found himself gulping at sight of an unwholesome pan of beans and a platter of half-consumed hash on the table.

That skeletal Scot could not have been interrupted from his dinner! Bill Shepherd had lost some of the *sang-froid* which had fortified his pursuit of the one-legged organist, but he was not to be panicked as he had been in the middle of the night. If there was food on that dugout table, some flesh and blood diner had been eating it, someone who had been inhabiting this trench in the forest.

He stumbled on in the rain, pausing at intervals to shout for Fielding, Arnoldo, Putinov and the others to follow him from wherever they were. Then as suddenly as he had found himself in it, he was out of the trench, breasting through a thicket of brambles on a path that led toward what looked like, screened by tall saplings, an abandoned stable.

Lightning blazed in the rain, and he glimpsed the building clearly—a small stone barn, roofless, vine-grown, isolated here in the forest. A haze of yellow lantern light outlined the barn window. Someone was there. Tightening his grip on the rusty weapon he had picked up in the trench, he scouted forward, aware now of the murmur of voices. Voices in German! Then a husky-throated protest in French!

He had found the girl!

26

SECOND WORLD WAR

SWIFTLY HE ADVANCED up the path, scouting the dim-seen barn with eyes narrowed to the rain, nerves throbbing, every sense alert. A voluble outburst of German reached his ears; a harsh-spoken, *"Nein, nein, nein!"* Then untranslatable French from the girl. One word detached itself from the low-voiced volley. *Espionne!* Bill Shepherd halted in his stride. The word stabbed into his brain, a verbal electric shock. That word had to do with espionage—spies!

"My God!" He had to grip his lips to keep from crying out.

Spies! In this fantastic jabberwok tonight, he had run the whole gamut of mystery-plot possibilities from Arson to Zombies; how the devil had he overlooked Enemy Spies? Espionage! It might explain every one of tonight's incredible angles. Might explain the recent murders in these woods, the ineffectuality of the police, the presence of these assorted and strangely various foreigners.

He saw now that their reasons for arriving at the *château,* their glib definitions of themselves might have been too pat. Suppose Fielding... suppose the others?... why had they scattered when he yelled for help?... where were they now? All at once the woods around him were full of agents and counter-agents, secret service men, foreign operators.

The Forêt de Feu was within cannon distance of Belgium. Europe on the edge of the next war, precariously balanced between Hitler, Chamberlain, Daladier and Mussolini, these old battlegrounds behind the French frontier were probably crawling with spies.

He wondered, "The girl, too?"

Behind that wall, she was talking vehemently. "I am not engaged in counter espionage! You are making a mistake! I have never betrayed the Germans!"

The words came clearly, and ended on a sob. Bill Shepherd glared at the faint-lit window of the stable, swallowing lumpy oaths. She had never betrayed the Germans? He gasped inwardly, "What the hell?" She was in this, all right. There were a couple of Germans behind that stable-wall, and one was accusing her of double-crossing. He could read angry accusation in the man's guttural snarls. Was it that fellow, Kull?

Another German was haranguing, *"Nein, Herr Leutnant! Nein! Gott in Himmel, nein!"* Bill Shepherd was able to translate the answer to that. "Do not be a fool, Fritz. I do not like to do this, either, but duty is duty. This woman has been cheating us all along."

Bill Shepherd's throat-muscles tightened. So that was it! A little game of spies. Arriving unexpectedly at the Château de Feu, he had probably blundered into a rendezvous of some kind. This forest, tabooed by the local peasantry, was a nice base for operations. The girl was in on the game.

He had wondered, climbing the stairs going up into the

tower, why the girl hadn't put up more of a scrap. Probably knew her one-legged abductor. He should have suspected that, but the crack that fellow had dealt him with the crutch had knocked him almost senseless, and he'd been pretty punch-drunk until he'd reached the open air.

He reached up and touched the lump over his temple. The lump throbbed viciously. Bill Shepherd put his teeth together. He was almost up to the barn. His assailant would pay for that crack on the head. He'd give him a couple of extras, compliments for Hitler and the Gestapo.

Clenching the broken sword, he crouched under the window. Too high to permit him a view of the stable within, and he couldn't risk chinning himself on the sill. There were two of them in there; his only chance would be a rush. He thefted along the wall, tense with caution. The downpour had thinned suddenly to a sifting brume; he could hear the voices in the stable clearly.

"You are making a mistake, *Herr Leutnant*. It will give us a bad name if you do this thing. They will blame the Fatherland. Let the woman go." It did not sound like the voice of Herr Kull.

The answer did not sound like Herr Kull's voice, either. Half gurgle, half snarl, it came in a guttural passion. "Duty is duty. I have my orders. The woman is guilty. The sentence against her has been passed."

The voice choked out. To Bill Shepherd's straining ears came that thin, eerie, peanut-whistling sound he had heard in the dark of the *château* mansard. The wheezy whistle made his teeth grind like the squeak of a rusty castor or the scrape of a file. It stopped, and the guttural voice repeated with finality, "There is nothing you can do about it, Fritz. The sentence has been passed."

Gabrielle Gervais sobbed, *"Ah, mon Dieu, mon Dieu!"*

There was a despairing cry of *"Lieber Gott in Himmel! The man is going to shoot!"*

Going to shoot! Leaping forward, Bill Shepherd rounded the corner of the barn in full career, raced around the wreckage of an overturned wagon, charged madly through the stable door. He skidded to a dead-stop across wet straw.

"Good God!"

HE WOULD NEVER forget the scene that paralyzed him there. The roofless barn full of cloudy mist. The streaky black shadows; the hand lantern spraying out yellow gleams from one corner. The figures posed like people playing a charade. Gabrielle Gervais standing against the backwall, her face in her hands. Five feet off and directly facing her, the one-legged man, his crutches braced to hold him upright, a rifle at shoulder-level, aimed to shoot the girl through the head. And in the corner opposite from the lantern, a man Bill Shepherd thought was sitting upright on the floor straw, his hands on the floor at either side, fingers spread flat as though he were trying to push himself up on legs that refused to stand.

These men were in German uniform, shabby tunics of field gray. The rifleman on crutches wore the scuttle-shaped helmet of German infantry; the soldier seated on the floor wore the goblet-shaped helmet of the Prussian cavalry Uhlan.

The girl backed against the wall—the soldiers in German uniform were enough to stun Bill Shepherd and rob him of power to move. Then with another shock of horror, he realized the German on the floor was a man without legs— the half of a man—head, arms and torso helplessly fastened to a little wooden platform which moved on roller skates.

This half-man wanted to get out of the corner, but the wheels of his platform refused to budge in the straw; he was panting heavily, face contorted with the effort to move himself, perspiration streaming down his jaws. He was like a human bust trying to throw itself from a shelf, and his struggling chilled Bill Shepherd.

But the one-legged rifleman on crutches was worse. As Bill Shepherd skidded almost to the middle of the barn to a stop, the one-legged man spun around with a hop and a twist; throwing up the rifle to draw a bead on Bill Shepherd's heart.

Bill Shepherd's heart was coated with ice. Not from the rifle aimed to kill him. Not from this German's face which contorted with hate and scribbled from mouth to ear by a livid, purple scar. Not from the source of that faint, elfin whistling—the little silvery button above the collar of his tunic—the peanut whistle imbedded in the wattles of his throat.

Bill Shepherd's heart was ice-coated because the rifle leveled at him was rusty-barreled, dirt-choked, with a mossy stock. Because the German tunic was a coat of fragments, the tarnished buttons clinging by threads. Because the coal-scuttle helmet was dented and fire-scorched, the crown full of little holes.

Once more the words of Madame Landru went tolling through his head. "The dead have not yet died in the Red

Zone." Again the night went flittergibbet and reason was askew.

Aiming the rifle left-handed, the one-legged man pressed a finger over the whistle-hole in his throat, and addressed Bill Shepherd in savage German gutturals.

"Halt! *Wer'st da?* How dare you interrupt the execution of a spy!"

"She is not a spy," the half-man in the corner cried hoarsely. "You are making a mistake, *Herr Leutnant!* A terrible mistake!"

"She is a spy, and the death sentence has been passed," came the wheezy answer. "You can see for yourself by looking at her. I was there in Brussels when Von Bissing passed the sentence. She is Edith Cavell!"

GABRIELLE GERVAIS CRIED, "He thinks I am a spy. He believes I am a woman named Edith Cavell—!"

Bill Shepherd yelled at the one-legged man, "Who are you, what are you doing here?"

The half-man in the corner cried desperately, "Quiet, *Mein Herr!*"

The girl screamed, "Take me out of here! I think I'm going mad!"

Bill Shepherd thought he was going mad himself. He stared at the gloomy visitation before him, at the moldy rifle, the scarred face, the threadbare uniform, wondering if it were possible to charge at a phantom. The whistle-throated man was grinning, the button in his neck creeing like a bos'n's pipe. He stifled the whistle with his finger and leered.

From the side of his mouth he said, "Regard this, Fritz. An American. So they're in the war at last."

Yes, Bill Shepherd was in the war at last. It was 1916. He was in a shell-torn barn. An execution scene. But the soldiers were dead; the trenches were dead; the girl herself was a specter out of the past. A nurse! On her own admission. And these German soldiers were carrying out the brutal orders of a General von Bissing long resting under his memorial monument.

Bill Shepherd clutched his eyes with his left hand and grasping his rusty sword, flung himself at the one-legged man. The rifle took him a glancing blow across the jaw; he went acrobating across the stable, landing a-cropper on the human bust of the Uhlan.

The half-man went over on his dreadful little platform. The girl screamed. The one-legged man whistled like a peanut wagon; grabbed his throat and gargled a laugh. Then, sitting up, in a daze of horror, Bill Shepherd beheld a new phantasm framed in the roofless stable door.

The man had arrived there like a conjuration out of the weeping mist. Another soldier. An officer in faded khaki. His British tunic trim on square shoulders, a Victoria Cross on his breast, the tabs of a Captain marking his rank, visor of an officer's cap aslant over his eye. He was balanced there on crutches; his left leg gone at the hip, his sleeves empty, both arms amputated just below the shoulder. He had no face! Merely a black mask with holes slit for lips and eyes.

The voice from the mask was hoarse, clipped, commanding in English, "Gustav! Fritz! What's going on here? Who is this girl? Who is this man?"

The half-man cried, *Herr Kapitan!* Gustav believes he has captured a spy! He believes this girl to be Edith Cavell!"

The black-masked officer started violently back on his

crutches. Bill Shepherd stared at this British specter stupi-
fied. He now saw behind this incredible figure a group of
figures even more incredible—four more apparitions from
the past, deformed in the gloom, who had gathered there as
if at some wizard's signal. The noseless man in the Cossack's
astrakhan—the one-eyed creature in the uniform of the
French Chasseurs—the hunchbacked cripple who wore
the feathered hat of the Italian Bersaglierie—the *poilu* with
steel hooks wing-like at his shoulders—this group might
have been the mutilated escort of all the Unknown Soldiers
killed in No Man's Land during the War.

GABRIELLE GERVAIS LAY on the straw in a fainted
huddle. Bill Shepherd's constricted throat could not utter
a sound. His brain seemed to swell like an empty balloon.
He heard the black-masked officer utter a harsh word of
command. The one-legged man with the whistle in his
throat lowered his rifle reluctantly.

The British officer was saying, "You know you ought not
to pick up those old guns, Gustav; they are liable to go off."

"I thought the girl was Edith Cavell," the man said
wheezily. "I had orders to shoot Edith Cavell. The girl
looks like Edith Cavell."

The black-masked British officer said to Bill Shepherd,
"Get up, young man." Tapping his forehead significantly,
"Gustav means no harm. The poor fellow has lapses. Do
not be afraid of him, the gun is useless, a relic he picked
up somewhere. Do not be afraid of us," the voice sounded
ironic, bitterly humorous, "you can see we are unarmed."

Bill Shepherd swayed dizzily to his feet. He stared at the
British officer, at the mutilated figures framed in the stable

door. Could there be some reason behind this fantastic charade after all? Was his vision sane?

There seemed to be sanity behind the armless captain's black mask. The clipped British voice was self-assured, in command of this ghastly situation. The apparitions behind the officer made no menacing move.

The legless Uhlan beside him was muttering in a relieved way, *"Herr Gott,* I'm glad the captain has come. On this cursed platform of mine I am too helpless to cope with Gustav when he has these spells." He apologized mournfully to Bill Shepherd, "Gustav is as good a man as any of us when he can forget the past. The thunder tonight, that is what upset him. They left me with him in the dugout. I could not stop him when he decided to go to the *château.* He cannot forget the War. That is the trouble with us Germans." The man brushed a sleeve across his forehead. "This conscience we have about the War."

Gabrielle Gervais was pulling herself to her feet, brushing straw from her face. She grasped at and clung to Bill Shepherd, gasping, "He forced me to go up into the tower. Made me come here with him. He said he would return and shoot you if I did not come. Then when we got here to the barn he said I was Edith Cavell, that I was a spy he had had orders to shoot from his commanding general in Brussels."

"That is right, *Herr Kapitan,*" the legless Uhlan said. "Gustav brought the girl here from the *château.* I had come here to get my horse. I was going to ride into the forest to your headquarters tent to tell you Gustav had run off. My horse was gone; it must have become frightened in the storm and escaped from its tether. Then Gustav came into the stable with the French girl. I could do nothing with him. Then the American civilian arrived."

Bill Shepherd said hoarsely to the black-masked officer, "I demand to know the meaning of this. What are you doing here? What are you and these miserable men doing here in the Forêt de Feu?"

But before he could get an answer to that enigma there was an interruption from the night. The one-eyed Chasseur in the stable door cried, "Somebody comes!" The Punch-and-Judy Italian in the feathered hat swerved clumsily around. The French *poilu* gestured his steel-hook arms. The Cossack rounded in a limpy about-face, challenging, "Who goes there?"

THEN FOUR MORE figures arrived in the gloom. Fielding. Professor Putinov. Doctor Arnoldo. The little Fiat-driver, Tac. They were there on the stable's threshold as ghostly, white-faced, dumbfounded as Bill Shepherd had been on his own arrival at this scene. Fielding cried, glaring from the grouped deformities to Shepherd, "Well, I'm damned! Who are these men? What the devil—!"

The black-masked British officer rounded smartly on his crutches. "Nothing is wrong here. Everything will be all right. We are only here for tonight to spend a last evening in the Forêt de Feu."

A crackle of lightning, splitting across the sky, sent a resounding thunder-clap through Bill Shepherd's brain. All at once he was shouting, finger aimed at the black-masked officer before him.

"Bertrand sent you here! The lawyer! He pulled this out of his sleeve! A plot to scare me away from the *château!*

He's trying to get control of the property! He hired you and these masquerading panhandlers to come here!"

The voice behind the black mask rasped like a file on iron, answering Bill Shepherd's blurted accusation.

"Masquerading panhandlers! You don't know what you're saying. The Uhlan at your side was decorated by the German Crown Prince himself. Poor Gustav, badly shell-shocked, was one of the greatest heroes in the German Army. These men behind me whom you have called panhandlers were all decorated for valor in the Battle of the Somme.

"Colonel Stefanovitch in the Cossack's shako was Russia's first ace. This Chasseur," the officer gestured an empty sleeve, "led the first cavalry charge on the Forêt de Feu. The *poilu* you see here once captured a machine-gun nest in that *château* single-handed. This Bersaglierie officer was an observer sent here from the Italian front. As a Marconi expert he detected the German wireless station secretly located in the *château's* tower. These are the men you have called panhandlers."

The armless figure came to attention on its crutches with a snap. "We were not sent here by any shyster lawyer."

It seemed to Bill Shepherd as if his mind had ravelled out like a string of yarn from Madame Landru's dowdy knitting. Once more the plot was burst. The jabberwok had returned. And at this climax the night itself seemed to explode. There was a blast somewhere in the forest like the Last Day. A red flare of fire spouted up over the trees, lighting the woods like the eruption of a volcano. Something whistled down the sky with a sound like the one-legged man's breathing amplified to an aerial shriek. The whistle ended in a crash.

A blast of light spurted from the underbrush not far from the stable. Iron fragment sang through the air. Unseen missiles hammered against the stable wall; there was a shower of pebbles and earth-clods; the detonations were deafening, banging away in the night like a succession of slamming iron doors. Those in the barn were thrown to the ground.

And the black-masked British officer was shouting, "Take cover! Take cover! The lightning has struck an ammunition dump! The whole forest is mined!"

The black sky seemed to come down crashing; the earth was rocked with a series of violent booms. Shrapnel tore bright holes in the sky overhead, flashing like splashes of quicksilver; the forest was livid where a pillar of fire mounted high above the silhouetted trees; the bombardment was on, and it was the Battle of the Somme.

27

THE MINES AWAKE

THEY WERE RUNNING. Out of the barn and through the underbrush and down the trench where Bill Shepherd had met the bony guardsman. Slipping and crying out and falling headlong in the stagnant water. Racing to escape the shell-bursts, the spurts of fire that blasted red holes in the blackness around them, the crashing sky bombs that lit the forest like rockets, spraying the trees with volleys of steel.

Running with his arm about the girl, Bill Shepherd expected momentarily to be blown to pieces. Doctor Arnoldo, little Tac, Putinov and Fielding were running directly ahead of him, their heads down, arms over their eyes, bumping and colliding on the zigzag turns.

Behind Shepherd came the armless officer, moving swiftly on his crutches, shouting to direct the way. He called to Bill Shepherd, "The dugout is not far! It should be ahead of us there! Do you need help with the girl? I do not see very well—"

The voice behind the faceless mask was lost under a din of explosions. That volcano in the forest's heart was erupting like Vesuvius. The whole wet sky took fire. The mist was red. Crimson smoke rolled over the woods like sluggish fog. Rockets criss-crossed high above the forest, soaring up like Roman candles. Sky bombs smashed pink holes through the storm-clouds, bursting like red electric-light bulbs hurled against a cosmic roof.

The aerial barrage echoed *crackety-crack-crack-crack!* Lower booms made the heavy ground-roar of cannon. Shells landed in the thickets near the trench, *whiz-bang!* There was a deep-bellied *whoom* that sent up a distant pillar of earth and shook the ground. Sticks, pebbles, bushes, clods of turf rained down into the trench for what seemed a dozen minutes afterward. In volcanic light the trench walls were stained vermillion, the water made a channel ol blood.

Close by, there was a tremendous crash. Bill Shepherd hurled Gabrielle Gervais against the trench wall; gripped her tight. His eardrums rang like gongs. He was blinded, for an instant stunned. Not too stunned to hear the winging flight of iron birds that swept across the trench; the *thud-thud-thud* of fragments spattering the earth wall at his back. There was a smell of scorched metal, burnt powder—a smell like electrocution. He was aware of the masked officer's voice as calm as though confronted with unimportance.

"That one must have been close."

Bill Shepherd opened his eyes to make sure. Yes, the officer was there. Upright on his crutches, his cap cocked and rakish, no more concerned with that shell blast than he might have been by traffic at a street corner. He turned to beckon at those coming behind him, gesturing a sleeveless arm.

"Are you all right, boys? It's that old ammunition dump, by the sound. The Fifty-first Artillery must've left a cache of shells under there, and figured the Germans would've carted them off. I'm worried more about the German mines—"

His voice was drowned out by another basso *whoom*—another tower of earth that soared up into the red sky and came down in a hail of clods.

A voice shrilled from around a bend in the trench, "We are coming, *Herr Kapitan. Ja, ja, ja,* those are our mines."

Around the bend of the trench came the freakish squad—the noseless Cossack, the hook-winged *poilu,* the humpbacked Italian in his feathered hat, the one-eyed Chasseur and the one-legged German with the whistle in his throat. They were bunched together, a dreadful huddle of figures that might have stepped out of some horrible *Guignol*—the noseless Cossack and the one-eyed Chasseur carrying between them the Uhlan on his little platform of boards and skates.

Through a crashing of shell bursts, the black-masked captain was crying, "Where is the dugout? These damned eyes of mine—"

The half-man on the platform cried, "Around the next bend!"

SOMEHOW BILL SHEPHERD got there. He tore aside the canvas curtain; flung Gabrielle Gervais down the steps into the arms of the English painter who, with Arnoldo, the bus-driver and the Russian, had gained the dugout ahead of him. Then, without quite knowing why he did it, he waited at the dugout entrance for the armless, masked officer.

The man was having trouble, struggling to extricate a crutch which had sunk below his weight in the mud. Bill Shepherd sprang back down the trench; yanked out the crutch with a cry. Seizing the officer about the waist, he dragged him to the dugout door, assisted him down the mossy steps.

"Thanks," came the voice through the mask. "Keep away from the door. Shell splinters. Otherwise bomb-proof. Rest of your party safe?"

A rataplan of explosions filled the underground chamber with din. The ceiling beams trembled. Earth slithered down the walls. The candles on the improvised table guttered.

Bill Shepherd saw Gabrielle Gervais, sitting in a rumpled bunk, smiling in fear, her features like frozen wax. Doctor Arnoldo slumped panting in a corner, mouth open, hands hanging limp, black eyes darting from side to side. Fielding was gripping the table, holding himself very stiffly, his expression tight-lipped, bleak. Professor Putinov, beside Fielding, was going through a mechanical pantomime of washing his hands, his face sickly.

When the near explosions stopped, Bill Shepherd was surprised to hear his own voice going. "That organ at the *château!* It was that one-legged German playing it! Don't be afraid; these fellows aren't ghosts! We can handle the lot of them. We—"

A hoarse-throated scream cut him off. "Did you think we were afraid of ghosts? *Sacré nom de Dieu!* An ammunition dump blowing up out there, and he thinks we are afraid of ghosts!"

Marcel Tac! Bill Shepherd had forgotten him. The little Fiat driver was under a bunk. There was a nearby crash, and the Frenchman's head disappeared like a turtle's, flicked back under cover. He began to wail like a baby, "Aaaah!

Aaaah! Aaaah!" kicking his heels and beating his hands in the dirt.

Gabrielle Gervais sobbed, "He's been hit."

"Hit!" the man under the bunk screeched. "No, but I am going to be! Cannot the rest of you hear those shells out there? They will kill us! Blow us to pieces!" His screaming went soprano. "Don't let them kill me! Don't let them kill me! Ah, God, don't let them kill me!"

The armless officer wheeled on his crutches. Through the faceless black mask his voice cut like a whiplash. "Put a stop to that! Somebody shut up that man!"

Bill Shepherd managed to say thickly, "Tac! That's enough of that!" Crossing to the bunk, he yanked the squirming Frenchman out from under by the scruff; jerked him to his feet. "Stop screaming! There's a girl here—"

It wasn't convincing, because a deafening blast sent something whistling in through the dugout entry; there was a thud on the rear will; the ground shook under him, and he could have screamed, himself.

Marcel Tac's mouth flapped open, and he went, "Waaaaaah!"

"Hit him!" the black-masked officer commanded.

Automatically obedient, Bill Shepherd slapped his palm hard across the little man's terrorized face. The bus-driver staggered back; plopped down beside the French girl; put his elbows over his eyes.

"He'll be all right," the officer snapped. "When I was first out here I did some screaming myself. The damned noise. It takes about six months to get used to it."

"Six months!" The cry was from Professor Putinov. His

face was tinged ptomaine-green. "You do not think these shells will be exploding for six months?"

The masked officer gave a dry, harsh laugh. "I was out here when they lasted that long. This is just some old ammunition that got mislaid in these woods. There wouldn't be enough to last half an hour."

BILL SHEPHERD STARTED at the clutch of Fielding's steely fingers on his arm. The Englishman's grip was like a tourniquet. He was behind Bill Shepherd; and he shouted into Shepherd's ear, in a pandemonium of detonations his voice hardly as loud as the metallic shouting of a telephone receiver: "For God's sake, man, what's happening? Those ghastly devils in the barn—who were they?"

"I don't know!"

"Who's this masked officer?"

"I don't know!"

"Shall we rush him?" Fielding's fingers squeezed meaningfully; he was yelling at the top of his voice, but tremendous explosions which seemed to be landing on the dugout roof reduced the yells to tiny echoes. "We can nail him—make him talk! What?"

Bill Shepherd yelled across a distance of three inches, "I don't know who he is, or where he came from!"

Fielding yelled back, "He was near the *château!* We saw him from a window! We were chasing him in the bush when you waved at us from the tower! Let's grab—" Bill Shepherd didn't get the rest of it.

There were five ear-splitting crashes on the dugout roof like gigantic blows on an anvil. The room shook violently, dim and deafened, befogged by an in-sucked draught of brown-black fumes. Raw earth slithered down the walls, poured from a crack in the ceiling timbers.

Everybody rocked, swayed. Professor Putinov grabbed at the table. In a corner, Doctor Arnoldo went down in a crouch. Bill Shepherd saw Gabrielle Gervais sitting with her fingers in her ears; little Tac with his head under a blanket. The masked, armless officer had swerved on his crutches; he seemed to be watching the dugout entry. Bill Shepherd had caught at a bunk-support to steady himself; Fielding was clinging to his arm, still yelling.

He couldn't hear the Englishman's voice. But Fielding was game. Ready for action. Didn't want to die like a rat in a trap—Bill Shepherd caught that much of the man's meaning. Then, his ear-channels clearing of the ringing, he was aware of shouting in the dugout entry. Figures at the top of the steps, creating a diversion.

The freakish soldiers! Grotesqueries in the bomb flares and smoke-fog. The masked officer was gesturing an empty sleeve at them. Had any of them been hit? The one-eyed Chasseur was laughing. *"Non, mon capitaine!* This is funny! It is nothing!"

The masked officer roared, ordering them to come down into the dugout. They jostled and cried out at the dugout entry, yells smothered by fiery blasts in the red night behind them.

Bill Shepherd was aware that Fielding had released his arm; staggered back. "No, no! Don't let them come down here! Those beastly horrors!" The Englishman's voice rose shrill. "Clear cut of here! My God! I can't stand the sight of you—"

In the candle flutter Fielding's face was twisted in

nausea. He reeled to the back of the dugout, his hand over his eyes.

But the creatures in the dugout entry did not come down the steps. Pandemonium behind them had blanketed Fielding's outcry; doubtful if they could have heard or understood the artist's words. Shells were blasting, the masked officer was raging, "Get down in here, you fools!" But they scuffled on the upper threshold, delaying to shove the Uhlan forward on his little platform.

It was terrible to hear Fielding's horrified cries, "I can't stand the sight of him! Take him away!" Squealing through his fingers from where he stood against the dugout's rear wall, face in hands.

The half-man couldn't hear it. Torso bent forward, he was shouting down the steps at the masked officer. *"Herr Kapitan! Herr Kapitan!* You must come up out of there! This trench is mined! Torpedoes linked by buried fuse! We can see the explosions coming! Quickly, *Herr Kapitan!"*

"Torpedoes!" The masked officer about-faced on his crutches. "Everybody out! This trench was mined! The shells have touched off the fuse-line! Up top with you! Into the woods!"

Bill Shepherd cried, "The *château!* The trench leads to a tunnel into the *château!* Gabrielle! Everybody! Run for the *château!"*

"No!" was that commanding roar. "If these mines are going up, it means that château goes up with them! The Germans would have mined the *château!"*

"German mines? German mines?" Professor Putinov might have just waked from nightmare to discover the dream real. Rushing for the dugout steps, he went by Bill

Shepherd in mad stampede, his mouth open in a bawl. "I knew the Nazis were behind this murder! That swine, Kull!"

It struck Bill Shepherd as a blow between the eyes.

Where *was* Herr Kull?

28

FUSILLADE AND FIRE

THEN, OUT IN the thundering bedlam of the trench, in the confusion of red smoke, shrapnel flares and earth showers, half blinded, deafened, choking in powder fumes and fear, Shepherd missed Fielding. Heaving Gabrielle Gervais up the mud bank, he had had a glimpse of Putinov, Arnoldo and Tac going over the top. He had struggled to aid the armless officer up the slippery wall, and the girl, kneeling on the parapet, had reached down a helping hand. Then he realized the English painter had not come out of the bomb shelter.

He dived back into the dugout, shouting.

Fielding stood at the back wall, fierce-eyed, white, defiant.

"I'm not going up there, Shepherd! I tell you, I can't go up there with those freaks!"

"You've got to get out of this hole! The explosions are coming this way!"

"I won't move! I'll stay here! That man without a nose—the one with those hooks—that horrible thing cut in half—my God!"

"They've gone into the woods! Damn you, do you want to be killed? Come on!"

"I'm not go—"

Bill Shepherd's hands, whipping to the Englishman's collar, choked the protesting yells. Fielding resisted wildly, the sanity gone from his eyes. Desperately, all his strength behind the uppercut, Bill Shepherd drove his fist into the man's jutted chin. Fielding's head snapped back; he slumped. Then he revived as Bill Shepherd wrestled him up the dugout steps.

"Are you coming?"

"Yes, yes, Shepherd. I'm with you. Bloody awful of me. Can't stand cripples. For a minute—lost my nerve—"

Bill Shepherd cried as they clambered up the boom-rocked wall of the trench, "Where's Kull? That bald-headed German—?"

"Don't know," Fielding moaned. "Didn't come out of the *château* with us. Left him there in that big empty hall!"

They were tearing through an acreage of underbrush, racing to catch the little group ahead—Tac, Arnoldo and Putinov running as an escort around the girl, the bobbing figure of the black-masked officer herding them from behind. The forest was flooded by a holocaustal light, a scarlet flush that streamed through the shattered trees like an unholy dawn.

A mile to the north, towering up out of the timber, stood a hundred-foot fountain of crimson flame. Rockets soared up from the vortex of this fire-fountain, arching high against the rainclouds and bursting like exploded planets. The zodiac was being shelled. Iron meteors rained down, crashing the nearby thickets. Aerial barrage was undertoned by the flash-crash of artillery shells which were bursting, now, around the *château*—the Norman tower and vine-covered upper walls plainly visible a quarter mile distant.

Shrapnel splashed like squirts of mercury in the tree-clumps under the tower, sending up funnels of white-gray smoke and savage, sharp bangs. Deep, basso booms which shook the ground underfoot were more terrifying. Most appalling in the bombardment was a terrific series of detonations traveling along the abandoned trench.

"Look!" Bill Shepherd seized Fielding by the wrist to halt him.

Blast after blast was advancing down the trench they had just deserted—explosions fifty feet apart and timed at one-minute intervals. The running torpedo bursts were blinding. Earth shot up in swirling funnels. Bill Shepherd watched a sandbag fly skyward like a beanbag taking off for the moon. The blasts were like concussions on the brain. There was a pause; then, at the bend where the dugout was located, a stunning blast raised up a sheet of earth that opened and closed like a fan. The blasts ran on in quick zigzag, traveling toward the *château.*

SHEPHERD AND FIELDING ran madly to join the others in a grove of decapitated pines. Doctor Arnoldo had located a footpath where the running was easier; he was crying, "We must get under cover! We must somewhere get under cover!"

Gabrielle Gervais was leading the black-masked officer, holding him by the sleeve. She cried, "This man says if we come to a gulley we must look for a concrete pillbox. He says there is a gulley and a concrete pillbox we can hide in. Ah, *mom Dieu!*" she sobbed at Bill Shepherd as he sprinted up to her side. "Who ever heard of a pillbox of concrete, or one big enough to hide in?"

"He means a machine-gun nest. I've been along this path! The gulley can't be far!"

The voice from the black mask snapped. "It will be at the left. Up the bank. I cannot see to hurry. Don't wait for me. Go on! Go on!"

Gabrielle Gervais cried to Bill Shepherd, "We've got to help him!"

The others were racing on ahead. Bill Shepherd snatched the unknown officer's crutches; flung his arm under the man's shoulder. The girl supporting him on the other side, they ran the one-legged man along the path. Then, out of the canning-factory bedlam in the burning night behind them, came the most appalling sound Bill Shepherd had ever heard.

It began like a rising of wind, mounted to a tempest shriek, and passed overhead with the rushing whistle of an invisible express train. A split-second later in the woods a half mile ahead there was a blast like an explosion in a boiler foundry. Logs, shattered timbers soared skyward like a flock of crows.

The mask-hidden voice at Shepherd's shoulder said carelessly, "Big Bertha shell. Must've been lying in the brush near that ammunition dump. Those demolition shells come tall as a man. Flying piece of shrapnel or heat probably sent it off."

He panted a moment later, "There's a lot of dud shells lying around here. Mind you don't kick any rusty hand-grenades."

They came up with Fielding, Tac, Arnoldo and Professor

Putinov in a frightened group at the mouth of the gulley. Bill Shepherd stared at a whale-sized obstruction of iron and cogwheels blocking the gulley where, by the looks of a steaming bank of raw earth, there had just been a landslide. Seen in black shadow and red flame-light, the iron engine resembled a giant bug that had been gouged out of the gulley-bank. It took Bill Shepherd a second to realize the thing was a tank.

Little Marcel Tac was hysterical. *"Nom du sacré cochon!* There was that thunder smash in the distance, then this monster came out of the hill. Right out of the hill in an avalanche of earth, and rumbling down straight at us it came!"

Fielding pointed a quivering finger. "Landslide. Bank collapsed from that big shell crash. That tank had been buried right there in the hill."

They had no time to marvel at that disaster. Yesterday's terrors paled before immediate emergency. No telling where the next stray shell might land; they were racketing in the forest all around, the air was alive with whistling missiles, flying shards of metal and hailing stones. The pillbox, dimly visible in the bushes up the gulley-bank not far from the unearthed tank, did not resemble a haven. Somehow they reached this objective; clawed through a casement camouflaged with weeds and brush, and huddled into a concrete-walled den in the earth, an airless, bowl-roofed igloo of stone that confined them like a trap.

CRIMSON LIGHT STREAMED in through a hooded lookout which gave a glimpse of the gulley mouth where it opened out into forest a hundred yards away. Explosions reddening the night were muffled by the pillbox's concrete walls, but in the narrow confinement of this machine-gun hideout, Bill Shepherd felt as if he were crowded in a tomb.

He was jammed in between Gabrielle Gervais and the Russian; the others were huddled at his back; the den was alive with their panting, muffled oaths, scuffling. Blasts lit the gulley mouth, and they crouched in tight-strung fear, listening to fragments ricochet from the lookout casement. There was a sharp order, words that cracked with authority.

"Keep your heads down! Shrapnel might fly through the gun-ports!"

Putinov, at Shepherd's side, stirred and squirmed. His face was like a cartoon of the face he had worn an hour ago. Lips loose and doughy. Slavic cheekbones accented by the hollows beneath. Eyelids shining with tears. He was groping around Bill Shepherd's ankles; looking up, agonized.

"Help me, my friend. I have lost something. A—a chain."

Bill Shepherd rummaged in dirt and dead leaves; pulled from under a heel a silvery trinket that glimmered as he dropped it in the Russian's palm. A crucifix on a chain. A rosary.

The Russian clenched it hastily. "Thank you, my friend, I—I had it wound about my wrist." His voice went husky. "I have carried it as a remembrance, and I would not want to lose it. My mother gave it to me—" The words were lost under a thundering detonation.

A hand crept into Bill Shepherd's. The fingers tightened in his. Gabrielle Gervais' eyes were dark, meeting his turned glance.

"Are you afraid to die, *mon ami?*"

He tried to grin an answer. "Sure. Everybody's afraid to

die. But nobody's going to." He gripped her hand reassuringly. "At least, not in here."

He thought she whispered, "I do not mind dying if I can hold your hand." She was blinking back tears. Her voice came through a distant shell crash,—"better than a man who can eat a horse."

He told her, squeezing her fingers, "I like that. Good girl. Stick to your guns. Be consistent."

Certainly she was, of all this night's madness, the only consistent character. That she could remember her confession-story romance throughout this maniacal nightmare! All hell was loose. In a woods of dead trees surrounded by cemeteries, the soldiers of the World War came back and brought a World War bombardment with them. Phantoms came and went in the night with the seeming reality of ghosts in Shakespeare's plays; an armless, one-legged officer in a black mask snapped orders to direct their actions. But this French girl who resembled Edith Cavell told a story and stuck to it.

"Beel! What is that?"

He had noticed it, too. Been half aware of it as something he might have imagined with his swirling thoughts. Somewhere out there in the forest beyond the gulley mouth a cat was squalling. The caterwaul had been going on for some time. Now the others in the pillbox were listening to the constant yowl.

Fielding asked hoarsely, "What the devil is making that sound?"

It was the voice from the black mask that answered. "There is a wounded man out there."

HORROR-STRUCK, THEY LISTENED to the wail. Waited

for the echoes of a shell burst to pass. Listened; heard it again.

Doctor Arnoldo said throatily, "It is someone in agony. I thought I heard a cry in German."

Bill Shepherd blurted, "Maybe it's Kull!"

The caterwaul reeled up to eerie soprano, died to a moan.

"Bloody!" Fielding gasped. "Sounds as if he's there in that thicket above the mouth of the gulley."

Marcel Tac was sobbing brokenly. "I cannot stand that. I cannot stand that wailing. I tell you, it is driving me mad!"

Bill Shepherd unlaced his fingers from the girl's. He said through his teeth, "I'm going out there." He called, "Doctor Arnoldo! Are you coming with me?"

Gabrielle Gervais gasped, "Regard! Beel! Look at that!"

No one had noticed the black-masked officer's departure. Through the narrow slit of the pillbox lookout, he had come into view, flickering down the gulley on his crutches, running at a one-legged skip toward the underbrush which gave issue to the caterwauls.

Then, up the bank not far from the crutching figure, there burst a ball of dazzling fire. The crippled officer stumbled forward and fell in an awkward heap.

Bill Shepherd spun about from the casement. "Come on, Arnoldo! That man was struck! We've got to reach him and the other!"

The Italian, squatting on his heels, made no move. Catching him by the lapels, Bill Shepherd jerked him to his feet. "You're a doctor, aren't you? You can't let men die out there! What the hell is the matter with you?" He flung the man at the pillbox hatchway.

Fielding moved forward. "I'm with you. Shepherd. You'll see I'm not yellow."

"Let's go!"

Out of the pillbox, they chased along the gulley in a wild dash to reach the fallen cripple. Behind Bill Shepherd there was a savage *whang!* Doctor Arnoldo dropped; floundered on his knees beside the path, screaming, "I've been hit! I've been hit!" His teeth were bared in agony; eyeballs glowing with fright.

Racing to the Italian's aid, Bill Shepherd found the man bent double, convulsed by a bleeding gash in the calf of his leg.

"Madre Maria! I will lose my leg! I am dying! I bleed to death! I have been struck by a shell!"

Stooping, Bill Shepherd snatched a rusty, weed-snarled army automatic out of the burdocks beside the path. "It's only a bullet scratch! You kicked this loaded pistol, you fool! Get up!" He hauled the whimpering Italian to a stand. "That officer's badly wounded. Get him back into the pill-box if you can."

But the others had come out of the pillbox to the Italian's aid; even the hysterical little bus-driver was running about. Bill Shepherd realized that the thunder of shellfire and the aerial bombardment had, as though at a signal, come to a stop. Red sky reflected a great fire, but there were no more explosions. In this silence, the caterwauling in the forest beyond the gulley echoed like the yowling of a banshee.

THERE IN THE bushes at gulley's end they found Siegfried Kull. The bald-headed German was snagged in a great net of barbed wire; held helpless like a large insect in a steel spider-web. His coat and britches were torn to rags; he was scratched and bloody from his struggles to extricate himself; and he hung sobbing and groaning in the tangle of strands, half mad with terror, his bald head wreathed in a crown of thorny barbs, his features like those of a man crucified.

"Save me! Save me!" he was screaming.

But, aside from the scratches on his legs, arms and hands, Herr Kull was unharmed.

His screams broke down into tears. Fielding had told him about the ammunition dump. *"Ach, Lieber Gott! Lieber Gott!* I thought war had been declared. I thought it was the war!"

Bill Shepherd, remarking the ashen face, thought, "That's no Nazi Terrorist—that's a frightened old man."

Weeping and groaning, Herr Kull was trying to explain how he had run into the forest to escape the bombarded *château;* the terrible experience of being caught and held helpless in an entanglement of barbed wire.

But everyone was more concerned with his own tortured nerves. With the wonderful quiet that had come over the forest after that fusillade of explosions. With the marvelous realization of personal escape from death. With bewilderment over the black-masked officer who was lying in a crumple, his armless sleeves askew; leg buckled under him—an alien and unknown stranger in their midst. And with the tower of the Château de Feu which was on fire and, reared against the fevered sky, was burning like a torch.

29

DAWN IS SANITY

GABRIELLE GERVAIS WAS trying to turn the wounded man on his back. "He is conscious, Beel! The blood comes from his chest. Ah, *Dieu!* we must stop the bleeding!"

Bill Shepherd shouted harshly at Doctor Arnoldo who was moaning and muttering, occupied in binding a handkerchief around his own leg. "Leave off fussing with that scratch of yours, can't you? This man will bleed to death."

The Italian doctor hitched forward with an exaggerated limp. His features writhed at each step. He snarled, "I have not got my surgical case. Without antiseptics I can do nothing. First it is my fingers in a door; now a wound in the leg. A bullet from a rusty gun such as that is almost sure to give one tetanus."

He winced, going to one knee beside the crumpled officer. *"Porca!* A miracle if I do not return to Italy in an ambulance, suffering from gangrene. And who is this masked one who masquerades in officer's uniform—a bandit?"

Fielding said, "That's right!" voice indignant. "Who the devil is he?"

There was a crowding forward as Bill Shepherd and the girl turned the wounded man over. Gently, Gabrielle Gervais was fumbling to unbutton the faded khaki tunic.

Bill Shepherd, straightening the helpless leg, discovered that it was hinged at the knee and encased in a steel brace, like that worn by paralytics, concealed under the pant.

He felt a twinge of pity. Whoever this fellow was—in the madness of the past thirty minutes, there'd been no time to ask questions—he'd undergone at some time in the past a barbarous butchery. Both arms and right leg amputated. Left leg in a brace. The man's uniform cap had fallen aside, and Bill Shepherd didn't wonder that the tousled hair which lay damply across the forehead of the black cloth mask was snowy white.

Gabrielle Gervais said tremulously, "Is it bad, Doctor Arnoldo?" opening the tunic to expose a bleeding gash under the heaving ribs. The wounded man was breathing heavily. Gusty breaths which billowed the mask that covered his face like an execution cloth and was tied by strings knotted tightly at the back of his head.

The Italian doctor grunted. "How can I tell? Has anyone a bandage? Before I work on this brigand, I would remove his face-cloth."

A groan escaped the prostrate figure. "No!"

Bill Shepherd, a hand behind the white-thatched head, hesitated.

Fielding cried, glaring down, "Go on! Go on! What are you waiting for, Shepherd?"

The masked head lifted itself from Bill Shepherd's supporting hands. The armless shoulders reared up as though in convulsion. Then the wounded man fell back panting. "Do not remove the mask! I appeal to you as gentlemen! There is a girl here—do not remove my mask!"

At the panic, the utter misery in that petitioning cry,

Bill Shepherd felt the hairs rise on his scalp. It was as if the wounded soldier, supernatural, feared exposure and extinction if his face were looked upon by human eyes.

AND THE EYES that arrived on the fringe of that scene just then were not human. Madame Landru's eyes. White-rimmed. Glowing like witch-shine in her gray-frowzed head. And the hobby-horse eyes of Archambaud peering wildly over the old woman's shoulder.

They created an interruption, charging out of the red-shadowed gulley, both galloping. In her arms Madame Landru was carrying her dog. The dog was dead.

Bill Shepherd bucked to his feet. "The *château!*"

"On fire!" Madame Landru moaned. "It is the Battle of the Somme that is still going on. Theophile has been killed."

Archambaud whinneyed, "The ghosts are in the halls. I saw them! My wife saw them! Run for your lives!"

Madame Landru, hugging her pet, came to a shrieking stop. "There is another, Landru! Look! The one without a face! *Ah, la, la!* The woods are full of them! Soldiers without arms! Soldiers without legs! Racing into the *château!* Up into the burning tower! The maimed ones! The corpses! The dog howled in death, and when we ran upstairs to find Theophile we saw the dead soldiers chasing a corpse with a whistle in its throat up into the tower." The old woman jigged in terror. "We saw the un-dead dead! The Forgotten of God!"

The growth on her throat strangled her. Empurpled, choking, she fell to the ground.

The voice behind the black mask was speaking. Harshly into the vacuum of silence left by the woman's outcry.

"Take me there! To the *château!* At once! Fritz has run up there—he is crazy with shell-shock—they have gone into the tower to save Fritz. I must call them back!"

Bill Shepherd gazed across the tops of red trees. A pall of luminous smoke hung over the *château.*

"We are only wounded veterans," the voice behind the mask spoke thickly. "Only poor *mutilées* left over by the World War. They called us heroes, then they imprisoned us in hospitals where we could not remind the good citizens of a time they did not want to remember.

"We—we are left-overs from the Battle of the Somme. We have meant no harm. We did not like the hospitals, and we walked out. Summers we have spent here in this forest, where no one comes. Winters we hide among the streets of Paris, and beg. They are only wounded veterans, those that you fear. Help me get them out of the fire. Help me save them—"

The voice broke off with a gasp.

Bill Shepherd, staring over the red-topped trees, was unable to look down. He tried to speak; could only shake his head. The tower was gone.

IT HAD FALLEN like a toppled chimney to make a great hill of scorched brick and broken masonry at that end of the wing. Only a lower bastion remained. Strange that tonight an unaimed shell from an exploding ammunition dump should fell an objective that the trained cannoneers of three armies had failed to demolish in months of firing. Queer, too, that the rest of that ruined manse should have suffered no demolition.

In the first gray creep of morning, the *château* in its shroud of vines—save for the toppled tower—stood silhouetted in dismal disrepair. Perhaps the ghostly artillerymen who had directed that aimless bombardment had scorned the already gutted ruins.

Ghostly artillerymen? Bill Shepherd was not sure, now, that there were not such things. In this forest cemetery surrounded by legions of white crosses the supernatural had happened. At least, viewed from the normalcy of life, they were not according to nature. That thirty minutes of bombardment, for example—thirty minutes by a clock, perhaps, but a terror that had lasted a whole lifetime.

Such things as that, and such things as Marcel Tac, as seen in this desolation of morning, moping about in the rags of his bus-driver's uniform like a plucked bantam beaten in the cockpit. Muttering over and over, "I was a coward. *Ah, Sacré Dieu!* Under fire I was a coward!"

And Professor Putinov, hobbling about on his sprained ankle, a man gone deaf and dumb, able only to stare and swallow and burst into dramatic Russian tears every time he looked at a silver rosary clutched in his hairy hand.

And Herr Kull, sitting on a bench in the decay and wreckage of the formal garden, his bald head bowed, his eyes on the vine-tangled fountain nymph in a fixed, unseeing stare. He had said once to Bill Shepherd on their approach to the *château,* "Do you think that horrible thing could have happened to—" then choked back the words, as if unable to bear the thought.

Such things as that, and such things as Fielding coming up from behind, spinning Shepherd about with a grab, then declaring in a sickly way, "Look here, old man. I know I seemed beastly about those—those veterans. I wish to God you'd try to understand."

Understand?

And there was Doctor Arnoldo, sleeves rolled to the elbow, working over that unknown officer whom they had carried into the one livable corner of the *château*. Doctor Arnoldo, self-assured once more, now that he had found his medical kit, cauterized that scratch on his calf and washed his hands in antiseptic. Altogether the surgeon, the best in Italy, professional, deft, dapper, fighting to keep an interesting specimen from hemorrhaging.

And Gabrielle Gervais, running to replenish the hot water, wringing out towels, quick and self-disciplined and gentle of eye and hand, like any good nurse—like Florence Nightingale herself, or Edith Cavell.

Such things as Gabrielle Gervais bringing sanity to the disordered brain of Madame Landru by commanding her to boil bed-sheets for bandages and be damned quick about it—"And wash that dead hound off your hands, you *bourrique!*" And getting fast action out of Archambaud, with, *"Sacré,* will you fetch the brandy, or shall I? Hurry quickly, lump of dirt! Lascar!"

And to Bill Shepherd, "Beel! Get yourself a drink of cognac and be off! We are going to operate! You are in the way! Go and assist the firemen! Be out of here!"

YES, FIREMEN HAD arrived—a comic opera company in brass hats, all sitting at attention in a little red hose-cart that had somehow come from Contalmaison. With them was the mythical Lieutenant Jaloux of the mythical Contalmaison *Gendarmerie.* Like extras at a carnival they blurred into the background and set to work digging in the tower ruins, bright birds scavenging for bodies.

On the heels of these clowns, a long-hooded, mud-spattered blue Rolls Royce skidded into the *château* driveway. Doors banged open, and there was the woman in black— the mysterious lady of the lawyer's office (how many years ago was that?)—and the lawyer, himself, dusty, vellum-faced Monsieur Bertrand.

"Monsieur Shepherd! Monsieur Shepherd! What in the name of God has happened here? I called your hotel and could not find you. They said you had not come in for the night. I thought you had come to this dangerous place. *Oui,* so I drove to Contalmaison last night: with Madame Mallarmier, hoping to find you at the inn. We heard the explosions, and—"

"Mother!" Gabrielle Gervais, towel about her head, came flying out of the *château.* "Name of God, mother! Why did you come?"

Gabrielle Gervais and the woman in black locked in each other's arms. The woman in black throwing back her veil, looking more like the French girl's twin sister than her mother, shaking Gabrielle by the shoulders.

"What is that which is this, Gabrielle? Your dress! Your hair! *Mon Dieu,* but Phillipe will never forgive you— running away from the wedding, leaving that mad letter that you were coming here to hide in this awful forest. Your father is on the verge of a nervous breakdown. Is it every day he could arrange a wealthy match? He phoned to me in Paris; I was just preparing to drive to Amiens.

"When I heard where you had gone! *Voilà!* I had seen an advertisement in the paper about this forest. I drove at once to the office of the good *avocat* handling the estate— this kind Monsieur Bertrand—told him he must arrange

at once for me to visit the property; that he must delay all
other visitors until I had found you—and that—"

Gabrielle Gervais cried, "Please, *maman!* I cannot talk of
this now. Poor veterans have been killed. A man is dying."
Disengaging herself from her mother's arm, she turned
to Bill Shepherd who was standing beside Monsieur
Bertrand, astounded.

"Beel! Beel! He is dying. The poor officer in there. He
asks to talk with you."

Ghostly artillerymen? Why not, when things like that
could happen in the Forêt de Feu? If the first pale banners
of sunup had not frightened them all away, they should,
Bill Shepherd thought, be there in the entry of that chamber where the masked officer was dying. Playing a ghostly
taps.

30

HEAR THE LITTLE PEOPLE

"CAN YOU HEAR me?" the voice behind the mask was very low. Bill Shepherd leaned over the shabby couch.

"Yes, I can hear you."

"I wanted to speak with you. You know I'm—washed up."

Bill Shepherd glanced at Doctor Arnoldo. Briskly professional, the Italian, now entirely recovered in demeanor, was closing his surgical kit. He caught Bill Shepherd's glance, and shook his head. "The man," he said aloud, heartlessly, "will not live."

The prostrate figure on the couch stirred slightly, chuckled. "Been living on velvet too long anyway. Damned public nuisance—big expense to the State. Interesting medical specimen to these sawbones; aside from that, no earthly use."

Bill Shepherd waited until the dapper physician was out of the room. He said huskily, "You—you'll pull through all right."

"Not a chance, fella. On my way West. It's about time, and not much left of me to go. That chunk of shrapnel broke about the last solid bone I had left. Besides, I want

to stick with my squad. Good fellows. Known 'em for years
in the hush hospital.

"We were all picked up after the same bombardment and
carted off in the black wagon, slated to be croppies. Instead,
we all lived. We've—we've stuck together for years."

After a period of heavy breathing the dying man
resumed, "They elected me captain. We had a sort of club.
There's a big batch of us in the hush hospitals in France.
Les Gueules Cassées.

"Ever hear of us? The Society of the Broken Faces. I
don't suppose you have—we aren't as popular as the Elks.
They don't like us in parades. Not in hotel dining rooms
or charity bazaars. Embarrassing at Cannes or Nice or the
race track, too." The faint voice was bitterly ironic. "They
chase us off the streets these days. They say we slow up the
recruiting."

Bill Shepherd waited as the dying man coughed.

"Are you still there, Shepherd?"

"I'm here."

"That's your name, isn't it? Shepherd?"

"Yes."

"The little French girl told me you owned this *château*
and the woods."

"I—I did."

"Say, Shepherd, take my hand, will you? No, damn it, I
haven't got any hand. Can't see very well. The little vision
I had is gone. That's all right, I don't need to see to know
you're a right guy. Listen, Shepherd, I'm sorry as hell—all
the trouble I've put you to. I know the rest of the boys were
sorry, too.

"If Gustav hadn't gone off the handle, there'd have been

no trouble. He never got over being in the execution squad that shot Edith Cavell. Fine chap when he was in his right mind. Thunderstorms sent him off. I—I'm certain the poor devil fired that ammunition dump. Must've found a detonator hidden in the woods somewhere. We've been around these woods a lot, you know. Camped out here in the summers. Good place for us. We never troubled anybody."

Bill Shepherd said chokily, "I'm sure you didn't."

"For a fact. We found some old tents. Nights we'd sit around a fire and talk the Battle of the Somme. Knew every inch of this sector, myself. Sometimes we'd pick up a little money gathering scrap iron. Didn't think anyone would care.

"French Government used to pay as high as a dollar for unexploded shells. So much a barrow for shell fragments. We'd load the stuff in a cart and the *chasseur* would put on his rags and sell it over in Thiepval. The peasants were sneaking in on the business, too. I figured if anybody was, we were entitled to it."

"Sure," Bill Shepherd whispered. "Sure you were."

"THE BOYS WERE all upset tonight about Gustav going off the handle. And they knew they wouldn't be coming to the forest many times more. I know they followed him into the burning tower deliberately."

"Why wouldn't they be coming to the forest?" Bill Shepherd whispered.

"The Uhlan read in the paper it was up for sale. Government was going to take it over for taxes if unsold. That's why we came out here tonight. Have a last fling. Camping on the old camp ground. The boys were all broken up about the sale. Didn't want to go back into confinement. Back among the basket cases. I guess we're all a little crazy. Of course, I don't think I am. When you are, you never think you are, eh?" The dying man chuckled a second time.

"Anyway, Shepherd, we'd left some clothes—old rags of uniform and stuff—around in the dugouts we'd lived in. I'd left a kitbag full of souvenirs and stuff up in that *château* tower. Figured we'd better get our things before the sheriff came in. And there've been some peasants killed in these woods—"

The faint voice choked off, coughing. Then:

"Are you listening, Shepherd? Peasants killed. We didn't want to be blamed for it. But we didn't have anything to do with it. That poacher—his dog stepped on the trigger of a rifle lying in the brush. Lots of old guns and junk around out there. The poor little girl kicked an unexploded hand grenade."

"I thought as much," Bill Shepherd said. "It was the blacksmith's daughter that bothered me."

"Poor Paulette?" Another faint chuckle. "Must've shot herself. Picked up a pistol somewhere—had it with her, maybe, when she went riding. Wanted the mayor's son nailed for murder. Anyway, she shot herself and threw the gun. The Cossack found a pistol lodged high in the crack of splintered pine not far from the place it happened. Anyway, it wasn't us. Hope we didn't scare you all half to death."

The dying man paused to draw a breath. Shadows were ebbing into the corners of the room; staircase, fireplace and grandfather clock were coming into view. The voice behind the mask was fading.

"Shepherd."

"Right here." He stooped low.

A gesture from the dying man's shoulder. "My cap. Is it on?"

"On the chair beside you. Want it on?" Then, as the black-masked head nodded and Bill Shepherd picked up the cap, he saw something he hadn't noticed before. Over the visor. A maple leaf.

"Captain!"

"Yes, fella."

"Were you with the—the Canadians?"

"Right you are. Went into action in these very woods. Stationed, matter of fact, here in this bloody *château*."

Bill Shepherd said in a tight voice, "Did you—did you happen to know a Captain Shepherd?"

"HUGH SHEPHERD?" THE figure on the couch stirred. "Sure, I did. Knew him well. I knew you must be the kid brother he thought so much of. Used to speak of you often out here. I remember. Kid brother named Bill who aspired to write novels. So you're Hugh Shepherd's brother—"

Bill Shepherd whispered, "I often thought of Hugh."

"He often thought of you, fella. Remember him once telling me he wished you'd write a novel some time and take the whole stinking lid off War. He was a good officer, your brother, but he hated the show like hell. Wished he could write against it himself. Write something that the underhanded diplomats and dirty propagandists and fat armament makers and hypocritical priests and ministers who send men out to butcher each other with their cheers and pious blessings—write something that would expose the whole lot."

"Hugh—Hugh said that?"

"Hell!" The fading voice roused. "That wasn't half. He—

he wouldn't even go home on furlough. Didn't want any part of the human society that could go off on such a murderous debauch. He felt that the people back home were as much to blame as anybody. Not the little people. The big people. The big people who stuffed the little people with a lot of poisoned propaganda and patriotic candy and sent them out to tear at each other's throats.

"He used to say if they could kill the big men at the top it would be just and fair. Kill what he called the upper scum. It's the bottom men who fight all the wars, he used to say—the little clerks and farmers and thirty-dollar-a-week factory hands who don't know what it's all about. What was the good of killing a lot of little German sausage makers, pastry cooks and carpenters when you didn't get the big boys at the top—the Prussian Junkers who had misled them.

"Did you ever get a shot at Bertha Krupp? At Fritz Thyssen, the millionaire armament king? At Eulenberg? At Von Bethman-Hollweg? At the men behind the German Government? At William the Second?

"You fired a rifle, and who did you kill? Some picayune nonentity who had no more voice in the show than Hindenburg's stable-boy. You fired a thirty-thousand-dollar battery of shrapnel, and you killed three pretzel bakers, a high school student and a chimney-sweep. You never got the men responsible.

"He used to say you could look all day through the sights of a rifle and you wouldn't see any kings, generals, prime ministers, bank presidents, steel-mill owners, bishops or Princes of the Church in the trenches.

"Personally," the dying man murmured, "I couldn't blame

him. He was only nineteen when he came out here, and he went into a battle that cost the British sixty thousand casualties the first day."

Bill Shepherd waited dumbly through a pause filled with the sound of the dying man's labored breathing. Who was this officer who had known his brother's innermost thoughts?

The masked head moved on the pillow. The fading voice roused again. "He used to talk with me a lot, your brother. He compared the War to a forest fire. It had started. You had to try to put it out. You had to blast a trench across Europe to stop it. You had to kill a lot of little men who hadn't started it. He thought the big men of all countries were responsible. The bankers. The clumsy diplomats. The men who owned and ruled. They threw the matches. They lit the tinder.

"Maybe they didn't mean to do it—maybe in some quarters it was deliberate—but the fire was burning and you had to put it out. Perhaps after it was over the incendiaries would have learned a lesson. Maybe all the little people had not died for nothing.

"Your brother thought nationalism was directly to blame. The selfishness of nations all trying to keep the best place in the sun. He hoped for a possible Democracy in which all nations joined together, formed a world nation—like the colonies joined together to form the United States.

"He used to talk about that. He said if that happened, this terrible human sacrifice might have some worthwhile meaning after all. As long as the German militarists were in the saddle they had to be beaten at any price, but Hugh

Shepherd didn't forget that other nations were partly responsible.

"He said that if he ever lived, he'd never go back and play golf in a world like that. He said his own father had made money selling bum steel to Russia in 1914; if he ever lived he wouldn't touch a penny of that kind of cash. He said there'd be only one thing worth living afterward for—a world Democracy, a new feeling among men, a new type of Christianity that practiced what it preached, honor among diplomats and unselfish, chivalrous, trustworthy, intelligent leadership. Ha—!"

BEHIND THE MASK there was a harsh, savage laugh. "Can you imagine what Hugh Shepherd would think of today? Hitler! Mussolini! Stalin! Madrid and China and the fate of Czechoslovakia and and the hate-campaign against the Jews! Oh, my God!" A terrible mirth shook the figure on the couch. The dying man was strangling. Convulsed.

Bill Shepherd cried out, unable to bear that agony of sound.

"Gabrielle! Doctor!"

"No!" the masked man cut him off, rearing his head. After a moment of panting, "I'm all right. I—I was just thinking what your brother would have thought, what all those soldiers out there in those War cemeteries would have thought—if they were alive today. I—I guess a lot of us felt as Hugh Shepherd did after the Battle of the Somme."

Bill Shepherd waited for the man's painful gasping to ease. Dimly he saw Gabrielle Gervais at the doorway; signaled her to go back.

Then, stooping over the couch, he whispered, "Captain?"

"Yes, fella."

"You know this forest; you knew the Norman tower! Are—are you my brother?"

The armless shoulders twisted in denial. "I only knew Captain Shepherd."

Bill Shepherd said huskily, "Would you—would you take off the mask?"

There was a long pause. "If you insist—"

But Bill Shepherd's fingers were already busy at the strings.

He lifted the black cloth expectantly; stood wordless, cold.

There were features beneath that crown of snow-white hair. Features, but no face. One ear and eye were gone— the left eye no more than a sliver of egg-shell gleaming from a slit above a dreadful, out-puffed cheek. The nose was broken, twisted, shapeless. The jaws, battered sideways, were a counterfeit of grafted bone and skin, blue-yellow in discoloration. The lips looked as if they had been sewed on with undertaker's thread, made of sausage peel and sewed down at one corner in a mocking, hideous grin.

Bill Shepherd could not repress a shuddery gasp. Shock-numbed, his fingers let the mask fall back into place.

The dying officer's voice was a faint, whispery snarl. "You can see I am not Hugh Shepherd. Hugh Shepherd was young, strong in body and heart, with honest and open features, and a certain integrity of mind. He was decent and democratic and forward-looking, anxious to amount to something and eager to do something with his life. He was proud of his intellect and proud of his physique. He was full of faith in the future, and hope and self-confidence.

Hugh Shepherd was killed in the tower of this *château* during the Battle of the Somme, and I saw him die. Hugh Shepherd is dead."

The figure on the couch went silent. Presently, waiting wordless, Bill Shepherd thought he heard a sigh. He placed his hand on the forehead under the thatch of snow-white hair. The masked Canadian officer was dead, too.

31

FAREWELL TO THE FORET DE FEU

HE STOOD AT a window with Gabrielle Gervais and looked out at a landscape hauntingly gray in the light of a morning that, after a brief appearance of the sun, had clouded over to rain. The day might have been mourning a prospect of neglect and ruin, shedding steady tears. In the Forêt de Feu the shattered pines stood up out of the second growth, black and ugly like the masts of sunken ships jutting from shoals of dark green surf. The gray paste wagon-road sloughed off between the tangled thickets and climbed an eastward slope jungled with weeds and briar and pitted with craters that still held segments of night.

At the slope-top where the road was banked on either side, Bill Shepherd could see the tilted barrel of the field gun which blocked the approach to the bridge— the cannon which had been exhumed by a bankslide, or dragged there by some furtive salvage-hunter.

Westward, where the road disappeared in the timber, he could discern the winding gulley where the pillbox had been. About a mile distant, in a forested hollow, a sluggish yellow steam cloud smoked up over the trees and was beaten down by the rain, as if a vast rubbish pile was smouldering there. It was a forlorn scene, and the sky over France and Belgium, and eastward toward Germany, wept. Only a patch of poppies thrown across a slope near the *château's* drive, like a quilt discarded on an ash-heap, made a bright smear of orange on the gray.

"Beel?"

"Yes."

"Mother and Monsieur Bertrand are waiting for us. Mother will become impatient."

"In a minute."

He wanted to remember this scene. He never wanted to see it again, but he would keep a mental photograph of it. Of this mouldy room with its great black fireplace and decaying stair, its shadowy corners and cobwebby, mummy-case clock. Of the wing of ruins beyond—the great, gloomy hall—the wreckage-strewn corridors and salons—the gutted mansards and demolished tower.

He wanted to remember the forest with its little German graveyard and weedy bypaths and dark thickets camouflaging crumbled trenches and rusted war machinery—these stale woods undermined with tunnels and ammunition depots and secret hideaways—a dangerous No Man's Land in a front of sleeping cemeteries.

He looked around at the room. He did not want to forget a detail of the setting or the people who had been there. Fielding and Herr Kull. Putinov and the little Marcel Tac and the doctor from Italy. He had shaken hands with them and said goodbye. What plain, unvarnished mediocrities they had seemed at daylight, taking their departure in the taxicab summoned from town—a physician, a business man, a bus-driver, a college professor, an artist.

At a time of danger and emotional stress they had been

no more undignified, panicky, demoralized and unheroic than he himself. He hoped he would never see any of them again.

But now they were gone they seemed as incredible as any other aspect of last night—identities as alien and strange as that squad of *mutilées* and their faceless captain from the hush-hospitals. It occurred to Bill Shepherd that the War had not only mutilated the soldiers at the front; it had mutilated the civilians who had stayed at home, and the younger generations that had followed—mutilated their minds.

Not the least incredible of last night's madness had been that brawl of hostile ideologies—Communism against Fascism—the next War argued violently in the midst of a dismal ruin still haunted by the last.

"Beel?"

"I'll go, Gabrielle. In a moment."

HE WAS THINKING, staring from the window, how strange it was. Those cemeteries out there—this shell-torn forest— Nature was doing her best to heal these wounded fields, hiding the deformities under moss and leafage, wiping out the scars with rain. Barbed wire and iron rusted and dissolved; cannon-wheels sank in the earth of their own weight; trenches shallowed into furrows; gunpits and undergrounds made burrows for the rabbit and the fox.

But the minds of men would not heal. Incredible to know that any day, now, the armies might be back; this very forest mined, uprooted, fire-blasted, blood-soaked again. The captains and the kings had gone, but their swords and cloaks merely passed to other men. Or had the Kaiser merely returned to Berlin with the tips whacked from his

mustache, the withered arm lifted in the air, the eagles
changed to a Swastika?

That bald-jawed man who shouted and made faces from
the Palazzo di Venetia—hadn't the Romans heard that
speech somewhere before? On the roof of the Kremlin the
same old Czar—shaved, yes, and in a workman's blouse,
but wielding the same iron fist?

Fascism, Communism—the words sounded different,
but didn't the meanings, if any, translate into the familiar greeds of empire, the familiar lusts for racial power?
Perhaps that clock had been keeping the correct time,
striking back to 1916. Little wonder that the black-masked
officer had laughed.

"Beel! *Maman* will be honking the horn."

He stared blankly at the raindrops spilling down the
window.

"All right, Gabrielle. I'm coming."

Yes, and in a way Madame Landru was clairvoyant. The
Battle of the Somme *was* still going on. It had never ended.
The armies had only retired to gather recruits. Tomorrow
or the day after there would be different generals named
on the roadside plaques—Gamelin, Voroshilov, Goering.
Two hundred thousand new names in those acres of little
white crosses—names like Fielding and Tac and Putinov
and Arnoldo, maybe his own.

"Beel! Please—"

"I—yes, yes; as soon as I get my hat."

"It is in your hand."

So it was. As well as the officer's cap with the maple
leaf over the visor. The captain's cap had dropped off as
they had carried him out to the police van to take him to

Contalmaison with his squad. Bill Shepherd had picked it up; meant to follow. Then he had hunted the name in the cap-band, because....

BUT THE NAME had been Enderby. *D. S. Enderby.* He had felt a great wave of relief—the maimed and broken-faced officer was not Hugh! And yet—? Admittedly these poor, unwanted reminders of the last War had been wearing such articles of uniform as they had been able to find in the hideaways of the forest. And his knowledge of the *château.* That kitbag in the tower!

But Bill Shepherd refused to think about it. He had no right to know. You could not question the dying, and the dead were entitled to their secrets. The captain had said he was not Hugh Shepherd. And he wasn't.

"Beel! I wish you would come."

He smiled as she grasped his hand. Gabrielle. Funny, wasn't it? In at the start and standing by to the finish. The only straight character-part in the show. Spoke her lines and meant them. Like most of the people in this world, he hadn't been able to recognize the truth.

"Beel, *maman* will think something is wrong. Please come while she is still interested in the *château* and—"

"Your mother?" he stared vaguely. "Interested in the—"

"Château de Feu!" the girl said, frowning and smiling at the same time. "Beel, you won't listen to me. I have been talking to *maman* about it. She has been talking to your lawyer, and Monsieur Bertrand is anxious for you to hear. *Maman* wants to buy the *château*—"

He started, hearing only the last. "Your mother? Wants to buy the Château de Feu?"

"And the forest also. Please convince her, Beel. I so much

want her to do it. *Maman* is very rich. From her second marriage to a Swiss. I did not approve her divorcing my father to marry a Swiss, but perhaps it will be nice, for the Swiss has left a great deal of money.

"My mother will not know what to do with it all. She would only lose it in silly investments. I want her to buy the *château* and give it to me. The *château* I would make into a fine veteran's hospital, and the forest would be a splendid grove for aged horses!"

He wanted to say something. You never could find a word that meant anything when you wanted one. Lord, if her mother did buy this place! Veteran's home, and a grove for grand fatherly horses! It would mean he'd be seeing the girl again, too!

He could only look down into her shining eyes and gulp, "Gabrielle—!"

BUT WAIT! NOT too fast, Shepherd! This was too much like Plot 61-D, Ending 23! This thing wasn't happening in a fiction magazine. Nice curtain-line for a story, but stories never bothered with Tomorrow. Why put up a veteran's home and a retreat for tired horses as a target for Tomorrow's cannon? For his own part, he had something first to do.

He was going to write that book Hugh had wanted to see written. It wouldn't be a great book or a best seller or even a well-written book. If you called it *Whither Are We Going* or *Economics Toward Armageddon* or some title like that, it would have to sell for three dollars, and the only people who might read it would be people who knew about it anyway.

But he would write it as a mystery story—stick to the

only technique he knew. Start it off with a murder, and then go back to that lawyer's office in Paris, and carry on out through all those moribund battlefields and World War cemeteries into the Forêt de Feu. All he had to do was tell the truth.

He would describe the forest and the grim *château*. He would introduce the characters as he had met them. He would try to convey the cold horrors he had experienced; tell the things he had imagined, the realities he had seen.

He would point the contrast between the cocky Marcel Tac of the fireside and the little man's hysteria at another kind of fire. Between Doctor Arnoldo's surgical detachment toward another's wounds and his intimate concern for his own. Between the agnosticism of Professor Putinov in a Soviet discourse, and his grasping for faith during emergency. Between Fielding's admiration for artistically ruined buildings, and his horror at the same artistry applied to man. Between Herr Kull's Germanic stoicism when it came to the death of his son, and his not so stoic acceptance of a similar demise for himself.

He would leave out no detail—Archambaud's horsy forelock or Madame Landru's parasite. He would describe the *mutilées* as he had briefly seen them—the *poilu's* shoulder-hooks and the Italian's punchinello hump—the one-eyed Chasseur—the halved Uhlan—the German with the peanut whistle throat—the masked captain's face.

Some readers would refuse belief, and others might criticize for morbidity and lack of good taste. When he told what Hugh had thought, a number would make charges of everything from pacifism to paganism.

But he would write what he had heard, felt, and seen.

Expound no moral—let the reader, if any, draw his own conclusion.

A happy ending? He wondered about it, walking hand in hand with Gabrielle out to the waiting car.

Then he had the ending for his story. At the point where, driving back to Contalmaison, the sleek Rolls Royce took the road across the landscape of cemeteries—white crosses marching in the rain—and Lawyer Bertrand, at his side, gave an inadvertent start. Bertrand supplied the end.

"Shepherd," he said, his sandy voice low, "I forgot to tell you—"

"What?"

"That which brought me out here seeking you in doubled haste." The pale eyes flicked sideways to the girl and her mother engrossed in conversation. Then, in the manner of a magician producing a secret and evil missive, the lawyer drew from his pocket a folded newspaper. A last-night edition of the Paris *Soir*.

Bill Shepherd stared, tight-throated, at the headlines.

GERMANY INVADES POLAND! FRANCE AND
ENGLAND SEND HITLER ULTIMATUM! NAZIS
PLUNGING EUROPE INTO WAR!

The car swerved, passing the police van laden with misshapen bodies. Was Democracy to perish with them? Who would remember them now?

He would call his story, *The Forgotten of God*.